TALLOW

Time to Pay

MJ Howson

Engine ❶❸

THE **TALLOW** SERIES

Published by Engine Thirteen

ISBN-13: 978-0-99961-66-7-3

Cover design by MJ Howson

Other books by MJ Howson

The Tallow Series:

Tallow – An Urban Legend (Book 1)

Tallow – Rosemary (Book 2)

for Lori

PROLOGUE

We can regret the choices and decisions from our past, but we cannot change them. We can try to learn from our mistakes and hope for a better future. But sometimes the past comes back to haunt us. When legends survive, destiny often steps in to determine our fate. In the end, someone has to pay.

Urban Legends of Cape Cod

Author – Unknown

ONE

Chatham

Emma Johnson sat in silence, staring out her kitchen window. The heat emanating from the coffee mug in her hands helped to lower her anxiety. Her guest, although pleasant as always, had arrived unannounced. Their brief chat at the front door had morphed into an impromptu breakfast of coffee and bagels.

"Em?" Jeff Jones asked. "Aunty Em, you there?"

Emma turned her attention back to the man sitting across the table from her.

"I told you I hate being called that," Emma replied, stifling a small grin. "It makes me sound so old."

"I know you're my mom's cousin, but growing up you always felt more like her sister. I wasn't trying to make you feel old. Why so pensive today? Is it the inheritance?"

"Inheritance? Oh, the house. Yes, my mother and that home have been on my mind these past months. I honestly don't know what I'm going to do with the place. Or Zeus."

"Zeus?"

"My mom's Doberman."

Jeff looked around the kitchen and toward the living room.

"He's not here," Emma continued. "Someone's caring for

him temporarily. I don't know what to do with him."

"Is he friendly? Maybe I could take him."

"He's getting old, Jeff. I'll have to think it over. The house. The dog." Emma let out a long sigh of frustration. "I didn't ask for any of this."

Jeff took a bite of his everything-flavored bagel. A smattering of poppy seeds, garlic flakes, and salt crystals fell onto his plate. He dabbed his finger in a dollop of cream cheese and used it to collect the tiny bits.

"It's going to take time for the courts to sort it all out, but she didn't have a will, and you're the only surviving child. In my opinion, it's way too much house for you, Em. Not to mention it's falling apart. Clearing out the debris from the barn fire is going to be a chore all by itself. You could just sell it as is and let someone else deal with the mess."

"Perhaps." Emma wasn't comfortable talking about her family's old Victorian home. Her mind raced as she tried to come up with a new subject to discuss. "Any plans for Memorial Day? It's another week away, isn't it?"

"I'm glad you asked. That's one of the reasons I stopped by. I'm all moved into my new condo. I'm going to throw a cookout. Nothing fancy. My mom is coming, along with some people from work. I was hoping you could make it."

"You didn't need to drive all the way out to Chatham to invite me to a cookout, Jeff. A simple phone call would do."

"I know, but ... well ... to be honest, Mom asked me to check up on you. She's worried."

Emma intensified the grip on her coffee. She forced a smile as she took another sip from the mug.

"What's bothering Susan?"

Jeff popped the last chunk of his bagel into his mouth and washed it down with the rest of his coffee.

"She said you've been a bit of a recluse the past several weeks. Ever since your mom and Sara perished in the barn fire. She said you refuse to talk about it. She's worried. So am I."

Emma looked down at Jeff's empty plate, relieved he finally finished eating. She took this as an opportunity to get him to leave. Emma reached across the table and collected his plate and mug. Jeff quickly stood up to help her.

"I've got it, Jeff." Emma brought the plate and mug to the sink and began to rinse them. She took her time so that she would not have to look Jeff in the eye. "I'm sorry I've been so absent. It was quite a shock when I heard about the fire and what happened in the barn. It's all been a lot to handle. I've just thrown myself into my work, taking on extra shifts at the hospital."

"I can understand that. Keeping busy helps to keep your mind focused so that you don't let yourself get lost in your thoughts. Trust me, Em, I was just as stunned as you were."

"Stunned?" Emma turned to face Jeff.

"I know you've read the papers. Seen the news. I've answered your questions about what happened with your mom and sister. But I still ... I ... I think back to the blizzard last December. Remember that storm?"

"Yes." Jeff's tone made Emma feel uneasy, and she turned her attention back to doing the dishes. "It was brutal."

"Remember the bodies found in Little Pleasant Bay a few months later?"

"I do."

"Those victims were first reported as missing the night the blizzard hit. Julie Perez knew them."

Emma stood in silence, staring at the soap covered dishes resting in the sink.

"Well, there was this old candle store in Truro," Jeff continued. "Julie said the owners were a mother and daughter that made candles in an old barn. I thought she was crazy because the store was owned by this sweet couple that had moved down from Boston. The Hamasakis. Anyway, I completely dismissed what Julie said about the barn. I thought her entire story was crap. I totally forgot about it. Then it turns out that she was abducted. Correction, allegedly abducted, by Sara and tortured by your mom in the barn."

"Where are you going with this, Jeff?"

"I just wonder what would have happened if I'd listened to Julie at the candle store last December. I knew your mom had that old house with the old barn. I just never made the connection, you know? What if I had? Would things have been different?"

"We can't change the past."

"I know. I just keep second guessing myself. I wonder, if I'd paid more attention, could I have connected the dots and pegged Sara as the culprit? I could have prevented her from abducting Julie and torturing her. Allegedly."

Emma clasped her hands nervously.

"Jeff, you're assuming that Julie told the truth. She and that guy were a mile away from the barn when they called the cops and told them what happened. Like you said, there were no survivors."

"So, you're calling them liars?"

"So, you're calling my mom and sister killers?"

Emma folded her arms and glared at Jeff. The house became extremely quiet as both stared at one another, waiting for the other to say something. Jeff stood up and walked over to Emma.

"Em, I didn't mean to ... I mean the evidence ... it ... well ...."

A thump resonated from the other room. Jeff instinctively turned and faced the open doorway. He took two steps forward into the living room and motioned for Emma to stay behind him. Another thump rang out several seconds later. Jeff pointed to the closed door across the room.

"That's the guest bedroom, Jeff. Please, it's a mess."

Jeff waved Emma back, motioning her to stay at a safe distance. He was not in uniform and did not have his gun with him. Jeff stood beside the door and twisted the handle. After a brief pause, he pushed it open.

Emma felt her pulse quicken, and her palms start to clam up with sweat.

"Jeff, I really wish you wouldn't go in there."

Just as Jeff was about to enter the bedroom, a shiny jet-black fur ball came bolting across the floor.

"Christ!" Jeff yelled.

"Gina!" Emma said with relief. The Bombay cat ran to Emma's feet and came to a halt. Emma knelt down and picked her up. "Did I close you in there? I'm so sorry."

Gina thrust her head under Emma's chin and began to purr.

"I forgot you had that stupid cat," Jeff said. He took a glance around the guest bedroom. The bed was made, and the floors were clean. He closed the door.

"Gina's not stupid. Apologize to her."

Emma held her cat up directly in front of Jeff's face. He looked at Emma and rolled his eyes. She swung the cat back and forth and waited for an apology.

"Sorry, cat," Jeff said. He smiled and walked back into the kitchen.

Emma followed, keeping Gina close to her chest.

"Listen, Em, about your mom and sister. I'm sorry. I truly am."

"It's OK, Jeff. You're right. It's been overwhelming for me. At times I just don't know who to believe."

"Who to believe?" Jeff paused to study Emma's face. She did not look up from her cat. "Who's telling you they didn't do it?"

Emma lowered Gina to the floor and used her foot to direct the cat back into the living room. She walked over to the front door and waited for Jeff to join her.

"I just can't believe they would do such horrible things. That's my struggle."

"I understand, Em. Look, I know you had a falling out with your mom and sister back when you were a teenager. You've never told me why. When I ask my mom about it, all she says is that your family disowned you."

Emma nodded silently as she stared at the floor.

"There has to be more," Jeff added.

"There is," Emma said softly. She looked Jeff in the eye. "Maybe someday I can tell you the whole story. Just not today."

Jeff kissed her on the cheek.

"Secrets and mysteries," Jeff said as he stepped out onto the front porch.

"It's a family tradition," Emma added with a grin. She watched Jeff walk away before closing the door and securing the deadbolt.

Emma made her way through the kitchen, into the living room, and back into the guest bedroom. She walked over to the closet and opened the door.

"I thought he'd never leave!" Laura Johnson vented. She pushed her way past her daughter and stormed into the kitchen. "I tried to keep quiet in there, but that closet is a very crowded space. These old bones aren't used to standing for such a long time."

"Sorry. I did my best to get him to leave. Could you hear our conversation?"

Laura poured herself a cup of coffee and took a seat at the kitchen table. She let out a groan as her hips and spine adjusted to the softly padded chair.

"No. Should I have? What did he want?"

"Nothing. He's planning a cookout Memorial Day weekend. He's also concerned. So is Susan."

"About?"

"About me. Needless to say, I've been a bit distracted since, um, well. The fire. And ...."

"My resurrection?" Laura chuckled. "Emma, dear, I know this has been stressful for you. It hasn't been a walk in the park for me either; hiding out here all these weeks. I only go out at night, and that's a rare occurrence. I'm going stir crazy in here. I know it's been a huge disruption to your schedule as well."

Gina made her way back into the kitchen and hopped up onto Laura's lap.

"At least I've had this little one to keep me company while you're working at the hospital. Remember dear, discretion is the key right now."

Emma refreshed her coffee and leaned back against the kitchen counter, keeping a comfortable distance from her mother.

"I'm still not happy with all of this."

"I know you aren't. I know I'm asking a lot. But I've been honest with you. I've told you everything."

"Have you?"

Emma's bagel remained half uneaten. The dough had grown soggy beneath the cream cheese, but Laura could not resist the smell of sesame, onion, and garlic. She took a bite.

"I don't like your tone," Laura said through a mouthful of food. "Why are you still questioning me?"

"I'm just tired of lying to Jeff and Susan."

"You haven't been talking to him about Sara and I, have you?"

"No."

"You need to listen to me, Emma. If you start asking Jeff questions, he's just going to get suspicious."

"I seriously doubt Jeff thinks you are alive."

"We need to be discreet. It will all be over soon."

Laura winced. A seed managed to wedge its way beneath her dentures. She sighed as she removed her top set of teeth.

"Will it?" Emma asked.

Laura kept her focus on cleaning her dentures, regretting her choice of a seeded bagel. After eradicating the offending kernel, she put her teeth back in her mouth.

"It will as long as you stick to the plan."

"But don't you think Jeff could help?"

"No. He may be family, but he's also a police officer. He was too involved with what happened in the past. He's too biased."

"But he's family."

"Yes, but I'm your mother!" Laura pounded her fist on the table. "We've spent weeks going over this. The police, including Jeff, will not believe me. I can't turn myself in. It's my word against those two kids."

Emma lowered her head, unwilling to look at her mother.

"Yes, Sara got out of control," Laura continued with a softer tone. "But it was only in self-defense."

"You told me."

"And how did she die, Emma? How did Sara die?"

Emma raised her head and stared into her mother's ice-blue eyes. She thought her mother looked tired. Old. Emma studied the lines on Laura's face, looking for an inkling of hope and honesty. She didn't know what or who to believe.

"Julie kicked her into the fire," Emma replied.

"And who started the fire?"

"Tom."

Laura stood up and walked over to her daughter. She grasped her chin and pulled her head up to look her in the eye.

"They came to Wellfleet seeking vengeance. I have no idea how they found us. They killed Sara and tried to kill me. I've explained it to you many times."

Laura released her grip and walked over to the box of bagels resting on the counter. She selected a plain one, sliced it open, and dropped it into the toaster.

"What about the attack at the condo?"

"I already told you, Emma. Those kids showed up at the candle store. Sara was there trying to sell our candles. They knocked over the display and destroyed her hard work. You know what a temper she has. She went back to that condo to demand payment. They burned her and threw her out a window."

"And the bodies at Little Pleasant Bay? Two were their friends, and the other two were the store owners."

"I've told you I have no knowledge of that. The store owners were the ones that hired Sara."

"But Jeff said the store owners were reported missing."

"For all I know, Tom and Julie killed them. Maybe they killed their friends as well, and reported them missing as a ruse."

Laura could see the doubt expressed in the cold stare she was getting from her daughter.

"I've tried my best to put the pieces together, Emma. Tom and Julie trashed your sister's candle display at the store. You need to realize your sister put so much love into those candles. It was the first time she'd mastered the family recipe. She blew her stack and followed them back to their condo seeking payment. Instead, they threw her out the second story window. Once the blizzard cleared and they had gone back home we thought it was over. Imagine our surprise when they show up on our property seeking revenge. We were in the barn when they attacked us. I was trying to save Sara when they ran out. I have no idea how they tracked us down. It will be my word against theirs. Two against one. That's why we need to stick with our plan."

Emma's heart was pounding hard in her chest. Her mother had told her this story a dozen times over the past several weeks. The story was always the same. Part of her hoped her mother would somehow stumble and provide a different set of facts. She was consistent every time.

"I watched her die, Emma. They burned your sister to death. Burned her alive!"

Emma closed her eyes as the image of her twin sister on fire seared itself into her mind. She threw her head into her hands and began to sob uncontrollably. Laura embraced her daughter and ran her hands across Emma's back.

"I've been honest with you, Emma. About everything. Even with how your Uncle Carl really died. I never wanted you to know that your father killed him. You've pulled every family secret out of me. I'm trying to make up for lost decades in a very short time. I've tried so hard to regain your trust. To rebuild our bonds."

"I know, Mom. It's just a lot to take in."

Laura released her daughter and brushed her hand across her wet cheek, wiping Emma's tears away.

"It all comes down to trust, Emma. That's a choice only you can make."

TWO

New Connections

The weather was unseasonably warm for the last weekend of May. The sun was blazing against a crystal blue sky, and the temperature had peaked at 88 degrees. Julie grabbed the front of her pink cotton tank top and fanned it back and forth. The wafting created a much needed cooling effect against her skin. The short walk down Hope Street to Tom's condo was a considerably stickier stroll than she expected. It was Friday, just after 1 p.m. She and Tom had taken a half day off from work to get an early start on the holiday weekend.

Julie paused at the entrance to Tom's driveway. She was surprised to see a moving truck parked along the side of his condo. The townhome above Tom's unit sold a few weeks ago; however, the new owner was a mystery to both her and Tom. She approached the moving van with curiosity.

I hope the new owner is hot, Julie thought to herself. *And single. And straight.*

Julie made her way around to the rear of the vehicle. The doors were open, and a loading ramp connected the bed to the ground. There was nobody inside. She made a brief inspection of the pile of boxes before heading over to the front porch. Julie pulled her keyring from her purple leather purse and flung Tom's condo door open. She expected to hear the soft thumping of Max's paws as he ran to greet her, but the dog was nowhere to be found. Instead, she was met with the sound of very loud music.

Julie looked around for either Max or Tom, but the place seemed empty. She walked over to Tom's entertainment center and flicked the receiver off. Max immediately came running down the hallway.

"Max! Max! Max!" Julie said with glee. Max immediately pounced on her. She was not ready and fell back onto the couch. Max jumped up beside her and rolled over onto his back. Julie took the hint and set about rubbing the dog's belly.

"Hey, Jewels," Tom said as he emerged from his bedroom.

"Why the loud music?" Julie asked.

"To drown out the movers. They are making a racket upstairs."

Tom sat on the couch, keeping Max between him and Julie. The dog was thrilled to now have four sets of hands to entertain him.

"Did you meet the new owner yet?"

"Not yet, but I saw four people out there. Two guys, a woman, and some kid."

"Oh shit, you've got a family moving in!"

"I guess."

"Why don't you go outside to meet them?"

"I only got home half an hour ago. Work was insane. I crammed a full day's work into four hours. You know I'm not the most personable when I'm cranky."

"No comment," Julie replied with a smirk.

Max was in heaven with Tom squeezing his two back paws and Julie scratching his stomach.

"Oh, but you are going to love the guys."

"Why is that?"

"They are tall, black, and built. Like your cop boyfriend in Provincetown."

"Trevor is *not* my boyfriend."

"Not yet," Tom said with a chuckle. "They've been unloading a ton of stuff. I don't know which one is the husband, but they are practically twins."

"Trevor twins?"

Julie shoved Max aside and ran to Tom's bedroom. Max followed, leaving Tom alone on the couch. Julie pressed her face up against the window overlooking the driveway. She could hear voices coming from inside the moving truck.

"We're wasting our time," Julie said with frustration. "Come on, Max, let's go meet the neighbors."

Julie marched down the hallway. Once in the living room, she pointed at Tom.

"Time for you to be friendly."

"Suddenly this is about me? You just want to go see the big black muscle guys."

"It's a win-win, Tom."

Julie opened the front door. Max hopped outside and onto the porch and looked around with confusion. Julie's running back and forth excited him, but without his leash, he didn't know what was going on. Max looked up as Tom grabbed his collar. The dog sat and patiently waited for Tom to secure his leash. Julie, Tom, and Max made their way toward the back of the moving van.

Robin Davis emerged from the back corner of the building. The townhouse occupied the top two floors of the three-story converted multi-family house. The main entrance was on the front porch next to Tom's door, but there was also a secondary entrance in the back. She was using that staircase to move her belongings into her new home. Robin smiled when she saw her new neighbors and jogged over to meet them.

"Hi, I'm Robin!"

"Julie."

"Hi, I'm Tom. I live below you."

"Oh, so you're the one making all that loud music."

"Oh, I'm sorry. I'm normally very quiet. I was just trying to drown out the banging."

Robin laughed and shook her head.

"I'm just bustin' on you," Robin said.

"You are gorgeous," Julie said. "Sorry, but you really are."

"That makes you my new best friend," Robin replied.

Robin smiled as she flung her red and white beaded dreadlocks behind her back. Her broad white smile contrasted against her deep auburn skin. At five-foot-nine she stood a few inches taller than Tom and Julie.

"Do you like my hair?" Robin asked.

"I love it!" Julie replied.

"Well, you can borrow it if you want. It clips on."

Julie paused, her mouth agape. Robin giggled at her reaction.

"You don't have many black friends, do you?"

"I don't have many friends period." Julie turned and looked at Tom. "We need to work on that."

Russell and Darryl Taylor descended the loading ramp. Robin's younger brothers made a striking pair. Darryl stood at five-eleven, and his older brother two inches taller. Russell was built like a rugged linebacker. Darryl was slightly leaner. Both were shirtless, showing off their complete lack of body fat.

Robin took note of the lustful look spread across Julie's face. She grinned as her brothers made their way over. Max began to growl as the men approached. Robin took a few steps back.

"Whoa, whoa, whoa!" Robin exclaimed. "Is that dog mean?"

Tom pulled Max closer to his side. The dog continued to emit a deep baritone growl but stayed on alert resting on his back legs.

"No. Max is actually quite sweet. He just doesn't know you yet. He can get protective when a bunch of strangers gets too close. He's the same way with strange dogs. This place has been empty for weeks, and now there are all these people around. He's simply defending his home."

Darryl and Russell slowed their approach and waited for Max to calm down. Tom knelt down next to Max and ran his hand across his ears.

"It's OK, boy," Tom said softly. "Relax. These are friends."

Tara Davis pushed her way past her mother and ran toward Max. The dog stopped growling and stood up to brace himself for the impending assault.

"Doggie!" Tara cried with joy.

"Tara!" Robin yelled.

The precocious six-year-old ignored her mother and threw her arms around the German Shepherd mixed breed dog. Max wagged his tail and began nibbling on Tara's nose. She laughed as she ran her hands across his sides.

"See?" Tom said to Robin. "They're already best friends."

Robin let out a nervous laugh as she watched her daughter fall to the ground and rub Max's ears.

"You damn near scared the shit out of me," Robin said. She twisted around to her brothers standing ten feet away. "Well, what are you waiting for? If my baby can handle that dog, you two shouldn't have much to worry about."

Russell approached first, keeping a concerned eye on Max. The dog continued to play with Tara. Julie was mesmerized by Russell's chiseled face and muscular, sweaty body. The man's shaved head glistened with sweat. Russell's skin tone was slightly darker than Robin's. He looked Julie up and down and smiled.

"This is my brother Russell," Robin said. "He's going to try and charm and smooth talk you. But I'm telling you right now that his wife would not approve of that flirty smile on his face."

Julie frowned as disappointment immediately set in.

"It's always nice to meet a beautiful woman," Russell said.

"See what I mean?" Robin added. "Darryl! Get your ass over here."

Darryl pulled a navy blue T-shirt from the back of his jeans and wiped his body down. He pulled it over his head and dried his hands across his pants. Unlike his brother, Darryl kept his hair buzzed short on the top and shaved on the sides. He extended his hand toward Julie.

"Nice to meet you," Darryl said.

"Likewise," Julie replied. She thought Darryl was just as handsome as his brother but found him much shyer. "So do you have a wife as well?"

"No," Robin answered. "He just got his ass dumped by his loser boyfriend. A breakup that was way overdue, if you ask me."

"Robin!" Darryl said with frustration. "Don't be talking about my business with strangers."

"These aren't strangers," Robin said. "These are my new neighbors."

"Oh I don't live here," Julie said. "Just Tom."

Robin turned and looked Tom up and down.

"But you two are together?"

"No. Tom rarely dates, but when he does they are usually loser men too."

"Jewels!" Tom cried. "That's not true."

"You're right, Tom. Sorry. Tom doesn't date losers. He usually dates nice guys that he smoothers to death until he scares them off."

Tom glared at Julie. Darryl glared at Robin.

"Oh we are going to be great friends," Robin said as she burst out laughing. She walked over to Julie and gave her a hug. Turning to Tom, she said "Darryl loves little white boys. Maybe if you both work through your relationship issues, you two can date."

Tom and Darryl briefly locked eyes before both looking away. Neither was sure what to say.

"As you can see, my sister speaks her mind," Russell said. He turned to look at Darryl, who seemed completely embarrassed by Robin. "We still have half a truck to unpack little brother."

Darryl nodded to Tom and Julie and headed back to the truck.

"It was nice meeting you both," Russell said as he looked Julie up and down one more time.

"The pleasure was all mine," Julie said. She sighed as she watched Russell strut away.

"Mommy, can we get a doggie?" Tara asked.

The girl was still sitting on the ground playing with Max. Tom leaned down and removed the dog's leash giving him more freedom to move around.

"No baby, you know Mommy travels."

"What do you do for work?" Tom asked.

"I do IT. Consulting."

"Oh great," Julie interjected. "Tom is a total geek."

"I work from home," Robin continued. "So, most of the time I'm here. But every now and then I have to go out to customer sites. It's only once or twice a quarter, which is more than enough. Tara is a handful for me to handle on my own."

"You're alone?" Julie asked.

"Separated. My husband is still in the picture but not for long. Irreconcilable differences, as they say. Luckily my mom lives in Johnston so she can take Tara when I travel."

"I do that with Max," Tom said. "He stays with my mom whenever I have to go away."

Robin looked over at her daughter. Tara was thoroughly enjoying playing with Max, tossing a stick for the dog to retrieve. Robin smiled at the instant bond the two had formed.

"Well listen, Tom, if you ever need me to care for Max just ask."

"Really? That's so kind of you."

"She already loves him. And to be honest, at first, he scared me. He's got such a deep growl for his size. But I already feel safer knowing he'll be downstairs."

"He's the best," Julie added. "I may be a cat person, but Max is the ultimate security guard."

"It was great meeting you," Tom said. "But we need to get going. We're heading to my mom's house. I'm going to store Ruby's doors there for the weekend. This heat is crazy. We plan on hitting the beach tomorrow before the weather cools off on Sunday."

"Ruby?"

Tom pointed to his bright red Jeep Wrangler sitting in the driveway behind the moving van.

"He names his vehicles," Julie said as she rolled her eyes.

"Oh, you and Darryl should definitely date. He's a dork too."

THREE

Home Sweet Home

Emma coasted her Subaru Outback Sport across the crushed stone driveway of her family's Victorian home. The sun was low in the sky, and the temperature was 70 degrees. Seeing her home with the barn no longer beside it still felt surreal to Emma. She reminded herself that the property was soon going to be hers. Emma parked her car next to the side porch and glanced around the yard, checking the pathways that led to the pond and ocean.

"It's OK to come out now," Emma said.

Laura Johnson was lying flat across the hatchback's rear seat. She groaned as she pulled herself upright, and tossed aside the blanket that had been covering her during the long drive from Chatham.

"Was it necessary for me to stay hidden?" Laura asked with frustration. "The road here is a rutted mess. I hit my head twice on the door."

"I wasn't sure if anyone would be here when we pulled up. The world thinks you're dead. I can't be driving around with you visible. Aren't you the one that keeps saying we have to be discreet?"

Laura sighed as she looked out the window. The debris from the barn fire had yet to be cleared. Weeks of rain and wind had transformed much of it into clumps of inky black sludge. The 120-gallon white propane tank was all that remained of the structure. It was only the second time Laura had been back to her home since her daughter's death several weeks ago. She couldn't help but feel tears well up as she recalled the image of Sara burning under the melted tallow.

"I suppose you're right, Emma."

Mother and daughter exited the car and made their way to the side of the house. Emma unlocked the door and flicked the light switch along the wall, smiling as the overhead light in the kitchen came on. Laura gave one look back at the mounds of charred wood and ash before joining her daughter inside.

"I brought most of your clothes back earlier," Emma said. "The power and water are back on, so you should be all set. I still need to get the propane tank checked."

"I had it repaired and filled last week."

"How?"

"Bobby."

"Oh."

Emma leaned back against the kitchen counter and folded her arms. Hearing Bobby's name caused her to immediately tense up.

"He's been coming to visit me while you've been at work. He wanted to know what he could do to help."

"I see."

"Don't look so glum, Emma. He saved you some money."

"You know how I feel about him."

Laura walked over to the stove and picked up the tea kettle that was resting on the back burner. She carried the pot to the sink and began rinsing and filling it.

"I know, Emma. You need to move forward. Look, I have a history with Bobby, and ...."

"Oh, I'm well aware of your history with him."

Laura slammed the kettle into the bottom of the sink. She turned to her daughter and pointed her finger at her.

"Drop the attitude, Emma. Bobby has done more for this family – more for me – than you will ever know. I've done my best to keep you two from crossing paths. The past is the past, and we are going to need to work together to pull this off."

"I'm still not completely comfortable with this plan. Ethically and morally I'm committed to healing, not hurting."

"That's exactly why I need you to do this. I'm not asking you to cause any harm. Your actions are meant to heal this family."

"It's not right, Mother.

The tension and angst on Emma's face were palpable. Laura diverted her attention back to the tea kettle. She filled it with hot water and set it back on the stovetop. A smile spread across her face as the propane-fired burner sparked to life.

"It's not right?" Laura asked. "So, you still doubt me? Are you saying you don't believe me?"

"Believe you? About?"

"Everything. Everything that I've told you these past two months. I promise you, Emma, I've been nothing but honest. Those two must be brought to justice. They must pay."

Laura walked past her daughter and opened the door to the pantry. She retrieved two tins. The first contained a mixture of different tea bags. Laura selected two chamomile flavored ones and brought them over to the stove. Emma took a seat at the far end of the table.

"Tom burned that barn down. Julie killed your sister. I can't be any clearer with you, Emma."

The two women remained at opposite ends of the kitchen, studying one another for several moments. Laura turned and retrieved two mugs for their tea. She walked back to the small dented maroon-colored tin resting on the kitchen table, and opened the top, extracting a luggage tag. Laura placed the tag on the table in front of her daughter.

"I know, Mother. I believe you. I just think we need Jeff. If you are telling the truth ...."

"If? So you don't believe me. After all these weeks of your endless questions, you still have doubts?"

The kettle on the stove began to whistle. Laura shook her

head in frustration and shot Emma a look of disappointment before heading over to the stove. Emma stood up and followed her mother.

"That's not what I meant," Emma said. She put a reassuring hand on her mother's shoulder. "Of course I believe you. Doesn't it make sense to have the police involved? Or at least consult a lawyer on how to handle it?"

Laura remained calm despite the last minute challenges her daughter was making. She set about filling their cups with boiling water from the kettle.

"Emma, dear, we've discussed this. It's my word against theirs. Two against one. I guarantee you they have worked out a fake story to protect themselves. There is no way for me to win. The minute I show my face to the world, I'll be arrested. We must get a confession from Julie. One that we can take to the police so that I can clear my name. That's our first order of business. Bobby and I will handle everything."

"That's the part that bothers me. How will you make Julie confess? I don't think a forced confession is admissible. See, this is why I think we should call Jeff."

"No!" Laura slammed her fist against the kitchen counter. She unclenched her hand and strained to force a smile across her face. "All I want to do is get Julie to admit what happened. I promise you I will be lenient with her. If she understands I'm not planning to charge her with murder, she should agree to confess. We'll come to a compromise. She clears my name. I go easy on her."

"I don't like it, Mother."

"I think your issue is with Bobby being involved. I know you don't like Bobby. And I know *why* you don't like him. You have my word that he will not harm her. Bobby is going to set up a hidden camera. I am going to confront her and get her to admit what really happened at the candle store. And the condo. And what she did in the barn. All you have to do is bring her to me."

Laura opened the fridge and frowned at seeing so many empty shelves. She closed the door and turned to face her daughter. Emma was leaning against the counter with her hands shoved deep into her pockets, and a frown still spread across her face. Laura crossed the kitchen and took Emma by her wrists, sliding her hands into her own.

"I know I'm asking a lot of you," Laura said. "Sara would do this, no questions asked. It's obvious that you are not Sara. This choice can't be an easy one. But I need you to trust me on this, Emma. Please. I can't stay in hiding forever. And I can't go to prison. We need this confession. It's the only way."

Emma stared into her mother's cold blue eyes. She wasn't sure who to believe. Who to trust. She just knew she felt trapped. Emma kissed her mother on the cheek and walked over to the kitchen table. She picked up the luggage tag with Tom Leblanc's address on it and shoved it into her pocket.

"That's my girl," Laura said with pride. "Thank you for doing this for me."

"I'm doing it for Sara just as much as for you."

Emma glanced at her phone and sighed.

"It's after three. I have no idea how bad holiday traffic is going to be this weekend. I should get going."

"Did you want to take your tea with you?"

"No thank you."

Laura walked her daughter to the side door. Emma opened it, and her mother grabbed her by the elbow.

"Remember to run silent, Emma. No calls or texting. And be discreet. We can't have any loose ends."

***

The knock at the kitchen door startled Laura. She looked up from the kitchen table to see Bobby Mason staring through the window. He smiled and waved to her. Time may have aged him, but to Laura, Bobby was still the same broad-shouldered, chiseled, handsome man she'd fallen in love with decades ago, exuding strength and masculinity. Laura quickly made her way to the door and opened it.

"Hello, Angel," Bobby said as he stepped into the kitchen.

Laura fell into his arms and buried her face in his chest. Zeus pushed his way between them and jumped up onto Laura. She kept one arm around Bobby and the other around her dog.

"It's so good to see you," Laura said as she released them both. "I can't thank you enough for taking care of my Zeus these past two months."

Bobby kissed Laura on the top of her head, closed and locked the door, and took a seat at the kitchen table. Zeus walked over to his side and sat next to him.

"He's been a faithful guard dog. It's been great having him around my house. He's been no trouble at all."

"Can I make you some tea?"

"No, I'm good. Thank you. But you need to get some blinds or curtains in these kitchen windows, Laura. You need to keep a low profile this weekend."

"You're right. I'm sorry. I should stay in the living room with the drapes closed. At least until this is over."

"What's going on with Emma?"

Laura sat next to Bobby and took a sip of her tea.

"She's on her way. She left about half an hour ago."

"Is she on board? Can we trust her?"

Laura drummed her fingers against her mug, sighing as she shook her head in confusion.

"Honestly, Bobby, I don't know. I'm pretty sure she trusts me now. I've spent the past two months trying to earn her forgiveness. That doesn't come easy. Especially in this family."

"I know, Laura. How many years did you keep me away?"

Laura slid her chair next to Bobby's and leaned her head on his shoulder.

"Too many. I'm glad you're here now."

"I told you I would always be here for you. I'm just not on board with how you are using Emma. I don't think we can trust her. I should be the one going. It's a risk using her."

"It's a bigger risk losing you. Trust me. She'll do what I want her to do. What *we* need her to do. I've convinced her that Tom and Julie are to blame for killing Sara. That loss and pain will consume her. Emma has no doubt they are evil. She's just not sure that forcing a confession is the right approach."

"Because it's not."

"We both know that. Look, this isn't easy for me. I'm lying to Emma. To my own daughter. But it's the only way to earn her trust and execute our plan."

"I understand." Bobby slid his chair directly against Laura's and put his arm around her. "This will all work out in the end, Angel. When the dust settles this weekend, you and I will be long gone. We will finally be together."

"So you've made the arrangements for our escape?"

"It's done. Cindy will be waiting for us."

Laura kissed Bobby on the cheek and allowed herself to collapse in his embrace.

"Then all we need is for Emma to do her part. I think it's best for you to continue to keep your distance from her as much as you can. I may have earned her trust, but she will never trust you. Or forgive you."

FOUR

The Drifter

1988 Monday 20-Jun 5:30 p.m.

Fred Johnson looked over at the young stranger in the passenger's seat sitting beside him. He could see how nervous the man was. Fred's Cherokee bobbed and shuddered as they made their way down the beaten dirt road that led to his house.

"Relax, Eddie," Fred said. "Everything is going to work out."

Eddie Ward managed a worried smile as he studied his dirt-encrusted fingernails. He picked at the small clumps of dead foliage caked to the tattered sections of his denim jeans. Staring out the window, he began to second guess his recent decision to get into the SUV.

"I really appreciate your offer, Mr. Johnson," Eddie said.

"Fred. Call me Fred."

"But I have no money. There's really no way I can repay you for your help."

Fred hauled the Jeep down to a stop and waited for Eddie to look at him.

"How old are you?" Fred asked.

"I turned twenty-three last month."

"And how long have you been homeless?"

Eddie paused as he tried to recount the rollercoaster of events that had transpired since the beginning of the year. He let out a sigh as some of the darker moments forced their way into his mind. He cleared his throat before speaking.

"Like I told you at the park, I lost my job in Dennis back in April. My girlfriend kicked me out shortly after that. I drifted around for a few weeks trying to find a job, but nobody would hire me. So, I started working my way east."

"And you've got skills?"

"I do," Eddie said with pride. "My dad was a master carpenter. I learned everything I know from him. I'm handy with electrical and plumbing, too. I can pretty much do it all."

Fred smiled as he lifted his foot off the brake pedal. The SUV began to crawl its way forward.

"We'll see about that."

Fred glanced over at Eddie and studied the man's tattered black and blue flannel shirt. He tried to imagine what it would be like to have no place to live, wandering from town to town.

"I'm going to do my best to get you a job with the state park, Eddie. I've been working maintenance with them for over a decade. It's good pay and benefits. We may be able to hire you for help with the rest of the season. Just part-time. But if it works out, it could lead to something permanent."

Eddie fought to suppress the tears he felt welling up inside. He turned his attention to the dense vegetation outside the Jeep's window.

"I really don't know what to say."

"Don't thank me yet. It's not a done deal."

"Why are you doing this?" Eddie asked as he looked over at Fred. "You don't know me. How can you even trust me?"

"Back at the park, you told me you have a record."

"It was minor. Honest. I promise I won't steal from you."

"That wasn't my point, Eddie. You told me you've had issues getting work because you have a record."

"Yes, sir."

"We have more in common than you know. Everyone

deserves a second chance. Someone gave me a break once. Time for me to repay that kindness. Besides, I have a good feeling about you, Eddie. But don't expect this to be all fun and games this weekend. I plan to put you to work. I need you to prove to me that you deserve that job."

"I won't disappoint you."

The Cherokee cleared the shrubs lining the narrow path, the roadway beneath it turning from dirt to crushed stone. Eddie's jaw dropped upon setting eyes on the grand Victorian home.

"This house is incredible," Eddie said with awe. "How much money does the state pay?"

Fred let out a hearty laugh as he parked the Jeep in front of the barn.

"This was my dad's house. I inherited it. Trust me, I wouldn't be able to afford to buy a place like this on my salary. But I sure as hell can maintain it. Come on inside."

Eddie popped his door open and stepped out into the cool 60 degree evening air. The sun would not set for a few hours. The breeze coming in from the ocean filled the air with the scent of salt and sand. Fred opened the back hatch and retrieved the young man's duffle bag. Eddie smiled as he took it from Fred and tossed it over his shoulder.

"This really is too kind of you," Eddie said. "I promise to repay you. Somehow. And you can give me anything to repair or fix, and I will do it. Anything. Just name it."

"I'm not the one you need to make happy, Eddie."

The kitchen door opened and Laura Johnson stepped out onto the porch. She ran her messy hands across her white apron, covering it with tomato sauce. The presence of the young man holding the giant bag sent a frown across her face.

"That woman right there is going to be your real test.

Laura descended the porch steps with trepidation, adjusting her blond hair as she made her way across the yard. Fred took a few steps forward to greet her. She kissed him gently on the cheek, all the while keeping her gaze fixed on the young disheveled looking man.

"You didn't tell me we were having guests," Laura said.

"It was sort of last minute," Fred replied. "Laura, this is Eddie Ward. Eddie, this is my wife, Laura."

Eddie lowered his bag to the ground and stepped forward, extending his arm to greet her. Laura cautiously raised her arm and shook hands with him. Eddie couldn't help but notice the look of disapproval on her face. His smile quickly faded. Fred immediately noticed the impending friction.

"Eddie is going to be staying with us for a while," Fred said.

"What?" Laura asked with surprise.

"Just until I can get him a job," Fred continued.

Laura looked Eddie up and down. Her frown turned into a glare as she took in his torn clothes and unkempt hair.

"I don't understand," Laura said. She turned to Eddie. "Who are you? Where are you from?"

Eddie shoved his hands into his pockets and looked down at the ground. He eyed his bag and considered picking it up and heading back down the road. Fred immediately positioned himself between Eddie and Laura.

"Can I have a word with you?" Fred asked Laura. "In private, please."

Laura shot Eddie one more look of displeasure as Fred took her by the elbow and led her into the barn. He kept the door open but walked far enough inside so that Eddie would not be able to hear their conversation.

"What's this all about?" Laura asked.

"I found him at the park."

"Found him? Like a lost dog?"

"I was doing maintenance on a pavilion at the National Seashore. I caught him stealing some candy bars from a food cart. He's homeless, Laura. But he's a good kid."

"How can you say that? You just met him."

"I'm trusting my gut."

Laura took a few steps away from Fred so she could see back out into the driveway. Eddie was standing between his bag and the Cherokee, staring at his feet.

"Why, Fred? You said it yourself, he's a thief."

"He was only stealing to eat. He needs help, Laura. He's had some bad luck. Trouble with the law."

"So, he's a criminal too?"

"Relax. It's nothing like that. Don't forget, I've had my share of issues with the law. He's a good kid. He deserves a fair shot. I told him he could stay here until I can get him a job working with me."

"He's a bum, Fred. Look at him. He stinks, too."

"I know. He's been drifting around since leaving Dennis. All he needs is a chance. We've had some rough times in our past, Laura. Can we try to do some good for a change?"

Laura sighed with frustration. She knew she would not be able to change her husband's mind.

"Fine. But I don't want him staying in the house. He's going to have to earn my trust."

"Understood. I told Eddie he needs to prove himself. I'm going to keep him busy doing some repairs around here for me. At least until I can get him a job. My boss is back from vacation next Monday. He won't be here for more than a week. Two the latest."

"He can sleep out here in the barn. Up in the loft. I'll get him blankets and pillows."

"Thank you for understanding."

"Dinner is ready. I'll put a plate out for him. But take him upstairs and clean him up first. I don't want his stench ruining our meal."

***

Eddie smiled as he dusted the golden hay off the sides of his denim jeans. Technically they were Fred's jeans. Everything he was currently wearing belonged to Fred. Laura had given him some of Fred's old clothes to wear last night. The jeans were a bit baggy, but he was more than happy to have clean smelling clothes. Last night's hot shower was the first he'd taken in three weeks.

"How are you making out up there?" Laura called out from below.

"All set," Eddie replied. He poked his head over the edge of the loft. "I fixed the lantern. The valve assembly was loose. But they really should be replaced. I can see these rusting out over time. It's a fire hazard waiting to happen."

"Thanks, I'll be sure to let my husband know when he gets home from work tonight. Are you hungry?"

Laura watched as Eddie rapidly descended the ladder that led to the loft. She felt her body tense up as his hands and feet skipped past the rungs. Even without a pitchfork to stop his progress, Laura still felt a cold shudder run through her body. She took a few steps forward to meet him as he reached the floor.

"Here, try a bite," Laura said as she handed Eddie a sandwich.

Eddie grabbed the sandwich and took a bite. He'd been running around the Johnson property for the past four hours and had worked up quite the appetite. As Eddie chewed the sandwich, he recognized a flavor and texture that he knew to avoid eating. His reflexes kicked in, causing him to spit the food out, catching it in his hands.

"I'm so sorry," Eddie said.

Laura recoiled at his reaction. She was holding the other half of the sandwich she had prepared for him and raised it to her nose. She sniffed the edges. It smelled wonderful to her – tomato, ham, goat cheese, and lettuce.

"I don't understand," Laura said. "I just made this."

"It's the goat cheese. Dairy makes me extremely sick."

Laura snatched the half-eaten sandwich back and shook her head in disappointment.

"It's disrespectful to be so inconsiderate. You're a guest here. I would think you'd be more appreciative."

"I meant no disrespect. Honestly. I'm sorry."

The clatter of an ill-tuned engine broke the tension in the barn. Laura twisted around and looked out the oversized arch doorway to see Bobby Mason's Ford F-150 pull into the driveway. The frustration and disappointment she felt toward Eddie quickly vanished. She turned and made her way to the exit.

Bobby smiled at the sight of Laura emerging from the barn. Fred was at work, meaning he would have some private time with her. He was about to embrace her when he noticed the young man walking behind her.

"Hi," Laura said as she leaned forward and kissed Bobby on the cheek. He did not return the kiss. "Bobby, this is Eddie."

Eddie approached Bobby somewhat nervously and extended his hand. Bobby gave him a vigorous handshake as he looked the lean man up and down.

"Nice to meet you," Eddie said.

"Fred found him at work," Laura said.

"Found him?" Bobby asked with confusion.

"He's going to be staying with us for a few days until he gets back on his feet. Fred's going to try and get him a job at the state park. He's pretty handy. He fixed that broken lantern in the loft. Earlier I had him working out on the dock at the pond, replacing some old boards."

"I see," Bobby said.

Eddie did not like the look of resentment he was getting from Bobby. He also felt his presence was not wanted. Bobby obviously did not like him.

Laura sensed the jealousy bubbling up in Bobby and let out a slight chuckle. She found it amusing that Bobby might feel threatened by this much younger man. Laura looked down at the plate with the half-eaten sandwich in it and quickly remembered the conversation she and Eddie were having before Bobby arrived. Her smile faded.

"Eddie," Laura said. "Since my food isn't to your liking do you mind running an errand for me?"

"The sandwich was fine. Like I said, I just can't eat the cheese. My sister is just like me. It's a family thing. If you can just take the cheese off? Or I can make one without the cheese."

"So your sister is just as disrespectful?"

"No, ma'am. That's not what I meant."

Eddie's face became flustered. He felt like there was no way to please her.

Laura reached into her pocket and pulled out a slip of paper along with a twenty dollar bill. She gave both to Eddie.

"I need you to go to the market for me. I put this list together for you earlier this morning. If you have enough left over you can buy yourself a cheese-free sandwich while there."

Eddie glanced at the list and the money.

"Well go on," Laura said. "You know where the market is, don't you?"

"I do."

"I know it's a few miles away. Is that too far for you to walk?"

"Not at all."

"And bring me a receipt. I know how you don't like to pay for your food."

"Sure thing, Mrs. Johnson."

Eddie shot Bobby a quick glance before heading toward the driveway. He shoved the list and money in his pocket as he walked across the crushed stone and through the dense shrubs that lined the entrance to the dirt road.

"Where are the girls?" Bobby asked Laura.

"They took their bikes over to my sister's house. They won't be back until after seven."

Once Bobby was sure the young man was out of sight he turned to Laura, picked her up, and kissed her passionately. Laura struggled to not drop the plate as she held onto Bobby with one arm. He slowly lowered her to the ground. She buried her face in his chest and laughed.

"What's so funny?"

"Green isn't a good color on you."

Bobby glanced down at the denim jeans and white T-shirt he was wearing.

"Green?"

"Envy," Laura said with a grin. She took Bobby by the hand and led him into the barn, dropping the plate onto one of the tables. "I've never seen you so jealous before."

"Jealous? Of that skinny kid?"

"He's quite handsome. You should have seen him yesterday. He was a filthy mess. Long scraggly beard. He cleans up nicely."

"Oh does he?"

Bobby pushed Laura up against the ladder. She slid her hands under his T-shirt and pushed her hands against his chest.

"You know I'm teasing," Laura continued. "You have nothing to worry about."

"Good."

Bobby removed his T-shirt. Laura pressed her nose into his chest, inhaled his musky scent, and groaned.

"Should we go up to the loft, Angel?"

"No. Eddie is staying up there."

"You put him in the loft?" Bobby chuckled as he started to unbutton Laura's blouse. "Your hospitality is questionable."

"Where should we make love, Bobby?"

Bobby bent down, slid his arms around Laura's waist, and lifted her into the air. He felt her head fall over his shoulder.

"How about my truck?" Bobby smiled an immoral grin as he imagined screwing Laura in the bed of his truck. Or perhaps on the passenger's seat. They had yet to have sex in his truck. It would be a first. "Well? Why so quiet?"

Bobby lowered Laura to the ground. As he did, he turned to face the entrance to the barn. There, standing in total shock, was Eddie. Several seconds passed before anyone spoke.

"I, uh, started to go through your list and realized I couldn't make out your handwriting," Eddie said. His voice shook with fear. "I'm ... I'm sorry. I can just go."

Eddie quickly spun around and exited the barn.

"Stop!" Laura yelled.

Bobby marched toward the front door, with Laura staying close behind him. Eddie could hear their footsteps grinding against the crushed stone driveway. He stopped and closed his eyes, fearing the worst.

"I won't say anything," Eddie said. "I swear!"

Just as Bobby reached for Eddie's shoulder, Laura grabbed Bobby by the elbow and yanked him back. She pushed Bobby aside and took hold of the young man. Eddie opened his eyes as Laura spun him around.

"You saw nothing," Laura growled. "Nothing! Do you hear me?"

"Yes, ma'am. I didn't see a thing."

"All it takes is one phone call to the police."

"No! Please. I'm not looking for trouble. Your business is

your business. It's got nothing to do with me."

Laura stepped within a few inches of Eddie and looked him dead in the eyes. Her initial panic at seeing him standing in the doorway subsided. She could see he was in a state of confusion and fear.

"Good. Then keep your mouth shut. If you mention this to my husband you will pay dearly. Am I clear?"

"Yes, ma'am."

Laura snatched the list from Eddie's hand and scanned the items on it. She knew her penmanship was far from perfect, but to her, it was an easy list to read.

"Tuna fish. Tomato sauce. Tomato paste. Baked beans. A loaf of French bread. What part couldn't you understand?"

"There is one more at the very end.'"

Laura looked at the list one more time and sighed.

"It says 'receipt.' It was to remind you to get one."

Laura handed the list back to Eddie. He slid it into his pocket and looked down at the ground.

"Take your time," Laura added. "Give us an hour."

"Yes, ma'am."

Laura headed back toward the barn as Eddie turned to go back to the dirt road. Bobby grabbed Eddie by the elbow and spun him around. Eddie felt his heart race as the broad-shouldered shirtless man glared down at him.

"Look at me," Bobby whispered. He waited until the young man locked eyes with him. Bobby stepped closer. "You seem like a good kid. I can tell you want to do the right thing. See that barn over my shoulder? The one you're staying in? It's got a long history. A dark history filled with death. Accidents happen. You fuck this up, and you will join that list. Am I clear?"

"Yes, sir."

FIVE

Ruby

Tom eased his foot off the gas pedal as he turned Ruby into his mother's driveway. Max stood up on all fours and stuck his head out through the Wrangler's roll-bar. The dog began to whimper and wag his tail in excitement.

The Leblanc family home was a traditional two-story Cape-style house. Located in Warwick, RI, the property was only a few blocks from Greenwich Bay. With three bedrooms and two and a half baths, the residence was much more space than his mother required. The 60-year-old woman cherished her home and was not yet ready to downsize or move away.

The home's exterior wood shingles were white, as was the trim. Eight perfectly manicured rhododendrons lined the front of the house, their pink flowers beautifully complimenting the maroon-painted front door. A white picket fence encircled the back yard.

"Sit, Max," Tom commanded.

Max ignored his master and began to bark.

"You've got him so well trained," Julie said with a chuckle.

Tom grinned as he parked his Wrangler in front of the garage. Julie opened the passenger door and walked around to the tailgate. Once she opened it, Max jumped out and ran to a towering maple tree sitting several yards away. The front door of the house swung open. Tom's mother stepped out onto the covered brick entryway.

"Max, don't pee on my daisies!" Mrs. Leblanc yelled out from the doorway.

"Hi, Mom," Tom said as he exited his Jeep.

Dorothy Leblanc frowned as she made her way along the winding weathered brick path that led to the driveway. She shot Max a look of disappointment before turning her attention to her son.

"Relax, Mom," Tom said. "It's good fertilizer for the flowers."

Mrs. Leblanc gave her son a kiss.

"I wish you called and told me you were coming. I would have made dinner."

"We already have plans for tonight. We stopped in so I could take Ruby's doors off and put them in your garage."

Mrs. Leblanc's eyes wandered across the jagged gouge running across the Jeep's driver's door.

"When are you getting that fixed? You never told me how it got like that."

Tom and Julie nervously looked at one another.

"Didn't I?" Tom replied. "I came out of the grocery store and found it that way."

"I told you never to park close to other cars. Why don't you listen to me?"

"Mom, I just want to leave my doors here. Like I always do. I can put them back on Monday after the cookout. It's just for the weekend."

"Where are you going with the doors off? Not the beach, I hope. You know I don't like you driving on the highway with those things off."

Tom looked over at Julie for help. She grinned and walked over to join the pair.

"No worries," Julie said. "We're taking my car tomorrow. We only go around with the doors off for bopping around town."

"Oh, that's good. I would hate for you two to have an accident. Why you bought such a dangerous vehicle is simply beyond my comprehension."

Their conversation was interrupted by Max. The dog wedged his way between everyone, burying his snout under Dorothy's hand. She allowed a smile to replace her frown and bent down to greet Max, giving the dog a brisk neck massage. As she did, she noticed something new hanging from his collar. It was black and shaped like a key fob for a car.

"Tom, what's this?" Dorothy asked.

"Oh, that's his GPS tracker."

"You put a tracker on your dog?" Julie asked as she knelt to inspect the device. Max's tail spun in circles due to all the attention he was suddenly receiving.

"I don't understand," Dorothy said with confusion.

"Remember last month when you thought Max had run away?" Tom said. "You'd left the gate open, and he got out."

"I remember," Dorothy replied.

"Well, this is a tracker. If he ever runs off again, I can find him on my phone."

"Is that the same way you track your tablet?" Julie asked.

"Yes and no. It's the same concept. It's a different app, but yes I can pull up a map and find him."

"Are you doing this because of me?" Dorothy asked. "You had to buy this PGS thing because I lost him? How much was it? I will pay you for it since it's my fault."

Tom sighed, disappointed that his mother changed the conversation to be about her. Julie had seen this happen many times and did her best to suppress a smile at the power struggle that was unfolding before her.

"Not at all, Mom. I use it at my place too. He's run off down the street a few times without me. Better to be safe than sorry. And it's GPS, not PGS."

Julie could see Dorothy did not believe Tom. An argument was about to ensue.

"Do they sell them in different colors?" Julie asked. "Maybe we could get a nice floral one for your mom?"

As Julie started to laugh at her attempt to defuse the situation she quickly realized nobody else was laughing. Tom's mother looked appalled.

"What am I, a dog?" Dorothy asked. "I don't need to be

tracked. I'm not so old that I am going to wander off and not know how to find my way home. My mind is quite sharp."

"I was only joking," Julie replied. "Tom already tracks your phone, so you don't need what Max has. It wouldn't make sense for ...."

"What do you mean he tracks my phone?"

Julie looked over at Tom. He was shaking his head in despair.

"I don't track your phone, Mom. Jewels is trying to be funny again. Isn't that right, Jewels?"

"Obviously my comedic timing is completely failing me today."

Julie could see the angst and frustration cascading across Tom's face, and realized she needed to pivot the conversation if she was going to prevent things from getting any worse. She placed her hand on Mrs. Leblanc's shoulder.

"Tom told me you started a garden this year?"

The frown on Dorothy's face dissipated, soon replaced by a smile. She turned to Julie and grabbed her other hand.

"Yes. It's become a passion of mine. I have a wonderful garden growing out back. Do you like to cook?"

"My skills in the kitchen would shock you."

Tom burst out laughing at Julie's response. Dorothy ignored her son.

"Would you like to see it?"

"I'd love to," Julie replied.

Dorothy led Julie toward the gate between the house and detached garage. Max ran past them, excited to explore the back yard. As they made their way, Julie turned and looked back at Tom and mouthed "you're welcome" to him. Tom blew her a kiss and quickly set about getting his toolset out to remove Ruby's doors.

***

Mrs. Leblanc's garden was much larger than Julie expected it to be. Tom had helped his mother with the heavy lifting earlier in the season. Together they had carved out a ten-foot by eight-foot section behind her garage. It was the ideal spot due to the amount of full sun it would receive. Dorothy planned to try different vegetables each season. During this inaugural year, she was attempting to grow tomatoes, spinach, and peppers.

"This is really beautiful," Julie said as she walked along the garden's edge.

The dark green leaves of the spinach plants took up a third of the area. They were almost mature. The pepper and tomato plants were short, thin green stalks, just starting to grow.

"I couldn't have done it without Tom," Dorothy said. "He dug this out for me and got the soil prepped. Unfortunately, most of this won't be ready for the cookout. I might be able to get some spinach tomorrow, but the tomatoes and peppers won't be ready until September."

"It's quite lovely."

"It keeps me busy."

Julie couldn't help but notice how perfectly aligned and spaced the rows of vegetables were. She grinned as she wondered whether Tom or his mother had been the one to insist on the near perfect spacing of each plant.

"Do you like herbs?" Dorothy asked.

"Herbs?"

Mrs. Leblanc pointed to six gallon-sized woven baskets hanging along the back wall of the garage. Each was overflowing with a different herb.

"I've got sage, parsley, oregano, two kinds of basil, and rosemary. Do you like rosemary?"

Max trotted up next to Dorothy and began to sniff along the edge of the wire fencing. The green metal boundary was only a foot high. The dog stuck his head over the top edge and glanced into the garden.

"Max, don't you even think about jumping in there!" Dorothy commanded.

Max let out a whimper as he flared his nostrils, taking in the earthy garden scents. His fascination with the plants ended with the appearance of a squirrel at the back corner of the yard. The dog bounded off across the grass, growling as he approached his prey.

"I'm sure he won't harm the garden," Julie said. "He's a sweetheart."

Dorothy watched Max as he chased the squirrel up a red oak tree. She let out a laugh as he attempted to climb the bark.

"I know he is. Don't tell Tom, but I feel so much safer whenever Max is here. I love caring for him."

"Do you feel unsafe? I thought this was a pretty safe neighborhood."

"It is. Now. Max is so protective. Any vehicle that enters the driveway he is at the window barking. He's got a big bark for his size."

"He does."

Dorothy stepped over the fencing and knelt to inspect one of the spinach plants. She was hoping to make a spinach bread for the Memorial Day cookout she was hosting in two days. Four plants looked hearty enough for her to harvest. Dorothy plucked a few leaves from the plant and held them to her nose. She stood up and joined Julie on the other side of the wire fence.

"Julie, we haven't had any time alone since you returned from Cape Cod several weeks ago."

"I know. It's all flown by so quickly since then."

"I have to ask. Why did you lie to me? About your plans."

"Lie? I didn't lie."

Max was still circling the tree at the back of the yard. Julie began to head there to meet him. Dorothy grabbed her by her forearm, halting her progress.

"You told me you were going to Hyannis. Instead, you went to Eastham. You went chasing after those killers, didn't you?"

Julie took a deep breath as she tried to compose herself before replying. She studied Dorothy's face and could see the anguish and anger spread across it.

"I'm sorry," Julie said. "Truly, I am. I didn't lie about taking Tom away for his birthday. I only lied about the city."

"Why? Why would you lie to me?"

"Because I knew if I told you where we were going, you would freak out. Just like you are now."

"Well, I'm sorry, but I told you how obsessive my son could be. He wouldn't let go of his father's murder. I warned you he would try to track down the killers. Didn't I?"

"You did, but ...."

"But what? Why didn't you listen to me?"

Julie's concern about Mrs. Leblanc's feelings began to fade away. She suddenly felt angry and defensive with Tom's mother.

"Why are you dumping this on me? You're as bad as your son."

"Excuse me?"

Dorothy finally released her grip from Julie's arm and took a few small steps backward.

"You were adamant I listen to you and not take Tom out to the Cape. Tom was adamant that I listen to him, insisting we would not run into any danger while there. The both of you are so fu ... so controlling."

"I was only trying to do what I thought was best for my son."

Dorothy lowered her head and looked away. Julie realized she might have gone too far.

"The weekend did not go as planned," Julie said softly. "I'm sorry I wasn't completely honest with you. I never expected us to run into trouble while out there. That's not why we went. Trust me, if I could change the past, I would. I was there too, you know. Or did you forget what I went through?"

"You tell me," Dorothy replied. She turned and faced Julie. "My son has been less than forthcoming about what happened out there. I called that police officer in Provincetown, and all he did was direct me to Tom."

"I have no idea what Tom told you. And, honestly, I'm not about to get in the middle of the two of you. Let's just say I'm lucky to be alive."

"I'm sorry." Dorothy reached out and put her hand on Julie's shoulder. "He told me about the fire and that you were injured. Are you doing OK?"

Julie was relieved the tension between them was subsiding. At the same time, she felt slightly trapped. Given how secretive Tom was, Julie was never sure what Tom shared with his mother.

Does she even know I, was almost killed? Julie wondered.

"I'm doing OK. Better. I hate to say it but, they're dead, right? That fire ended everything. I feel like it's finally all behind us. You knew about those nightmares I was having after we got back in December?"

"Yes, I remember Tom telling me."

"I haven't had any since we returned home last month."

"I'm glad to hear that, Julie." Dorothy reached out and took Julie by the hands. "I'm sorry I yelled. It's just that my Thomas can be so ... so obsessive."

"Just a bit."

The two women began to laugh, releasing some much-needed tension.

"He obsessed so much about his father's murder. I hope he's finally able to let go of what happened out on Cape Cod."

"I can tell you he has. He never brings it up anymore."

"Really? Are you being honest this time, Julie?"

"I am. Trust me. His obsession with everything in Eastham shocked me. It was a side of him I'd never seen before. At least not to that extreme. He simply wouldn't let it go. I won't let it happen again. I've learned my lesson."

"Good. Tom means well, you know?"

"I do."

"I don't know where he gets it from."

"Gets what?"

"Being so obsessive."

Julie chuckled, but her laugh quickly subsided as she realized that Mrs. Leblanc was serious.

***

Julie banged her sneakers against the edge of the porch step, trying to release the dirt packed in the soles. Her shoes were caked in soil from spending so much time in the garden.

"Can you please remove those before going in?" Dorothy called out from the backyard. Max was by her side, enjoying an ear massage.

"Sure thing," Julie replied. She quickly kicked her shoes off, opened the back door, stepped into the kitchen, and closed the door behind her. "There you are!"

Tom was sitting at a barstool at the island in the center of the kitchen. The island was six-by-nine feet, taking up a large portion of the middle of the room. A beautiful flower bouquet sat in the center of the countertop. Tom's back faced the rear door. His attention was focused entirely on his tablet.

"I was wondering where you disappeared to," Julie said. "I went out front to see if I could help you with the doors, but they were already off."

"I've got that down to a science."

"Your mom was getting deep into the art of maintaining a successful garden. She kept shoving the rosemary in my face. Rosemary! If she only knew. I told her I had to pee. What are you doing?"

Tom closed his tablet as Julie approached.

"Nothing. I was just cooling off and enjoying the AC in here."

Julie locked eyes with Tom. His crossed arms and painfully fake smile alarmed her.

"Bullshit. Show me."

Tom sighed as he flipped the lid open on his tablet. He spun it around so Julie could see the browser page he was reading.

"What is this?" Julie asked as she leaned forward to study the screen. "What am I reading? Is this ... Oh my God! Tom! Why are you reading this obituary?"

The tablet screen showed an obituary for Sara Johnson, detailing her burial last month.

"Remember the cousin? The one in Eastham?"

"What the fuck, Tom? I swear! I was just telling your mother how you have finally let go and stopped obsessing about what happened out on the Cape. That conversation was literally ten minutes ago. Ten minutes! And here you are reading up on the people that died. Why?"

"Mrs. Closed. Sara. The one that died in the fire. She has a twin, Jewels. Her name is Emma, and ...."

"No, Tom. No. Cut the fucking cord."

"I'm not obsessing, Jewels. I was just ...."

"Just what? Not obsessing like you didn't obsess when we were in Eastham? Every time you said we were done you would say 'but just this one more thing,' and it would go on and on and on. Is this what it was like after your dad was killed? Is this the obsession your mom worries about?"

"It's not the same, Jewels. Honest."

Julie slammed the tablet's cover closed.

"Closure, Tom. Literal closure. Let. It. Go."

Julie walked around to the other side of the island. She rummaged through a few cabinets before finally finding a drinking glass. She filled it from the faucet and chugged the water down. Julie spun back to face Tom, relieved to see the tablet was still closed.

"I'm sorry I snapped," Julie said. "We just need to move on. Correction, you do."

"I'm an obsessive guy," Tom replied. "No idea where I get it from."

"Are you kidding me?"

Tom burst out laughing.

"Of course I'm kidding you! Have you met my mother?"

Julie shook her head and laughed.

"She has no clue," Julie said. "I seriously think she has no clue how bad she is."

"She just considers herself a perfectionist."

"She's a control freak. Just like you."

"Thanks, Jewels."

Julie turned back to the sink to get more water. She couldn't help but notice how heavy the glass was. It was a crystal goblet with faceted edges along the bottom. The cabinet was filled with similar glasses, in multiple sizes.

"Your mom may be a control freak, but she does have impeccable taste. The garden out back is amazing, and this kitchen is stunning. The whole house is. Every room is not only immaculate but also beautifully put together."

"Her attention to detail is unmatched. I think it comes with being a control freak."

As Julie's eyes wandered around the room a sense of

dread washed over her.

"Tom, is this .... Is this your childhood home?"

"Yes. I've told you that before. Why?"

"That means that this ... this kitchen. Your ... your dad."

"Oh," Tom said solemnly. "Yeah. Yeah. I forgot my mom told you the details. This room is where my dad was murdered."

"And you saw it."

A chill ran down Julie's spine as the hairs on the back of her neck stood up. She suddenly found herself short of breath. Her heart began to reverberate in her chest.

"I'm sorry, Tom," Julie said softly. "I didn't mean to .... I mean .... I only found out the details last month."

"It's OK, Jewels. There's no need to apologize. I always kept the specifics from you. You've been in this house dozens of times and never knew. I never liked to talk about it. I'm not going to tell my friends 'hey check out the kitchen where my dad was killed.' Right?"

"And they never caught him?"

"No. He was wearing a hoodie. I saw my dad fighting with him, and then ... then the knife." Tom paused to hold back the tears that were slowly building inside of him. He allowed a single tear to fall. "The killer ran off before I could see his face. There was no way for me to give the police a description. They had very little to go on."

Julie took a few small steps forward and leaned across the island. She extended her arms as far as they could go and motioned for Tom to do the same. He obliged, allowing Julie to take him by his hands.

"Is it still weird for you? To come into this room?"

"Not really," Tom replied as he let go of Julie. He folded his arms and leaned back in the barstool. "I was twelve when it happened. Back then it was a completely different kitchen. This island wasn't even here. It was just a big table. Within a year after his murder, my mom had the kitchen completely gutted and replaced. I barely remember the old one. I just remember it all being very dark. I think that's why my mom went with these cream cabinets. Light and airy, you know? She threw out all the pictures we had of the old kitchen. Most of my memories here are with the newly renovated one. Other than, well, you know."

Julie looked around the kitchen, studying the cabinets, flooring, and walls. The French Country décor chosen by his mother was perfectly executed.

"Wow. That's a lot to change. I probably would have done the same. Or moved. I'm surprised it still doesn't rattle her. You know, to walk in here and think about it."

"She wasn't here the night he was killed. A storm had grounded her flight home. By the time she finally got here the next day, the blood had been cleaned up. For her, walking into the kitchen was not a big deal. But she knew how much it upset me. That's why she had it all torn down and replaced. The table was gone the next day."

"She moves quickly, doesn't she? That was sweet of her to do that for you. I'm still surprised she hasn't moved. It's such a big house."

"My mom's in no rush to move. I think she feels like if she moves the killer wins. She doesn't want to give up her home. Instead, she just erased everything associated with that night. The den used to have a safe with his gun. Both are gone now."

"I never knew your dad had a gun. What does she think of you doing archery?"

"She doesn't know."

Julie walked around the island and stood next to Tom.

"What is it with you and secrets, Tom?"

"You know how my mom is, Jewels. The less she knows, the better."

Julie closed her eyes and recalled the story Mrs. Leblanc had told her of Tom witnessing his father's murder.

"I'll never be able to understand what it must have been like. At that age."

"I definitely carry it within me. Time does heal wounds, but something like that is different. That memory I have of seeing my dad killed will never go away."

"My nightmares may have stopped, but I'm sure I'll always be haunted by what happened out on the Cape. There's no way to escape it. We both need to move forward, Tom.

Dwelling on the past only slows the healing. Stop reading obituaries, OK? That woman and her mother are dead."

"I know, Jewels. I can't help it. I lost my dad. We lost Marc and Chris. I just want to make sure all of this is finally over. And I feel like I'm the one that can to do it. I mean, the cops never found who killed my dad. And as much as you love Trevor, he didn't save you in the barn. I did."

"True, but if you had listened to Trevor in the first place, I never would have gotten captured. He told us to not get involved."

"True, but if we hadn't followed her, they would still be alive right now."

Julie sighed and shook her head.

"There's no winning with you, is there?"

***

Hope Street was quiet this evening. Tom guided his Jeep along the two-lane road. With the doors off, the warm air rippled its way throughout the vehicle.

"That restaurant was fantastic," Julie said. "I'm glad you recommended Italian."

"Are you sure you don't want me to drop you at your place?" Tom asked.

"No," Julie replied. "It's a beautiful evening. I want to enjoy the walk home and work off all that bread I ate."

Tom flipped on his directional and turned into his driveway. The moving van that had been there earlier this evening was gone. The second and third story windows were filled with lights. Robin's daughter Tara was looking out the corner window waving at them as they arrived. Julie waved back.

"I like your new neighbors," Julie said. "Robin seems like a lot of fun."

"She does seem nice. I want to pick her IT brain and see how geeky she really is."

Tom killed his engine, and he and Julie exited Ruby. Tom opened the tailgate and let Max out.

"I think she could be a good friend, Tom. And don't lose

this one."

"What's that supposed to mean?"

"Whenever you date someone you drop your latest friend. You've lost many friends. We both have. We need to broaden our circle."

"Are you getting tired of me?" Tom asked with a snicker.

"No. It's just that seeing Robin with her daughter earlier got me thinking. I turn thirty in November. Will I ever get married? Have kids?"

Tom stopped at the base of his front stairs. Max ran off to the side fence to follow a scent. Julie was next to the Wrangler, leaning against the front fender. Tom could tell this was a serious topic for her.

"You've never talked about settling down, Jewels."

"I know. I've been in party mode since college. But the clock is ticking." Julie walked up to the stairs to join Tom. "We both know my family is a bit of a mess. We joke that I'm the normal one. But I look at my screwed up siblings and see how my parents fight all the time. Is that the life I want?"

"Jewels, you are still plenty young enough to settle down and start a family. If that's what you really want. Besides, your family is far from normal. I think you can set the bar higher for yourself. Don't benchmark them and think that if you get married and have kids, your family will end up like them. What about your grandmother out in Greece? She seems to have her shit together. Aim higher."

Julie smiled, stepped forward, and kissed Tom on the cheek.

"Thanks for that, Tom. You're right about my family. Bad role model. Speaking of which, we need to go see her."

"Who?"

"My yaya! Escape to Santorini."

"Greece?"

"Two words, Tom: Greek men."

Tom laughed and shook his head.

"We can talk about Greece tomorrow while we bask in the sun at the beach. I'll text you in the morning to figure out what time to leave, but we should head there early to beat the traffic."

"Sure thing. I have to run some errands first."

"Errands? You aren't doing kickboxing training, are you? I know that's your normal Saturday morning routine. Because if you are, then I can hit the archery range."

"No, I canceled it. I just need to get a few things – girl stuff. Plus, I'm getting low on cocoa butter. Chat tomorrow."

Julie looked around to say goodbye to Max, but he had wandered off into the backyard. She made her way down the driveway and turned to head home. Julie paid no attention to the Subaru Outback Sport that was parked across the street from Tom's condo. The occupant had been watching Tom, Julie, and Max ever since they'd gotten home.

Emma Johnson opened her car door and crossed the street to follow Julie home.

SIX

Accidents Happen

1988 Friday 24-Jun 8:00 a.m.

Fred Johnson gazed listlessly at the plate of bacon and eggs sitting in front of him. His wife always prepared them exactly the way he liked, and today was no exception. The eggs were fried, but the yolks were very runny. The bacon was crisp and just shy of being burnt. At any moment she would place a single slice of lightly toasted wheat bread, cut diagonally, along the plate's edge. The toast would be dry because Fred enjoyed running it through the yolks. After seventeen years of marriage, Laura didn't even have to think about the steps needed to prepare the meal.

"Why so down?" Laura asked.

"What?" Fred replied.

Laura sat in the chair next to her husband. She placed his toast on his plate and topped off his coffee. Laura then poured a cup for herself and set the carafe back on the table.

"You've been in a fog all morning. That food isn't going to hop off the plate into your mouth. Eat."

Fred bent a bacon strip against the plate, snapping it in half. The aroma of salted pork brought him little joy as he took a bite.

"I just get down this time of year. Or did you forget what tomorrow is?"

"Tomorrow?" Laura looked over at the calendar hanging on the wall next to the telephone. There was a circle around the box for the twenty-fifth, along with a purple star. That was the symbol Laura used to mark birthdays. "It's Susan's birthday. Already? Oh …."

It had been four years since Susan's thirteenth birthday party. That was the weekend that Rose, Mary, and Carl died.

"That drifter you brought home has completely distracted me," Laura continued. "I forgot. I'm … I'm going to have to call my sister. And Bobby."

"Bobby? Why him?"

"What do you mean? Did you forget he was the one that covered up your mess?"

Laura shoved her hands against the edge of the table and pushed herself away from the conversation. The chrome chair legs rang out as they dragged across the kitchen floor. She grabbed her coffee and walked over to the stove.

"How many times do I have to apologize for Carl?" Fred asked. "For everything? This has haunted me forever and will do so until the day I die. I never meant for any of that to happen."

Fred stared at Laura. His cheeks turned bright red, as he fought to control his anger and guilt. Her ice-blue eyes were like daggers filled with judgment. He gradually turned his attention back to his breakfast, sopping up some egg yolk with his toast.

"It's your temper, Fred. That nagging jealousy."

"I know, Laura. I know."

Fred stood up, wiped his lips dry, and walked over to the calendar hanging on the wall. In addition to the purple star marking Susan's birthday, the box contained three small black circles. Fred felt his eyes well up.

"I think … I think we should stop by the cemetery some time tomorrow," Fred said. "To pay respects to our Rosalyn."

Our Rosalyn, Laura thought to herself. *Our? If he only knew.*

Laura walked over to her husband and rested her hand on

his shoulder. He kissed her on the cheek and pulled her close.

"You know how sorry I am," Fred whispered into her ear.

"I know. Let's discuss it tonight."

Their conversation was interrupted by the sound of the porch door opening. Eddie Ward smiled nervously as he stepped into the kitchen.

"Good morning," Eddie said. "It smells amazing in here."

Eddie was dressed in jeans and a plain white T-shirt, ready to start the day. He did not bother to ask to use the shower. After only four days he still felt uncomfortable being in the Johnson home. Especially around Laura.

"Laura can fix you something," Fred said. "I have another punch-list for you to tackle today. I left it on the workbench in the barn. Bobby is coming over again today as well."

"Happy to help," Eddie replied.

"Excuse me," Laura said.

Eddie stepped aside to let Laura exit to the porch. He waited for the door to close completely before walking over to Fred.

"Can I ask why Mr. Mason is coming by?"

Laura paused outside next to the open kitchen window.

"He said he has something to drop off."

"I see."

Fred studied the young man's face. Eddie looked down at the floor and shoved his hands into his pockets.

"Why?"

"It's nothing."

"I want you to feel comfortable here," Fred said. "My boss will be back Monday. It won't be long before we get you that job, and then find you a place to live."

"I appreciate that. I do. It's just ... Mr. Mason ... he ... he bothers me."

Fred chuckled as he walked over to the kitchen counter. The keys to his Cherokee were next to the coffee maker. He scooped them up and shoved them into his pocket.

"He can be an intimidating man," Fred said. "But you have no reason to fear him."

"He just ... he ... never mind."

"What?"

"He seems to come around here a lot. I mean, doesn't it bother you that he comes here and spends so much time with your wife?"

Fred felt his blood pressure begin to rise. His mind filled with images of his brother-in-law Carl, and the fight they had over Fred's misplaced jealousy.

"Listen, Eddie, Bobby has been a very good friend to this family. He's taken care of us in ways you can't imagine. He and Laura are close. We all are."

Eddie looked around the room nervously. He was not sure how to respond, or what Fred was trying to tell him.

"OK, my apologies. I didn't mean anything by it. I just …."

The porch door swung open. Laura smiled as she walked past Eddie and Fred on her way to the refrigerator.

"Are you hungry, Eddie?" Laura asked. "You have a lot to do today. We don't want you working on an empty stomach."

"Thank you," Eddie replied.

Fred squeezed Eddie by his shoulder and gave him a nod of approval.

"I'll see you tonight," Fred said.

Fred went into the hallway and headed toward the front door. As he reached the end of the hall, Emma and Sara came bounding down the staircase from upstairs. They hugged their father before running into the kitchen.

"Hey Mom," Sara said.

"Good morning," Emma said. "Hi, Eddie."

Emma felt her cheeks redden at the sight of Eddie. She was beaming. Her infatuation with the young stranger was apparent to everyone in the room, especially her mother. Laura found it all to be a bit amusing.

"Good morning," Eddie replied. "What do you two have planned today?"

"We're riding our bikes over to see our cousin," Sara said. "That's still OK, right Mom?"

"Just be home by five," Laura said.

Emma stood frozen in the kitchen, admiring Eddie. He was almost as tall as her father. His green eyes popped against his pale skin. Her father's baggy T-shirt did it's best to conceal his sinewy toned body. Emma found the scruff at the end of his chin mesmerizing.

"Are you girls going to have breakfast?" Laura asked.

"No," Sara said, eyeing her awe-struck sister. "Aunty Jen is making pancakes."

Sara grabbed Emma by the hand and dragged her past Eddie. As the porch door closed behind them, Emma waved a shy goodbye to the drifter. Eddie grinned at the girl's obvious crush. He turned to see how Laura was handling it.

"My daughter is only fifteen," Laura said.

A wave of embarrassment consumed Eddie.

"Ma'am?"

"I'm just reminding you," Laura said with a grin.

"I would never ...."

"Fred barely touched his breakfast," Laura said. She pointed at the plate sitting on the kitchen table. "Help yourself. But eat it in the barn, please. I have to make a phone call."

"Of course."

Eddie grabbed Fred's fork, knife, napkin, and plate. He briefly considered taking Fred's cup of coffee but decided it was best to make a quick exit.

"Thank you," Eddie added.

Laura watched Eddie cross the driveway and enter the barn. She picked up the phone and called Bobby Mason's house.

"Hello?" Bobby asked.

"It's me," Laura replied.

"Hi, Angel."

"I think we may have a problem with our little drifter."

"How so?"

"I overheard him talking to Fred about you."

"Me? What did he say?"

"Nothing serious. Just that he didn't like you coming here and being with me when Fred wasn't around."

"That little shit! I told him to keep his mouth shut. What did Fred say?"

"I interrupted them before the conversation went any further. Fred seemed to ignore him. I laid into Fred earlier this morning a bit about his jealousy over Carl. You do know what tomorrow is, don't you?"

There was a slight pause before Bobby replied.

"Our precious Rose."

Several seconds passed in silence. Neither Laura or Bobby spoke. They both needed a moment to remember Rosalyn's passing.

"I'm worried he's going to say something, Bobby. He saw us in the barn. What if he's already tried to talk to Fred about it and I just haven't seen it yet? I just don't trust him."

"I'll be by soon. Don't worry, Angel, I'll handle it."

"What are you going to do?"

Bobby did not respond and simply ended the call.

***

The engine in Bobby's Ford F-150 rumbled loudly as he pulled into the Johnson's driveway. His truck shuddered across the uneven crushed stone surface. The heavy cargo in the bed sent several shimmies through the steering wheel. Bobby swung the vehicle around, aiming the rear of the truck toward the barn.

Laura opened the side door and stepped onto the porch. A sense of joy welled within her. Seeing Bobby always brightened her day. She ran to the driver's door to greet him.

"Hi, Bobby," Laura said. She waited patiently for Bobby to kill his engine. The thrumming and clatter of the struggling engine echoed throughout the yard. Laura coughed from the oily fumes coming from the exhaust. "Are you coming out?"

"Where's the kid?" Bobby asked.

Laura glanced around the yard, taking a few moments to inspect the paths and areas around the barn. She frowned and turned her attention back to Bobby.

"I have no idea," Laura replied.

"The girls?"

"They're over at my sister's for the day. They left earlier this morning."

"Good."

The Ford's engine sputtered one last time before it shut

down. The mechanical clattering was soon replaced by the cries of birds circling overhead. Laura waited for the cloud of exhaust smoke to clear. The bitter soot clouded her eyes. Finally, she was able to inhale the sweet salt air from the nearby ocean.

Bobby exited his truck and immediately swept Laura into his arms, lifting her off the ground. She giggled with delight and kissed him on his chin. Laura paused to drag her nose across the beads of sweat running down his neck. The musky scent was both familiar and arousing. Laura tilted her head back and welcomed Bobby's passionate mouth against hers.

The cracking of tree branches interrupted their embrace. Bobby lowered Laura to the ground and took a few steps into the driveway. He spun his head around trying to pinpoint where the noise had come from. The creak of the barn door broke the silence. Bobby turned around to see Eddie emerge from inside.

"Good morning," Eddie said.

"Was that you?" Bobby asked Eddie.

"Was what me?"

Bobby glanced around the area one more time. There was a light breeze, and the only sounds to be heard were from a pair of seagulls circling above. A gust of wind rolled through, causing several branches in the pine trees towering over the barn to bang together. Bobby sighed and looked back over at Eddie.

"I'm going to need your help, kid."

"Sure thing."

"Laura, do you mind getting us some iced tea?"

"Of course," Laura said. She nodded and smiled as she excused herself.

Eddie felt knots begin to take shape within his stomach. A new one formed with each step Laura placed between them. When she entered the kitchen and closed the door behind her, Eddie couldn't help but feel trapped. He was standing on acres of unfenced land, but the stare he was getting from Bobby pinned him to the ground.

Bobby walked to the back of his truck and flipped the tailgate down. It landed with a rattle. The Ford was several years old and had seen endless days of hard work. There was no bed liner installed, leaving the cargo area dented and scraped. Leaves and dirt covered the bed, surrounding the payload that was strapped inside.

"What is that?" Eddie asked as he approached the truck. "It looks like a cauldron."

"That it is," Bobby replied.

Eddie walked around the truck, inspecting the three-foot-wide polished metal crock. Four steel hooks gripped the top rim of the curved sides. They were attached to straps that were anchored to the bed's corners. The pot was resting on two-by-fours that ran front to back.

"What's it for? It looks too big to fit on a stove."

Bobby nodded as he started to loosen the tie-downs.

"It's for the barn."

"Is it heavy?"

Bobby jumped into the bed and took a position between the cauldron and the back window of the truck.

"I'm guessing less than a hundred pounds. I need you to help me get it to the ground. Then we can roll it into the barn."

"Oh, OK. Sure thing."

Eddie stood at the back of the tailgate. Bobby was wearing a loose fitting blue T-shirt. He removed it, exposing a tight white A-shirt. He squatted down low and leaned against the pot. After a brief moment, it began to slide toward Eddie.

"The slats are moving!" Eddie called out.

Bobby stopped and looked down at his feet. The two-by-fours were getting dragged along with the heavy iron crock. Bobby knelt down lower and leaned his shoulder a foot below the rim to get a better grip on the cauldron.

"Hold them in place, or they will snap off when we try to lower it. Keep them at the edge of the tailgate for me. Let me know when I'm at the end."

"Understood."

Eddie clasped his hands together and pulled them close to his chest, making his arms form a solid barrier. He braced them against the wooden support beams. Bobby began to push again. Eddie threw his right leg back to keep the planks from sliding. The pot grew closer and closer.

"You're almost there," Eddie said. His right leg quivered from the immense tension he was using to hold everything in place. "Another foot. Let me know when you are done pushing."

"Hold still."

With one swift move, Bobby stood up and grabbed the base of the cauldron, tilting it back toward the tailgate. He let out a primal scream as he launched the pot backward. Eddie flung his hands up to try and deflect it away. His right leg collapsed as the iron crock came crashing down on top of him, compressing his waist and lower torso. Eddie cried out in agony. His arms flailed in desperation as he tried to free himself.

Laura opened the back door and stepped outside. She stood speechless at the sight of the young drifter pinned beneath the cauldron.

Bobby leaped from the bed and knelt down next to Eddie's head. The young man's screams quickly faded as his mouth filled with blood. Eddie reached out toward Bobby, his fingers trembling in terror and confusion.

"Help me," Eddie sputtered.

Bobby stood up and walked to Eddie's feet. The pot faced open side down and stretched from just below his ribcage down to his knees. Eddie's feet were twitching. Bobby straddled Eddie's legs, squatted, grabbed the edge of the rim, took a deep breath, and flipped the cauldron forward. The heavy iron bottom of the crock crushed Eddie's skull, ending his cries for help.

A high pitched gasp rang out. Bobby looked up to see Laura running across the driveway. She stopped a few yards from Eddie's body. Crimson red blood permeated across the white crushed stone surrounding the young drifter.

"Bobby!" Laura cried. "What happened?"

Bobby stepped forward and pulled Laura into his arms. She buried her face into his chest and began to shake.

"Accidents happen, Angel." Bobby pressed his lips against her ear. "I told you I'd take care of him."

Laura's body continued to tremble as she pulled herself

away from Bobby's embrace. A sharp gust cut through the space between the barn and the house. Several branches let out thunderous cracks in protest.

"What now?" Laura asked. "The blood ... there's so much blood."

"Don't worry. Remember how we handled Carl, Rose, and Mary? I cleaned up after them. I will clean this up too."

Bobby slid his finger under her chin and tilted her head up. He gave Laura a gentle kiss on the lips. The lovers gazed at one another for a brief moment, silently acknowledging they were in this together.

"I need to build a fire pit in the barn," Bobby said. "Come with me."

Laura slid her arm around Bobby's waist. She couldn't bring herself to look at Eddie. Part of her was repulsed by what just happened. Yet, she couldn't help but feel safe and protected in Bobby's embrace.

The crunching of the crushed stone beneath their feet masked the whimpering cries coming from the dense vegetation several yards away from Bobby's truck.

Emma's hands shuddered as she stared through the parted branches of the shrubs across her driveway. She watched through tears as her mother and Bobby disappeared into the shadows inside the barn. Her body would not stop shaking. Emma released the foliage that concealed her and retreated behind a cluster of nearby pine trees. She wiped the tears from her face, smearing her cheeks with grease.

Emma looked over at her bicycle leaning against the oak tree across from her. The broken chain dangled from the bike's front chainring. She looked at her trembling greasy hands. Her simple plan to come home to fix her bike did not turn out the way it was supposed to. Tears fell harder. She covered her mouth to muffle her cries. Her heart raced as she tried to figure out what to do next.

He killed Eddie, Emma said to herself. *Why did my mother kiss him?*

***

Fred pulled his Cherokee alongside Bobby's Ford. He was surprised to find Bobby here. He looked at his watch. It was 3 p.m. Fred felt a sense of unease wash over him. He recalled Eddie's concern about Bobby always being around when Fred was away. He tried to shake it off as he headed to the kitchen door.

"You're home early," Laura said.

The kitchen was filled with the aroma of garlic, onion, and tomatoes. Laura was standing at the stove, stirring a pan filled with homemade pasta sauce.

"It's always good when the boss is away," Fred said. He walked over to Laura and gave her a kiss on the cheek. "What's with the stain?"

Laura looked down at her white and yellow apron. The smock was covered in tomato sauce.

"Not that," Fred continued. "The driveway. There's a huge black stain next to Bobby's truck. How long has he been here? I thought he was dropping something off. Where is he?"

Laura immediately picked up on Fred's overly inquisitive tone and decided it was best to stick with the plan she and Bobby made earlier.

"That stain was Bobby's doing. He brought us something for the barn. I think you'll like it."

"A gift?"

"You could say that."

Fred scratched his head and looked around the kitchen. It dawned on him how quiet the house was.

"Where are the girls?" Fred asked.

"They've been at my sister's since this morning."

"Have you heard from them?"

Laura leaned forward and paused a few inches above the bubbling scarlet sauce. She ran her finger across the hot silky surface and slipped her gravy covered finger into her mouth. She frowned at the bitterness. Laura opened a small glass sugar jar, thrust her hand inside, and withdrew a large pinch of sugar. She tossed it into the pot and began to stir it.

"The twins will be sixteen this year, Fred. They don't need their mother checking in on them."

"Oh. Right. Of course."

Laura took one last whiff of her pasta sauce before putting the cover on the pot.

"Where's Eddie at?" Fred asked.

Laura felt a lump rise in her throat. She smiled and wiped her hands across her apron.

"He left."

"What do you mean? He's gone?"

"Bobby and I ran into town to get some supplies. When we came back, he was gone. His clothes. Bag. Everything."

"Why would he leave?"

"He's a drifter, Fred. You should be glad he didn't steal anything. Trust me, the first thing I did was look to make sure he didn't take any valuables."

Fred sat at the kitchen table and lowered his head. He ran his hands across his face and let out a very audible sigh.

"But he knew I was working on getting him a job."

"What can I say? I warned you he couldn't be trusted."

"He was a good kid, Laura."

"He was a drifter, Fred. A common thief. He admitted it."

"That was just food. Eddie was only trying to survive. He had no money. He couldn't pay."

"We all have to pay at some point."

Laura walked over to the door that led to the porch. The hinges squeaked as she opened it. She raised her hand and pointed to the barn.

"Bobby's waiting for you."

Fred groaned as he stood up. His body ached from a very long work week. He nodded to Laura and made his way outside to the porch. The fresh salt air was a drastic change from the smells of Italian food circling around inside the kitchen. He gave the large stain in his driveway a disapproving look before entering the barn.

"What on earth is that?" Fred asked.

Bobby was standing in the center of the barn. Fred frowned, disappointed to see that Bobby had rearranged his two tables. The metal table that used to be in the back of the barn was now at the front, leaving a four-foot space between it and the wooden workbench. In between them sat the iron cauldron, perched atop a circle of stones. The stainless steel tabletop glistened and smelled of bleach.

Fred approached Bobby with caution. As he got closer, he picked up the scent of what seemed like a stew. Flames thrashed and beckoned throughout the firepit. Fred paused a few feet from the metal pot, the intense heat signaling him to keep a safe distance.

"What's this all about?" Fred asked.

Bobby was busy stirring the contents of the cauldron. He withdrew the ladle and placed it on the metal table.

"It's for your cows."

Fred glanced past Bobby and let his eyes wander across the stalls that ran along the back of the barn. He smiled as he noticed the cows quietly pacing within their pens.

"How so?"

"You need to think beyond milk and cheese, Fred. You've got a full butcher shop back there just waiting to happen."

"Butcher? Never. My girls are for dairy use only."

Fred inched closer to the pot. The boiling walnut-colored liquid inside smelled odd to Fred. The texture wasn't that of soup stock. It was thick and heavy.

"What's in there?" Fred asked.

"I brought a goat over to christen it. Sorry about the stain out front. There was an accident. I'll get that cleaned up for you."

Fred frowned as he studied the cauldron. He glanced back at his cows.

"I can't chop up my cows, Bobby."

"Not now, Fred. But someday. This cauldron can come in handy. If you don't want to eat them, I can show you other uses for them."

"I'm fine with milk and cheese. Besides, Sara would never forgive me."

"A couple of those cows are getting old, Fred. No sense in selling them off to some butcher. You really should use as much of the beast as you can. I make soap and candles with my goats."

"Really?"

"Really. In fact, Laura said she wants to learn the recipe."

***

Sara was pedaling as fast as she could. She gasped for air as she turned her bicycle onto the dirt path that led to her house. Beads of sweat seeped from beneath her bike helmet. The road became uneven. She stopped pedaling and let her bike coast for a bit. The entrance to her driveway was several yards away. She hit the brakes to make the turn. Suddenly Emma jumped out from the side of the road.

"Stop!" Emma yelled. "Stop!"

Emma was positioned directly in front of her sister's path. Sara slammed on the brakes and swerved to avoid hitting her.

"What the hell?" Sara cried. She brought her bike to a halt and hopped off the seat. "Where have you been? You were supposed to meet us at the beach near Aunty Jen's. You totally missed out on seeing the new lifeguard."

"Did you call the house?"

Sara unlatched her helmet and tossed it to the ground. She took a moment to study her sister's face.

"No. Why are you covered in grease? Have you been trying to fix your bike all day? Is dad home yet, maybe he …."

"Shut up, Sara!" Emma burst into tears. "You have no idea what happened."

Sara dropped her bike to the ground and pulled her twin into her arms. Emma's entire body shook as she struggled to compose herself. She squeezed Sara for a few seconds before releasing her.

"I saw something," Emma said. "Today."

"Where?"

"At the house. When I got back. I was walking my bike home. I got to the end of the path before it clears. Bobby was here."

Emma took a few steps back and stared longingly into Sara's eyes. She held her hand up in front of her. Sara instinctively raised her arm and took her sister's hand.

"You want to do the poem?" Sara asked with confusion. "Now?"

"I don't know what to do, Sara."

Sara took Emma by the hand and pulled her close.

"Tell me, Emma. There are no secrets between us."

Emma closed her eyes and remembered what Bobby said to her mother.

"Accidents happen," Emma said softly. She wiped her runny nose and gave Sara a kiss on the cheek. "I can't tell you, Sara. For your own safety."

Emma walked over to Sara's bike and pulled it upright. She wheeled it over to her sister.

"Bullshit, Emma. You've been gone for hours. Something's upset you. Tell me what happened with Bobby."

"Trust me, Sara. It's safer this way. You have to trust me. Remember our blood oath?"

"Of course I do."

"Well, that's why I'm doing this now. I need to keep you safe. I'll tell you when I know you won't be hurt."

"Emma, you're not making any sense."

"I know I'm not. All I need you to do right now is to tell everyone that we had a great day with Susan. And we need to call Susan once we get home. She needs to know the story."

"The story?"

Sara grabbed her bike from her sister. Emma picked up her helmet before pulling her own bike away from the oak tree. The sisters turned into the opening of the long winding family driveway.

"I was with you all day. We left together. Halfway home my chain broke. We tried to fix it but couldn't." Emma stopped. She realized her story needed to be convincing. She bent down and ran her fingers across Sara's bike chain. Emma smeared grease on her sister's cheeks and the palms of her hands. "We walked home together with my broken bike."

"Emma, I don't understand."

"Trust me, Sara, there's no other way. If they ask any specifics about our day, I will let you tell them what happened. Be honest. Tell them everything you and Susan did after I left. I will just play along like I was there. Please do this for me."

SEVEN

Beach Day

Mr. Fluffy was spread out on his belly, his front legs fully extended ahead of him. His eyes were fixated on Julie, who was fast asleep in her bed. The cat inched his way closer and closer to her face. Mr. Fluffy's ears twitched in unison with Julie's snoring.

The cat stopped inches from Julie's chin. He purred quietly, patiently waiting for her to wake up. Julie let out a yawn. The rhythmic thrumming coming from Mr. Fluffy put a smile on her face. She opened one eye and groaned.

"What time is it?" Julie asked.

Mr. Fluffy crawled closer and shoved his head under Julie's neck. Julie chuckled and pulled him closer. She propped herself up on one elbow and gave him a gentle kiss on his head. Julie's eyes drifted up and across the room to the window. The blinds were raised a foot above the windowsill, the pull strings jammed into a knot Julie had long abandoned unraveling. She was shocked to see someone staring back at her.

"Oh my God!" Julie yelled.

The figure outside ran off. Julie shoved Mr. Fluffy aside and kicked the bedsheet away. The cat meowed in protest, leaping to the floor and running out of the room. Julie quickly followed him, running to her front door in a panic. As she made her way down the hallway, she could not get the person's face out of her mind. What she saw terrified her.

Julie reached the front entrance, unlocked the deadbolt, and flung the door open. Her face bright red and filled with fear and confusion as she stepped out onto the porch and looked around. No people were wandering the street. She ran to the end of the porch and stuck her head out so she could see down the side of the house where her bedroom window was. The alley, just like her street, was empty. She ran to the other side to check the driveway. Nothing

A chime rang out from inside her apartment. Julie gave one last look around before stepping into her hallway and securing the front door. The chime rang out a second time. She went back to her bedroom and picked up her cell phone to see a text message from Tom.

You up yet? It's after 8. Beach day!

Julie did not bother to text back and instead called him. The phone rang twice before Tom answered.

"Wow, I'm impressed," Tom said sarcastically. "I figured you would still be asleep."

"No. Tom, listen. I'm sort of freaking out here."

"What's going on?" Tom's wise-ass tone from earlier became much more serious. "You sound out of breath."

Julie looked around her room for Mr. Fluffy. She dropped to her knees and found him hiding under the bed. She shoved her arm under and fumbled around until she was able to get a good grip on him. The cat pawed at the floor as she dragged him out. Julie clutched him to her chest and kissed him on his head.

"When I woke up I saw someone staring in my window."

"Someone?"

"I was barely awake. I glanced over, and this person was watching me."

Julie walked over to her window and peered through the upper half of the blinds. After double checking the lock was secure she made her way to the kitchen with Mr. Fluffy crushed against her chest. The cat kept his front legs wrapped around her arm and began to relax and purr.

"Did you recognize them?"

"That's the freaky part, Tom. It looked like ... like Sara. It looked like Mrs. Closed."

"Sara? What the hell are you talking about?"

"I know! I know! It looked like her, but not her. You know?"

"No, I don't. This sounds like Eastham all over again, Jewels. Except now we know she's dead."

"I know. But ...."

"What was she wearing? Why do you think it was her? Was she in a hoodie?"

"No."

"Then why do you think it was her?"

Julie bent down and released Mr. Fluffy. She then walked over to her stove and grabbed the teakettle from the back burner. She filled it with tap water and returned it to the stove, setting the burner to high.

"She had on a baseball cap and glasses. But it was her nose. Lips. Jawline. It just ...."

"Are you sure you weren't dreaming?"

"No, I was up. Mr. Fluffy woke me and I was half awake. Listen, there was definitely someone looking in my window."

"What was her hair like, Jewels?"

"I never got a chance to see it."

Julie waited for Tom to respond. Several seconds passed before he spoke.

"You know what I think, Jewels? I think our discussion yesterday spooked you. When we were in my mom's kitchen, and you freaked out about me reading the obituaries. What was Sara's sister's name? Emma."

"Tom, I didn't imagine it. Someone was outside my window."

"I don't doubt that, Jewels. We both know it couldn't be Sara. She's dead. And do you really think her sister Emma would be out here? Even I'm not that obsessive."

Julie let out a nervous laugh.

"Oh my God, am I turning into you?"

Tom laughed.

"Before you know it you will stop having sex and become a fantastic cook."

"I hope not. I love you, Tom, but I don't want to turn into you."

"Ditto on that, Jewels."

The whistle on the teakettle began to escalate in volume. Julie ran to the stove and moved the pot to another burner.

"Maybe you're right, Tom. I'm being paranoid. I did lecture you from my soapbox yesterday. Maybe I was just overly anxious when I went to bed last night. I didn't have any nightmares, though."

"It was probably just a nosey neighbor, Jewels. Or maybe some drifter saw the open blinds and was looking to see if anyone was home."

Julie opened the cupboard next to her stove, revealing four different instant cocoa boxes – dark chocolate, mint, raspberry, and marshmallow. She reached into the marshmallow one and frowned as she realized it was empty. Julie opted for mint flavored.

"Let me have my cocoa, Tom. I need to calm down."

"Will you be ready for nine?"

Julie looked at the clock on her stove. It read 8:15 a.m.

"Nine? I told you I have errands and shit to do. It will be more like ten. Maybe even eleven."

"We can't go that late, Jewels. Holiday traffic is going to be insane."

"Then let me go so I can get my day started. I'll text you."

"But ...."

Julie ended the call and set about making her instant hot chocolate. Her cupboard was filled with mugs she had collected from various vacations around the country. She grabbed one shaped like an apple. The letters "NYC" were emblazoned in white across the glossy crimson colored cup. Just as she was about to take a sip her phone rang.

"What the fuck?" Julie cried. She grabbed her phone and angrily looked at the screen. Her frustration quickly turned to joy. "Yaya!"

Julie ran to her kitchen table and flipped her laptop open.

She debated taking the video call on her phone but knew the laptop would be more convenient. Once the computer was awake, she logged in and saw the video chat request. Julie immediately accepted it. After a few moments, her grandmother's smiling face appeared on the screen.

"Tzoúli!" Helen Perez cried out through the computer.

Julie laughed as she reached for the volume control to lower it. Mr. Fluffy jumped up onto the table and sat in front of the screen.

"Well, hello Mr. Fluffy," Helen said. "I see you are both awake."

Julie dragged a reluctant Mr. Fluffy onto her lap.

"Hi, Yaya," Julie said. "We've been up for a bit. How are things in Santorini?"

"Just another day in paradise."

Julie smiled as she sipped her cocoa, taking in the sweet minty scent. Helen squinted as she inspected the oversized ceramic mug in her granddaughter's hand.

"New York?" Helen asked. "Where is your mug from Greece?"

Julie's smile faded. She looked over her shoulder at the cupboards surrounding her stove. With a heavy sigh, she turned to face her grandmother.

"I don't have one."

"My point exactly. When are you coming to visit?"

"I want to Yaya. I really do. I'm thinking later this year."

"Why not this summer?"

"That's a big trip. I need to save up for it."

"Why do you do this?" Helen asked with frustration. "You are so much better."

"Better? Do what, Yaya?"

"You're almost thirty, and you can't jump on a plane to come to visit me? I don't like seeing you live paycheck to paycheck. Why did you drop out of law school?"

"Oh, well, it was a lot of time and work. Years, really."

"Nonsense. You let your family talk you out of it. Trust me, I know your father. That man can be a real downer. Just because your other brothers and sisters are all failures doesn't mean you have to be one."

Julie sat there stunned. This was not the upbeat conversation she was hoping to have with her grandmother. She lowered Mr. Fluffy to the floor and pushed her chair back. Without excusing herself, she walked back to the stove and turned the burner on beneath the kettle.

"Can we talk about school and family another time?"

"I just worry. When will you settle down and raise a family? What are you waiting for?"

"You know, I was just talking to Tom about that yesterday. Are you psychic?"

Helen smiled, rolled her eyes, and shrugged her shoulders.

"I like to think I've got a gift."

"My clock is ticking. I need to get serious about dating."

"And go back to school." Helen watched her granddaughter buzz around the kitchen. "But that's not why I called. We can talk about your future education when you are here in Santorini. I called to convince you to come visit."

Julie reached into her cupboard and instinctively thrust her hand into the box of marshmallow flavored cocoa. She sighed again, this time opting for raspberry.

"Convince me?"

"Well hello there."

Julie did not recognize the deep tenor voice coming through her laptop. She turned to see Mr. Fluffy back on the table staring at the screen. She flicked off the burner and walked back to the table. As she got closer, the screen came into view. Julie's jaw dropped.

An extremely handsome man was staring at her through the display. His golden brown skin wrapped tightly over high cheekbones. Long wavy blond hair was parted on the side and styled perfectly. His piercing crystal blue eyes remained fixated on Julie. Helen Perez stood a foot behind him, smiling.

"Remember I told you about Adrian?" Helen said with pride.

"You must be Julie," Adrian said, revealing an impeccable set of dazzling white teeth.

Julie was speechless. Almost without realizing it she

began to run her hands across her frazzled hair. She looked down and noticed she was still in her pajamas. Julie ran to the kitchen chair and pulled her cat closer, to cover her clothing.

"Yes, um, yes. Wow. Sorry. I just. Wow. Seriously? Oh my God. I'm not really dressed for company. I just woke up. Sorry."

Adrian let out a hearty laugh as a wry smirk spread across his chiseled face. He scratched his classically straight Greek nose and lowered his chin into his palm.

"You have nothing to apologize for."

Helen stepped forward and rested her hands on Adrian's broad shoulders. He leaned back and allowed the old woman to rest her head next to his. Julie was entranced by Adrian's face.

"Adrian knows all about you," Helen said. "I told him what happened to you last December. And last month."

"Yaya!"

Julie felt her cheeks become flush. She was embarrassed at both her appearance and her grandmother's boldness. Yet she could not help but find the handsome man spellbinding.

"It's OK, Julie. Helen cares deeply for you. That's why she called me to tell me what you've been going through. How are you? Are you doing OK?"

"I ... I am. Thank you."

"My dearest kósmima," Helen said. "I told Adrian you needed a vacation and I would not take no for an answer."

"I'm working on it. I want Tom to come along, too."

"Tom?" Adrian asked. "Helen mentioned him. Is that your boyfriend?"

"No. God no."

"Good," Adrian said, flashing his blinding smile at Julie once more. "Then it's settled. You just let me know when you want to come visit, and I'll take care of it."

"Take care of it?" Julie asked. "I assumed we'd just stay with you, Yaya."

"Of course you will," Helen replied. "I have plenty of room here in my villa."

"I'm talking about the flight out," Adrian said.

"The flight? Oh. Oh! Oh my God! No, you can't pay to fly us out."

"I'm not buying tickets for you."

"Then what are you talking about?"

"I have a plane. A few, actually. Different sizes. We have offices around the world, including Boston. There's always a jet flying from Logan. It won't be a problem to make room for two more."

"But they're down in Providence, Adrian," Helen interjected. "Can you send a car to shuttle them up to the airport?"

"Easily."

Julie stared at the screen, debating what to say next. Adrian folded his arms and smiled. Helen wrapped her arms around Adrian's neck and kissed him on the cheek.

"It's settled," Helen said.

"Adrian," Julie said. "This is awfully kind of you, but I can't ask for this."

"And you didn't. Your sweet, wonderful grandmother did. You must know she's impossible to say no to. I'll have her send you my details. I can connect you with my assistant to get it all booked. No rush at all, Julie. I'm excited to have you come visit. From what Helen has told me, you've earned it. An escape to Greece is definitely in your future."

Adrian turned his head and gave Helen a gentle peck on the cheek. He glanced back at Julie and winked at her before standing up and walking away. Helen sat back down in front of the screen, exposing a smile that would not go away.

"Well?" Helen asked. "What did I tell you?"

"Is he gone?"

Helen glanced over her shoulder and watched Adrian disappear around the corner. She turned back to the screen and nodded.

"He's gorgeous," Julie exclaimed. "But look at me. I look like shit. Sorry. Like crap. Warn me next time, Yaya."

"Nonsense. You are ravishing. Even first thing in the morning."

"But Yaya, you shouldn't have asked him to fly me out there. And Tom as well? I mean ... wow. He has a plane?"

"Apparently he has a few."

"It's too much, Yaya."

"Adrian said it best. You've earned this. You both have. Too much suffering and pain. This is not up for discussion. Do you have passports?"

"I don't. I doubt Tom does."

"Well, then that's the first thing you need to do. Talk it over with him. I'll email you Adrian's information."

Julie lowered her head and pressed her nose against Mr. Fluffy's ears. He purred in appreciation.

"Tzoúli, don't overthink this. Greece is calling for you. You will fall in love here. Trust me, it's impossible to resist the call of the deep blue waves.

"Or those deep blue eyes."

Helen let out a hearty laugh and nodded in agreement.

"I told you he was handsome. His brother is just as tempting. You will meet him when you come out. But don't be seduced so easily. Those boys are known to misbehave far too often."

"I can't think that far ahead," Julie said. She glanced at the clock in the computer screen's corner. "I need to get going, Yaya. I'm spending the day at the beach with Tom. I can't wait to tell him about Greece. I don't know how to thank you. Or Adrian."

Helen did not reply. Instead, she smiled and blew a kiss toward the screen.

***

Emma Johnson twisted her torso as she attempted to stretch the muscles in her lower back. She spent last night sleeping in her car's hatchback. Folding the seats down and spreading several blankets out did not make for a comfortable bed. Her mother's instructions were quite clear, however. No hotel rental. No use of credit cards. No calls or texting on her phone.

Emma checked the silver watch her mother had given her before leaving Wellfleet. It was 9:45 a.m. She peered out her windshield, keeping a close watch on the three-story house that Julie Perez lived in. The cars parked behind Julie's apartment began leaving over an hour ago. There was only one car left – Julie's. Emma fired up the Subaru's engine and pulled the car forward. She came to a stop just across the street from Julie's driveway.

A dark navy blue canvas bag sat on the passenger's seat next to Emma. The sack contained a change of clothes, toiletries, and other items she had packed for her trip. She reached in and retrieved a small case. Emma opened the box and inspected the sedative-filled syringe packed away inside. She immediately snapped it closed.

"What am I doing?" Emma said aloud to herself.

The front door to Julie's apartment opened. Emma turned to see who it was. A lump formed in her chest as Julie stepped out onto the front porch.

"This isn't right," Emma said with angst. She watched as Julie descended the porch stairs and turned to head down the driveway. "Dammit."

Emma grabbed the syringe, adjusted her aviator style sunglasses and set a baseball cap atop her head. She tucked her hair beneath the hat and exited her car. Emma shoved the syringe into her pocket as she jogged across the street and headed down the driveway.

Julie was standing at her car, fumbling through her purse. Emma slowed her approach as she got closer to Julie. Once she was only a few feet away, she stopped. Emma's heart pounded loudly in her chest. She took a deep breath.

"Julie," Emma said, her voice cracking as she spoke.

Julie spun around, completely startled by the person standing behind her. She immediately recognized the baseball cap and glasses as the face from earlier this morning.

"Who ... who are you?" Julie asked.

Emma did not immediately answer. The two women, now standing only three feet apart, stood motionless. Julie instinctively clenched her fists. Emma kept one hand in her pocket, wrapped tightly around the syringe.

"I just want to talk," Emma said.

"Why? Who the hell are you?"

Emma sighed and used her free hand to remove her sunglasses. Julie's eyes widened, and she felt her knees begin to tremble.

"Oh my God," Julie whispered.

"I'm Emma. Emma Johnson."

Julie looked on in disbelief. The woman standing in front of her looked like a slightly leaner version of the person that had twice tried to kill her. Her nose, eyes, and complexion were so familiar to Julie, yet also somehow eerily different. Julie couldn't quite place what it was that was off.

"I just want to talk," Emma said. "Please."

"What the fuck are you doing here?" Julie said. She felt overwhelmed by fear and anger. "Did you come to finish the job?"

"Finish? What? No. I want to understand what happened. With my mother and sister."

Julie dug her heels deep into the ground, locking her body into place. She looked Emma up and down. The woman's similarity to her sister was startling. However, it was obvious to Julie she weighed at least ten pounds less than Sara.

"Understand what?" Julie asked. "Those psychopaths tried to kill me."

"I know that's what the news reported."

"The news? You must be joking."

"I want to hear it from you."

"Hear what? As if you aren't part of that urban legend."

"Legend?"

"Waxed in Wellfleet. From the book. Your mother confessed it to me when I was tied up in the barn. Or should I say *your* barn?"

"What book?"

"The book of urban legends that your sister had at the store."

"Julie, I honestly have no idea what you are talking about."

The adrenaline flowing through Julie began to slow as she studied Emma's bewildered look. Her eyes and ears struggled to separate the face of her attempted killer with the voice of a clearly confused woman.

"I don't believe you. Your mother knew all about the Wellfleet legend. They killed that Asian couple that owned the candle store and turned them into candles. Then they killed our friends Marc and Chris. Your mother showed me the blue candle she turned them into. It's all true."

"Candles?"

"Why are you playing stupid? You probably helped them."

"Julie, you don't understand. I've had no contact with my mother or sister for decades. This is all new to me. Trust me."

"Trust you?" Julie shook her head and groaned. Her nails were beginning to dig deep into her palms. She uncoiled her fists slightly and tried to slow her rapidly pounding heart.

"I'm telling you the truth."

"Why should I believe you? Your sister tried to kill me at the Seabreeze condo. Then again last month in the barn. How do I know you aren't a killer, too?"

"I'm no killer, Julie. I'm just trying to understand what happened. The Sara I knew could never kill anyone." Emma paused to recall the decades that had passed since she and Sara used to ride their bikes and play at the beach. Those teenage years were a distant memory. She remembered that Sara was always the hothead with the short temper.

Could she? Emma wondered to herself.

"Just ask the store owners she turned into ginger and sesame candles."

"You mean the store in Truro?"

"Why am I even bothering to explain this to you? I want you to leave."

Julie stepped forward. Emma took two steps back.

"But I want answers," Emma continued. "I need to understand everything that happened."

"I just told you."

"But I know there's more. A lot more. Please. I'm just trying to square this up with what my mother told me."

"Your mother?" Julie felt her throat begin to close up. "You just said you haven't seen her in ages. When did you talk to her?"

Emma suddenly realized she said too much. She stood

motionless, refusing to answer the question.

"Is she alive?" Julie asked, her voice hoarse with fear. She felt her legs begin to tremble again. Julie stepped back against her car to try and steady herself. "You need to leave."

Emma did not respond or move. She was dazed, trying to process everything Julie said. There was too much information from Julie. It was overwhelming. So much of what she heard was a complete contradiction of what her mother had told her. Emma closed her eyes to try and square up the conflicting stories swirling in her head.

"Fine," Julie continued. "We'll let the police settle this."

Julie reached into her bag and retrieved her phone. Emma opened her eyes and lunged forward, knocking it from Julie's hand. Julie instinctively hurled her right fist at Emma, hitting her dead center in her gut. Emma collapsed to the ground.

Julie took a brief moment to appreciate seeing Emma bent over gasping for air before looking around for her phone. It landed in front of her car. She let out a sigh and went to get it. After taking three steps, she felt a pinch a few inches below her waist. She spun around to see Emma standing upright, with one arm hidden behind her back.

"I'm sorry," Emma said softly.

Julie spun around to retrieve her phone. She took a few steps forward and knelt down to pick it up. A quick inspection revealed the case was intact and the screen did not shatter. Julie wiped the grime from the back of the phone and stood up and turned to face Emma.

"Sorry? Tell that to the police." Julie looked at her phone and was surprised to find herself having trouble focusing on it. She wiped her eyes to clear them, but it did no good. Julie tried to get closer to Emma but realized her equilibrium was off. "What's going on?"

Julie's vision began to blur. She grabbed the hood of her car for support, dropping her phone to the ground. Her knees quivered as they started to buckle. Julie stepped forward and attempted to throw another punch at Emma, but she immediately lost her balance and fell to the ground. She crawled back to her car and pulled herself upright.

"What did you do?" Julie asked, her speech slurred as she grappled with staying focused.

Emma surveyed the front entrance to the driveway to be sure they were still alone. Her heart raced as she watched Julie bob and weave, struggling to keep herself upright.

"You're just like your sister," Julie said.

"I'm the opposite of Sara."

Julie fell against the car's fender. The world around her was beginning to fade away. She found it difficult to stand up.

"How did she die?" Emma asked. "Did you kill her? Did you kick her into the fire?"

"She got what she deserved."

Julie could see multiple sets of her phone a few feet away. Her eyes were tearing up, causing everything to streak and blur.

"Why are you doing this?" Julie asked. "Why are you …."

Emma stepped forward and caught Julie just as she passed out. She dragged her body over to the back of the house and propped her up against a garbage bin. Emma looked around to make sure they were alone. The rear of Julie's apartment building was heavily secluded by two large maple trees that anchored the back corners of the yard. They were alone.

"You gave me no choice," Emma said.

Mr. Fluffy watched from the back window as Emma picked up Julie's phone and tossed it into Julie's purse. She threw Julie's pocketbook over her shoulder and went back to the street to get her car.

EIGHT

Broken Bonds

1988 Saturday 2-Jul 6:00 p.m.

Emma dragged her fork across her plate, swirling the utensil in a figure-eight pattern. The tines repeatedly cut their way through the white rice and buttery peas heaped on her dish. A roasted chicken leg sat in a puddle of grease and spices, barely touched. Emma preferred to be lost in her food than engaged in any conversation with her family. A week had passed since she witnessed Eddie's murder. Each day left her feeling more and more trapped – a prisoner in her own home.

"Are you going to eat any of it?" Laura asked. "Or just shove it around?"

Fred, Laura, Sara, and Emma were seated at the kitchen table for dinner. Sara's plate was already half empty. Fred studied Emma's movements with concern. She'd been in a dour mood ever since Eddie left a week ago.

Laura frowned at Emma's emotional distance. She looked around the table at her family and let out a long sigh.

"We have two days until the holiday," Laura said cheerily. "Tomorrow is going to be a hectic day. We're going to have yard work to do to get the picnic area cleaned up. I've got a lot of cooking to do as well. But if we all work together, we can be sure to make the fourth a lovely day."

"Is Aunty Jen going to make her rosemary chicken?" Sara asked. "She never makes it anymore."

"Well, I don't know," Laura replied. "Maybe she will surprise us."

"Aunty Jen stopped making it after Susan's thirteenth birthday party," Emma interjected. "She's never been the same since Uncle Carl, Rose, and Mary were killed."

"That was an awful day, Emma," Laura said. She lowered her head as she remembered walking into the barn and seeing the carnage. "Your Uncle Carl had an accident. They all did."

"Did they?" Emma replied in a condescending tone.

"Emma!" Fred bellowed. "What kind of question is that?"

"Never speak ill of the dead," Laura said. "They aren't here to defend themselves."

Emma let her eyes roam across the table. Her entire family was glaring back at her in disapproval. She folded her arms and leaned back defiantly in her chair.

"What were they doing at the beach?" Emma retorted. "The waves were awful that day. We were all warned not to go. You told us they all went swimming and drowned. Last month Aunty Jen got drunk and told Susan that Uncle Carl committed suicide with a knife. You told us he drowned in the ocean with the girls. Why the lies?"

Laura leaned forward and with her palm struck Emma hard across her right cheek. Emma recoiled and let out a gasp. Sara dropped her fork on her plate, letting it bounce off and hit the floor.

"Laura!" Fred said. "Enough. Everyone calm down."

Sara sat in silence. Her mother had never hit them before. She could see tears forming in Emma's eyes.

"I'm sorry," Emma said. She looked down at her plate and attempted to eat her dinner. The sting on her cheek tingled repeatedly. It was a blow Emma would not soon forget.

"I'm sorry, too," Laura said. She reached over and took Fred's hand in hers. "Carl, God rest his soul, was an ill man. Your aunt is correct. He did kill himself. You kids were much too young to know the truth. Your uncle let the girls run off to the ocean, and they drowned. I don't know if it was the medication he was on or the guilt of letting them drown or a combination of both, but for whatever reason, he took his own life. The past is the past, girls. We need to let them rest."

Emma was surprised her mother confirmed what her aunt had admitted. Her support only made Emma more confused over where her mother stood regarding Eddie's death. She wondered what other lies she may be hiding.

Sara found herself to be both stunned and mesmerized by the conversation that was unfolding before her. Emma had been in such a sour mood all week. Distant. Closed-off. Their usually close sisterly bond was gone. She reached down and picked her fork off the floor, wiping the tines across the paper napkin in her lap.

When did she get like this? Sara wondered to herself. She turned to her father. "Dad, have you heard from Eddie? He left last weekend, right?"

"No, I haven't heard from him," Fred replied.

"You were getting him a job, weren't you?" Emma asked. She looked over at her mother. "Why would he just up and vanish into thin air?"

Laura was about to bite into her chicken but stopped. She lowered the fork to her plate, picked up her napkin, and wiped her chin. She fixated on Emma with a long icy stare. Emma did not blink.

"I've been asking myself that all week," Fred said. "He was such a good kid. Talented too. He did some great work here around the property."

"He was a drifter." Laura chimed in, her tone was dismissive and uncaring. "A freeloader. A thief."

"Now, Laura, that's not fair," Fred said. "He meant well."

"He was a thief, Fred. We're lucky he didn't rob from us."

"All he did was take food. The kid was only trying to survive."

"What's it to you, Emma?" Laura asked. "Why do you care?"

"Emma had a crush on him," Sara blurted out. She pointed across the table at her sister and began to laugh.

"She thought he was cute."

"Stop it, Sara!" Emma yelled back.

Laura's concern over Emma's inquisitive attitude subsided. She'd forgotten about Emma's fondness for the handsome young stranger. Laura realized she might be overreacting to her daughter's barrage of questions.

"What's the big stain in the driveway?" Emma asked.

The smile spreading across Laura's face came to an abrupt halt.

"I'm not sure," Fred replied. He looked over at his wife. "When I asked Bobby about it he said it was an accident. Do you know what spilled?"

"I think it was from his truck," Laura said nervously.

"Why did he bring that big pot here anyway?" Emma asked. Her mother's stumbled response gave Emma a sense of courage. "What's it doing out in the barn? That's when that stain got here, isn't it?"

"What's that pot for, Dad?" Sara asked.

"Bobby brought it for the cows," Fred replied.

"My cows?" Sara cried. "Are we going to kill them? You promised me they were just for milking."

"Relax, Sara," Fred said soothingly. "I don't plan to butcher our cows. Bobby said he has other recipes for soaps and things. He said he would teach your mother."

Laura smiled and reached out and took Sara by the hand. She gave her daughter a reassuring squeeze.

"You never know when a pot that size can come in handy," Laura said.

"That's true," Fred said. "But I want to run a propane line out to it. I don't like the idea of a raging wood fire in that barn. A formal grill with a safety valve is what we need in there."

Laura looked around the table. Everyone had cleared their plate except for Emma. Her daughter was still pushing her food back and forth. Every now and then she would slide a few bits of peas and rice onto her fork and take a bite.

"Well we won't be using it for the cookout," Laura said. "Enough talk about the cows, that drifter, and your Uncle Carl. Am I clear?"

"Yes, Mother," Sara replied.

Laura looked on as Emma silently stared at her dish.

"Emma?" Laura asked.

"Sure," Emma said flatly.

Laura stood up and began collecting the dishes from the table. Sara and Fred joined her. Emma remained seated, sulking.

"I want Monday to be a lovely cookout," Laura said. "Emma, you cannot bring up your Uncle Carl, OK? Or Rose or Mary. My sister is fragile enough these days without someone digging up the past. This needs to be a fun family affair."

"Is Bobby coming?" Emma asked.

"Of course he is," Laura replied. "He always does."

"But he's not family. Why is he always here?"

Laura did not respond. She continued to collect the dishes and silverware from the table. Laura grabbed hold of Emma's plate and leaned closer to her daughter.

"Help your sister with the dishes."

Emma sighed, but obeyed, meeting Sara at the sink. Emma plugged the drain and turned the hot water on. She squirted dish soap into the basin and let her mind get lost watching the foam bubbles form. The lemon scent of the detergent brought her no comfort.

"What's with you?" Sara whispered. She looked back at her parents on the far side of the kitchen. "You've been in a mood ever since Eddie left. Did you really have that big of a crush on him? Why won't you talk to me about it?"

"It's for your own good," Emma replied. She glanced over her shoulder to make sure her mother was out of earshot. "Trust me, Sara, I'm doing this for you."

"For me? How? You've been pouting and sulking all week."

"I'm sorry, Sara. It's for the best."

"I can't believe Mom hit you. Those questions you were asking really upset her."

Emma turned off the hot water. Sara passed her the first dish, and she submerged it into the sink and began to wash it.

"You came home early last weekend," Sara continued. "Did you see something?"

"Drop it, Sara."

"I want to know." Sara was doing her best to balance a whispering tone with her rising temper. "You made Susan and I promise to cover for you and your broken chain. We did. Did you forget the three of us have a blood bond? That trust swings both ways. You were here for hours. What happened?"

"Is everything OK?" Laura asked.

Emma and Sara both jumped at the sound of their mother's voice. Laura was standing mere inches behind them, directly between the two girls.

"Everything is fine," Emma replied.

"No it's not," Sara countered.

"Sara, don't," Emma said.

"Emma came home early last week, and she's been making Susan and I cover for her. She's been a total bitch since then but won't say why."

"Sara!" Fred said. "Watch the language."

Laura rested her hands on Emma's shoulders and slowly dug her thumbs deep into her T-shirt. Emma winced but did not make a sound.

"The cows need milking," Laura said coldly. "Sara, go outside with your father. Fred, be a dear and show Sara that you won't be putting her big animal friends into the cauldron. I'll finish things with Emma."

Sara snatched a hand towel from the countertop, dried her hands, and flung it at Emma's head. The blue and white checkered cloth tumbled onto Emma's shoulder, coming to a rest on Laura's hand. Laura waited patiently for Fred and Sara to leave. As soon as the porch door closed she spun Emma around to face her.

"I've had enough, young lady. Your attitude tonight has been unacceptable. Now I think I know why. What time did you get home last week? The day you were supposedly out biking with Sara and your cousin."

Emma could not look her mother in the eye. Her cheek, still stinging from the hit it took earlier, became swollen and pink. Emma looked past her mother, out the window, and watched as Sara and her dad entered the barn. Laura grabbed Emma by the chin and snapped her head frontward.

"Answer me, Emma. What did you see? No more lies."

Emma suddenly felt consumed by anger and resentment. Her desire to stay quiet and hope things would simply go away was no longer an option for her.

"Lies? Are you kidding me?" Emma leaned forward, forcing her mother to take a small step away. "I saw what happened to Eddie, Mother. He didn't run off. Bobby killed him!"

Laura was stunned. She studied her daughter's face to see if there was any sign of concern or confusion. All Laura could see was rage.

"That's not true, Emma."

"Bullshit."

"Watch that tongue of yours. I want to know everything. Everything."

Laura turned to make sure Sara and Fred were still in the barn. She figured they would be out there for quite some time. Laura took Emma by her elbow and led her to the kitchen table, forcing her into a chair. Laura remained standing.

"Talk," Laura said.

Emma's mind raced as she debated what to say. She looked out at the barn, hoping her father would come back to stop the impending interrogation. Her heart told her she was trapped and the only person she could now trust was herself.

"My bike chain broke. I had to walk my bike home. I was at the edge of the driveway when I saw Bobby and Eddie unloading the truck."

"And?"

"I saw Bobby push the cauldron out, dumping it on top of Eddie."

"Then what?"

Emma stared deep into her mother's icy blue eyes, searching for any sign of trust or remorse. All she could see was the look her mother gave to Bobby when she kissed him after Eddie's death.

"I ran."

"You ran?"

Emma felt tears burst from her eyes. Her tears weren't for Eddie's death, however. It was at this moment she realized she could no longer believe in her mother.

"I saw the blood. I heard Eddie screaming for help. So, I grabbed my bike and ran away."

Emma lowered her head into her hands and sobbed uncontrollably. Laura did not reach out to embrace her daughter. Instead, she simply studied Emma's sounds and motions, searching for the slightest hint of pretense.

"Why?" Emma continued. She lowered her hands and looked up at her mother. "Why would Bobby do that?"

Laura looked into Emma's emerald green eyes. Her eyelids were red and swollen. Laura held Emma by the chin and used her thumbs to wipe the tears from her daughter's cheeks.

"That's not what happened," Laura said cautiously. "Eddie was helping Bobby unload the cauldron."

"I know. I saw them doing it together. But then Bobby ...."

"But then the planks supporting it gave way."

"What?" Emma was both confused and surprised by this explanation. "But I saw Bobby push it off onto Eddie. Then he jumped down to the ground. I heard Eddie screaming. That's when I ran."

"Then you left too soon. Bobby jumped down to save him, but his injuries were too severe. It was an accident."

"An accident?" Emma gently took hold of her mother's hands, pulling them away from her face. "But then where did Eddie go?"

Laura took a few steps back and turned her attention to the barn. Fred and Sara were still inside. She glanced over at the blood-stained crushed stone in the driveway.

"Bobby took care of things."

"I don't understand."

"Of course you don't." Laura walked back over to Emma and knelt down in front of her. "You're too young to. Emma, dear, where do I begin? What happened to that drifter was awful."

"Eddie. He had a name."

"What happened to Eddie was a horrible accident. But we couldn't call the police."

"Why not?"

"Well, for one thing, Bobby could have been arrested."

"So what?" Emma's confusion began to subside as she reminded herself of the kiss. "Why do you care what happens to him?"

"It's not just Bobby. Eddie supposedly had a record too. And your father, well, let's just say it's best not to have the police snooping around here. There are things about him that you cannot and will not ever know. When your Uncle Carl and sister and cousin died four years ago, we had week after week of the police here. Do you remember that?"

"I do. Every time the cops showed up you made us leave the room."

"And now you know why. We didn't want you to know the truth about what happened to your uncle. The police were very suspicious about how he died. There were no witnesses, so they had many questions for us."

"What's that have to do with Eddie?"

"Imagine if the cops come back here four years later for yet another dead body on our property. Trust me, there was one detective that didn't believe our story about your uncle's death. If he came back here, it would have caused too many problems. Your father, Emma, has a history with the police. The less we have them around here, the better. They can't be trusted."

"So, what happened to Eddie?"

"Bobby took care of Eddie's body. That's all you need to know. Maybe someday when you are older I can tell you more. I've already told you too much. Don't tell your father you know he has a bad history with the cops. This all stays between us."

"Doesn't Eddie's family deserve to know what happened to him?"

"Family? I know you were fond of the boy, Emma, but he was a thief and a drifter. His family obviously never cared for him, or he wouldn't have been homeless. Let it go."

Emma closed her eyes and recalled the entire conversation that her mother and Bobby had exchanged in the driveway. She played it over and over again in her mind and did her best to reconcile it with everything her mother was now telling her. Emma felt like the stories of Eddie and Uncle Carl were a giant jigsaw puzzle with too many missing pieces.

The silence in the kitchen was broken by the barn door creaking open. Emma looked past her mother's shoulder and smiled at seeing Sara and her father returning to the kitchen.

"Does anyone know what you saw?" Laura asked. She grabbed Emma by the chin. "Sara? Susan? Anyone?"

"No. That's why Sara's so angry with me. I didn't say a word. Honest."

"And you never will. Am I clear?"

"Yes."

Laura stood up and looked out the window. Fred and Sara were almost at the porch stairs.

"One more thing, Emma. You better make right by your sister. Repair whatever damage you did from lying to her about what happened. But never tell her the truth."

***

It was just before noon, the following day. The forecast called for a mild July day, with temperatures in the low 70's. The wind was pleasant today, carrying the crisp scent of salt air in from the Atlantic.

"Is it fixed?" Sara asked with hope.

Emma cranked the pedal on her bicycle, keeping a close eye on the newly installed chain. She stopped spinning the crankset and watched the rear wheel spin freely. Emma looked up at Sara and nodded. Sara's hands were locked around the bike's seat, holding the bicycle off the ground. She lowered it until the wheel hit the dirt. The bike shuddered before the wheel came to a halt. Emma did a final inspection of the chain, giving it several tugs to be sure it was set at the proper tension.

"Thanks, Sara," Emma said.

"I could never replace a bike chain. You did that with surgical precision."

"It's not that hard."

A roll of paper towels sat atop the picnic table a few feet from the siblings. Beside it was a coffee mug filled with a mixture of sugar and water. Emma poured the sweet syrup over her hands and began to scrub them vigorously. She then walked over to the water hose hanging against the barn and started to rinse them. When finished she tore a few pieces of paper towel off and finished cleaning her hands.

Sara stepped up onto the seat of the picnic table, spun around, and sat on the tabletop facing her sister. She watched as Emma methodically scrubbed each finger. The two had exchanged very few meaningful words since last night's explosive dinner.

"How's your cheek?" Sara asked.

"It's fine."

"I've never seen Mom explode like that."

Emma inspected her nails for grease. Once she was satisfied they were clean enough, she turned off the water faucet and walked back over to her bike. She started to wheel it away when Sara jumped off the table.

"Why won't you tell me what happened?" Sara asked. "What did you and Mom talk about when Dad and I went into the barn?"

"Sara, I told you last night before we went to bed."

"You told me not to worry about it. That you were protecting me."

"Because I am. Look, Sara, I know this is hard for you to understand right now. You need to trust me on this."

"How can I trust you if you won't tell me what happened?"

Emma could see her sister was not about to let this go.

"Sometimes trust requires faith. I would think after all these years you would just believe me. Remember our blood bond by the pond?"

"Of course I do. Why do you think I'm upset? Family forever. Remember?"

"We are, Sara."

"What did you see?"

Emma gripped the rubberized handles of her bicycle and took a deep breath. She wanted Sara to understand how upset she was that she couldn't be truthful with her. But she feared that if she shared that with her it would only make Sara continue to pressure her for information.

"It's not that I don't trust you, Sara. I just ... I just don't want you to get hurt. It's best that you don't know. I promised Mom."

Sara stared at her twin sister in disbelief. She realized Emma would never tell her what happened last weekend.

"Have it your way, Emma. I thought our blood bond was forever. I guess it's not."

"Sara, don't say that."

"That blade can cut both ways."

Sara turned and marched past the picnic table toward the front corner of the barn. She crashed directly into her father as he came around the corner.

"Where are you going?" Fred asked Sara. She did not answer him and simply maneuvered her way around him and continued trudging back to the house. Fred looked over at Emma and frowned. "I see you two haven't patched things up."

Fred walked over to the picnic table and took a seat on one end. He tapped his hand along the peeling mahogany painted plank beneath him. Emma leaned her bike against the closest tree, lowered her head, and sat next to her father.

"I've tried to. But she's being stubborn."

"Sara?" Fred said with feigned surprise. He smiled at the sound of Emma laughing. "Some things just take time."

"I know."

"I didn't realize you were still so upset about what happened to your sister, Uncle Carl, and Mary. All those questions last night. How long has this been bothering you?"

"Well, like I said, Aunty Jen told Susan the truth about how he died. I couldn't understand why you guys would lie about it. Then I started wondering if maybe we didn't know the truth about Rose and Mary. Did they really drown in the ocean?"

Fred clasped his hands together and closed his eyes,

searching for the proper response. The lies and deceptions were piling up and eating him away from the inside out. He needed to be honest with his daughter, without telling her the truth.

"We told you what happened, Emma. The girls suffered a terrible death. It was ... It was an accident. A horrible accident."

Accident, Emma said to herself. *Another accident that had to be covered up like they did with Eddie?*

A sense of dread washed over Emma. She had no idea what her father did and did not know about Eddie. She began to wonder if he could be trusted. Emma now doubted there was anyone she could confide in.

Fred glanced back at the house. He could see Laura and Sara in the kitchen talking.

"Tell me, Emma, what did you mean last night about Bobby coming here too much? You seemed very upset with him."

"It's just that Mom talks about family all the time, but then he's always here."

"He's done a lot for this family, Emma. Bobby ...."

The clatter of Bobby's F-150 engine echoed against the trees as the big Ford truck emerged from the path.

"Bobby's here," Fred continued. He turned to Emma and kissed her on the cheek. "You finish cleaning up. But don't get too clean. We have a lot of work to do to get ready for the cookout tomorrow."

Fred stood up and walked away to greet Bobby. Emma grabbed the garden hose and began to coil it around the stand attached to the barn. The rubbery tube was covered in leaves and mud, quickly dirtying her hands again. Emma sighed and returned to the picnic table to clean up. She proceeded to use the paper towel and soap-filled mug to wash up again. As she did, she couldn't help but replay the conversation she just had with her dad.

I wonder what he knows? Emma thought to herself.

"Hello, Emma," Bobby said.

Emma spun around, startled at Bobby's appearance. He was at the corner of the barn, with his shoulder leaning up against the siding. His arms were folded defensively across his black T-shirt. Bobby was directly in the line of sight of the entrance to the kitchen.

Instead of responding to Bobby, Emma turned and grabbed her bike. She took a path several feet away from him. Bobby took a few steps forward, intercepting Emma's escape. She quickened her pace, but Bobby seized the handlebar just as she tried to pass him. He pulled both the bike and Emma closer.

"I talked with your mother, Emma. She told me you think I'm some kind of killer?"

Emma could see the entrance to the kitchen several dozen yards away, but it felt like miles. She could see her entire family inside. Her heart raced, and her throat became dry like sandpaper. All she wanted to do was scream.

"Now, your mom explained to you that it was an accident. And it was. An accident. I want to make sure you are clear on that."

"I am," Emma managed to say.

"You won't be telling anyone what you saw, will you?"

"No."

Bobby released his grip on Emma's bike. She started to walk away. Bobby held his arm out in front of her neck.

"You seem like a nice kid, Emma. I've always liked you and your sister. You've got a real nice family here. But I want to be very clear with you. Accidents happen. I clean them up. You turn sixteen later this year. I want you to have a beautiful birthday. A great life. And you will. As long as you keep your mouth shut."

Bobby lowered his arm. Emma refused to look at him. It took all her willpower not to scream at the top of her lungs. Emma pushed her bike forward and slowly made her way back to the house. Tears ran down her face as she watched her parents and Sara laughing and having fun in the kitchen.

There's nobody I can trust.

NINE

Revelations

The traffic on Route 195 eastbound slowed to 45 miles per hour. Emma was approaching the city of New Bedford. She did the math in her head and estimated there would be another ninety minutes left in her journey. Given the holiday traffic, she could see that timeframe extending by an hour, if not longer. Emma considered pulling up a traffic map on her phone, but her mother had given her strict orders to avoid using her phone while away. Emma knew if their plan fell apart, it was possible the GPS data on her phone could be used to implicate her.

Since leaving Providence, Emma could not stop thinking about what Julie told her. The store owners. The book. The attack at Seabreeze. What Sara and her mother had done to Julie. Emma glanced over her shoulder as her Subaru crossed the Acushnet River.

"Fuck it," Emma said.

Emma's navy blue canvas bag was resting beside her in the passenger's seat. She shoved her hand inside and fumbled around until she found her phone. It felt like an eternity waiting for the device to power up. Once on, Emma went through her contact listing and dialed Jeff Jones.

"Hey there, Aunty Em," Jeff said. "You must be psychic. I

was just about to call you."

"Is everything OK?"

Emma tightened her grip on the steering wheel. She immediately shook her head at her nervous reaction to Jeff's call. Although Jeff was a police officer, he was also her cousin's son. Emma took a few deep breaths to try and calm herself down.

"Not really. I just got off the phone with Bob. Unfortunately, the cookout is canceled."

"Bob?"

"Sorry, Robert. Robert Grant, my boss. The Chief of Police. He insists I call him Bob lately, but it just feels weird to me."

Emma ran her fingernail along the edge of her phone. Robert Grant may have been Jeff's boss, but he also headed up the Truro police force. Bobby Mason lived in Truro. Her mind raced as she wondered if Jeff's change of plans might somehow be connected to Bobby.

"Why did the Chief of Police cancel your cookout?"

Jeff laughed at the serious concern in Emma's voice.

"I have to work, Em. I'm the junior guy, so I got pulled in for holiday coverage. It's fine. I mean, I was looking forward to having the event, but I can throw something together another time."

"Oh, OK. Sorry about that."

"So what are you up to?"

"Excuse me?"

"You called me, Em. Geez. What's going on? Are you driving? It sounds noisy."

"Yes, sorry. Look, Jeff, I was thinking about our chat the other week. At my place. When you told me about the store owners and that girl Julie."

"What about it?"

Emma glanced in her rearview mirror and let her eyes settle on the headrests in the back seat.

"I thought I heard something about a book."

"What kind of book?"

"A book of, um, urban legends?"

"Urban legends? In connection with what happened at the

store?"

"Yes. Does it ring a bell?"

Emma waited patiently for Jeff to respond. The thrum of the tires over the blacktop highway reverberated throughout the car's interior. A small dangling tree-shaped piece of cardboard hung from the front mirror, filling the car with a very unconvincing evergreen scent.

"Vaguely. That girl Julie Perez mentioned it a few times to Trevor. Officer Stevens in Provincetown. I remember him asking me about it. Where did you hear about it?"

"I don't recall. Maybe she gave an interview somewhere. What did she say?"

"She was adamant that there was this book of urban legends local to Cape Cod. Trevor and I both thought she was crazy. She insisted that one of the legends was about these candle makers that would put the bones of their victims into candles."

"Do you know who wrote the book?"

"That was one of my issues. Julie claimed there was no author. And she didn't have a copy to prove it was true."

"Odd."

"I know, right? A mysterious book with a mysterious legend about candles with bones inside. You know, it's so weird that you brought that up. Shit. I just got a chill. Did you talk to my mom?"

"About?"

"She told you about the candle, right?"

"What candle?"

"The rosemary one."

Emma stared blankly at the vehicles ahead of her. The average traffic speed was now around 40 mph. The SUV to her left blared its horn as Emma's Subaru drifted out of the lane she was in. She quickly corrected her course.

"The one she kept next to her bed? What about it?"

"OK, well brace yourself. Supposedly, grams – your Aunt Jennifer – told my mom, just before she passed, that the candle contained the bones of Rose and Mary inside it. Those are the kids that died at the beach in the eighties, right?"

Emma looked at her rearview mirror again, focusing on

the headrests.

"Em?" Jeff continued. "Did I lose you?"

"Sorry. I'm here. Rose and Mary. Yes, I remember."

"Of course you do. What am I saying. Rose was your sister."

"She was. And Mary would have been your aunt."

Emma frowned as the traffic came to a halt. Her journey, both on the road and with this phone conversation, was proving to be filled with surprises.

"So, Jeff," Emma asked. "Did you, um, check?"

"Check what, Em?"

"The candle."

There was a slight pause before Jeff burst out laughing.

"Of course not," Jeff replied. "Well, my mom did give it a long hard look. Grams never lit the wicks. Mom doesn't want to dishonor her memory, you know. I'm not about to crack the thing open looking for bones. You know my grandmother was not well, Em. Her brain was pretty much toast at the end."

"I know. It's just odd. I mean, isn't that what Julie said about the candle legend? That people were in the candles?"

"I guess so. Huh. I never really made that connection until you brought it up. I forgot all about that mystery book. But there's more to this story, Em. Unfortunately, my mom won't tell me. I figured she would've told you."

"No, Jeff. Your mom never told me what Aunty Jen told her on her death bed."

"That's not what I meant. There was something else, Em. Supposedly grams told my mom the truth about how her dad died."

"The truth? About Uncle Carl?"

"Supposedly he didn't kill himself. Mom seemed rattled by what she was told. I pressed her on it, but she didn't want to talk about it. Maybe you two should have a talk sometime. You were both there that day, weren't you? When they all died at the beach."

"It was your mother's birthday."

The traffic began to move again. Emma quickly accelerated to 50 mph. She turned up the fan speed and aimed a vent at her face. The fresh air washed over her beaded brow, bringing her some much-needed relief.

"Oh, right. See, I never knew that until Mom told me last month. It was a birthday party. What is it with this family, Em? So many secrets."

Emma did not reply. Her mind was adrift, and her eyes were fixated on her rearview mirror and the backseat of her car.

"Maybe someday you will tell me yours," Jeff added.

"Mine?"

"I know that you lived with my grams and mom for a short time. You moved in when you were only sixteen, right?"

"I did."

"Nobody will tell me why. Just that there was some big falling out. It's like pulling teeth with you and mom. It had something to do with your dad, right?"

Emma could not stop thinking about the rosemary-scented candle her mother kept hidden in the bunker. Despite weeks of rebuilding their trust, her mother never told Emma the story behind that candle.

"I need to go. Sorry, Jeff, but the traffic is getting crazy. I'm sorry you have to work on the holiday. We'll talk more another time. I promise."

"No worries. Drive safely, Aunty."

Emma ended the call and immediately dialed her cousin Susan. As the call went through all Emma could think about were the bones of her sister and cousin being in the rosemary candle.

Is that why my mother refuses to talk about that candle?

"Emma?" Susan asked. "It's so great to hear from you. I feel like you've been avoiding me since my mom's funeral. Is everything OK?"

"I'm fine. I just talked to Jeff."

"Did he tell you about the cookout? What a shame. He's so proud of his new place and was looking forward to having everyone over."

"I know. Perhaps another time. Susan, I need to talk to you about something."

"Sure."

"Jeff told me what your mom said about the candle. About the rosemary candle."

"Oh."

Emma waited a few seconds for her cousin to continue. It was apparent she was going to need to push Susan to discuss it further.

"Do you really think our sisters' bones are in that candle?" Emma asked.

"Of course I don't. Why would you think they were? My mother was not well, Emma. You know that."

"What else did she say? Jeff said she told you something about Uncle Carl's death. It wasn't really a suicide? What was it? Jeff said you wouldn't tell him."

"Emma ... I don't really think ...."

"Please, Susan. That was your thirteenth birthday. It was a nightmare for everyone. Family holidays in our teens were absolute tragedies."

"They were, weren't they? Remember your sixteenth? God, you were such a wreck that day."

"Christmas was worse." Emma paused and took a deep breath. The sterile scent of evergreen brought back Christmas memories she buried decades ago. She reached out and ripped the air-freshener from the mirror and tossed it to the floor. "We know our moms kept secrets from us. I fear we're becoming just like them."

"Why would you say that?"

"Jeff reminded me that we never told him why I moved in with you."

"That was *your* decision, Emma, not mine. You were adamant that he not know the truth. I was simply abiding by your wishes."

"I'm sorry, cousin. You're right. That was my call. I own that. And someday we need to come clean with Jeff. He deserves to know."

"Agreed."

"So tell me what your mom said. Please?"

"She said ... Jesus, I can't believe I'm even saying this out loud. Emma, you know how they told us that Rose and Mary drowned in the rough waves? And that my dad blamed himself and committed suicide over it?"

"Yes. But when we were kids, they told us all three had drowned at the beach. It was only later when we found out about your dad's suicide. So what's the real story, Susan?"

"According to my mom, my dad ... Emma, we really shouldn't do this on the phone."

"I need to know."

"No, really. I think this is more of a face to face discussion."

"Tell me. Please."

Emma and Susan both released a long sigh of frustration.

"Don't shoot the messenger," Susan said. "My mom said that ... that ... God. She said that your dad killed my father. The whole beach thing was a huge coverup."

Emma did not know what to say next. Ever since her sixteenth birthday party she wondered how her uncle had died. Then, just last month, her mother told her the same story – that her father had killed her uncle. Her aunt's confession to Susan seemed to confirm everything.

My mother was being honest with me. Can I trust her? Can I trust Bobby?

"Emma?" Susan quickly became frustrated with the silence coming from her cousin. "Emma?"

"I'm here."

"See," Susan said. "I told you we shouldn't discuss this on the phone. Look, Emma, I know it's not true. Your dad was a wonderful man. The Uncle Fred I knew never would have committed murder. You have to believe that, don't you?"

"Of course," Emma said flatly.

"Don't be mad, Emma. Please. This is why I never told you. It's just the ramblings of a sick old woman. My mother was deep into dementia. She wasn't well. Jeff never should have said anything."

"Was there anything else?"

"Anything else? Like what?"

"If my dad really did kill your dad, then how did Rose and Mary die? Did they really drown in the ocean?"

"Why would you ask something like that? My dad was not right. He killed himself. My mother was mentally ill and didn't know what she was saying. I don't want to talk about this anymore."

The traffic slowed to a halt. The smell of evergreen wafting from the cardboard laying on the floor, although mild, seemed to engulf Emma. She turned the fan up another notch.

"I'm sorry, Susan. I'm slowly remembering stuff from our childhood. It comes in bits and pieces. Our family seems to have so many lies and secrets."

Emma was exhausted. Her body ached from spending last night sleeping in her car, and her mind was a wreck from the conversations with Julie, Jeff, and now Susan. She looked at the clock on the car's dashboard. It wasn't even close to noon.

"I need to get going," Emma continued.

"I'm sorry if our chat was a downer."

"Trust me, you have nothing to apologize for."

"Hey, with Jeff canceling his cookout maybe we could get together on Monday for the holiday. Do you have plans?"

"Can I get back to you?"

"Sure. We can do something simple at my place. I can pull out the photo albums, and we can take a walk down memory lane. Talk about happier times."

"That sounds great, Susan. Enjoy your day."

"Goodbye."

Emma ended the call and tossed her phone back into her bag. She briefly considered powering it down, but figured at this point it didn't matter anymore. Emma gave another look at her rearview mirror. All was silent from the compartment behind her rear seats. The dose she gave Julie should last another two hours, if not longer. Plenty of time to get her back to Wellfleet.

TEN

Sweet Sixteen

1988 Saturday 1-Oct 1:00 p.m.

Fred stood at the end of the hallway that led to the kitchen, assessing the chaos running back and forth between the living and dining rooms. The twin's sweet sixteen birthday party was underway, and the house was overrun with over two dozen teenagers. Bobby Brown's "Don't Be Cruel" was blaring from a portable stereo perched atop the mantle over the fireplace. The dining room table was filled with cookies, chips, and dips, surrounding the girl's birthday cake. The cake contained four sections. Two were shaped like the numeral one, and the other two were shaped like a six. They were arranged in a mirrored pattern.

"I don't remember being this out of control at their age," Laura said.

Fred turned to find his wife standing by his side. He let out a soft chuckle.

"I think we were worse," Fred said.

"I suppose." Laura studied the two rooms, looking for the birthday girls. Sara and Susan were busy stealing bits of pink frosting from the edge of the cake. Emma was nowhere to be found. "Fred, where's Emma?"

Fred took a few steps into the pandemonium and pushed his way through to the dining room. Sara smiled as he approached, sucking the sweet buttercream from her fingers.

"Where's your sister?" Fred asked Sara.

"That grouch?" Sara replied. "Who knows."

Susan tapped Sara on the shoulder and pointed at two boys standing across the room by the fireplace. The taller one looked over and smiled.

"Bye, Dad," Sara said. She grabbed Susan by the hand, and the two left the room, heading toward the fireplace.

Fred grabbed a handful of potato chips before navigating his way through the maze of partiers on his way back to the hallway. There was now a line to get into the bathroom. He sighed, spun around, and headed to the foyer. Fred opened the front door and was surprised to find Emma sitting on the porch steps. He took a seat beside her.

"Enjoying your party?" Fred asked.

"Sure," Emma said quietly. She stared at her white laced sneakers, paying no attention to her father.

Fred took a deep breath, taking in the refreshing, salty air. It was a pleasant day with the temperature spiking to the upper sixties, making for an unseasonably warm October weekend.

"You don't seem to be having fun. Why are you out here all alone?"

Emma glanced over at Bobby's Ford F-150 parked at the end of the driveway. Jennifer was sitting in the passenger seat, talking with Bobby. The windows were lowered, but they were too far away to allow Emma to hear what they were discussing.

"It's just a lot of people, Dad."

"But you two asked for this big party."

"Sara wanted it. Not me."

"What's going on, Emma? You've been distant for months. Ever since the fourth of July. You were a downer on that holiday. Then again at your aunt's birthday. All the holidays and family events."

Fred waited patiently for his daughter to respond. Emma sat motionless, slumped forward with her elbows on her knees, resting her chin in her palms. Her focus was on Bobby's truck. Fred leaned over and kissed Emma just above her ear. He stood up and stretched his lower back.

"I'm always here for you to talk with, Emma. Just because I'm your father doesn't mean you can't confide in me."

Emma responded with a half-hearted nod. She leaned forward slightly, straining to hear the conversation happening in the pickup truck.

***

Bobby's knuckles whitened as his hands tightened their grasp around the steering wheel. Despite having his truck's windows lowered, the cab still reeked of alcohol. He tried not to stare at Jennifer as she took a large gulp of wine. Bobby glanced at his watch. He was growing impatient.

"Just tell me," Jennifer said. "Who is she?"

"For the last time, Jennie, there's no other woman. How many times do we have to go through this?"

Jennifer glared at Bobby's profile. Despite their fractured relationship, she couldn't help but drink in how handsome he looked. He gazed out the window ahead, refusing to look her in the eye. She took another swig of chardonnay.

"I don't believe you. You promised me we would eventually be together. Carl died years ago. You said …."

"I said it wasn't the time, Jennie. Remember? I'm sorry, but that was a long time ago." Bobby finally turned to face her. Jennifer's skin was pale, and she looked much older than her age, having put on twenty pounds since Carl's death four years ago. "People change."

Bobby looked past Jennifer and focused on Emma and Fred on the front porch. He knew Emma was watching them but was surprised to see Fred now outside. He was relieved when Fred turned to go back into the house but wondered what he and Emma might have discussed.

"Is this about my drinking? Don't worry, I have it under control. Susan's my designated driver."

Bobby did not respond. He was too busy keeping an eye on Emma.

"Do you not find me attractive anymore? Is that it? I can lose the extra weight, Bobby. Just tell me."

"It's not the weight. Look, I've changed too, OK? We have no future together. I've told you this many times. I'm sorry, Jennie. Can you please stop this?"

Jennifer stared longingly into Bobby's eyes. She reached out and ran her fingers across his chiseled jawline. The stubble scraping across her skin brought back memories of a passion lost long ago.

"Can I ask you just one thing?"

Bobby nodded, relieved the conversation was finally ending.

"Who is she?"

Bobby sighed and lowered his head. He did not bother to answer her. Instead, he opened his door and stepped out onto the driveway. The sun's rays felt like a warm embrace across his face. He took a deep breath of salt air and exhaled, letting the tension leave his body. The laughter of two girls near the barn brought a much-needed smile to his face. That smile faded as he noticed Emma staring at him. Bobby slammed the truck's door shut and marched toward the front porch.

Emma felt a sense of panic cascade from the top of her head down to her feet. She stood up and started walking to the barn. The sounds of laughter could be heard in the distance. Emma quickened her pace, but Bobby jogged ahead, running past her and then turning to halt her progress.

"Excuse me," Emma said sternly.

"Where are you headed?" Bobby asked.

"Just to see some friends."

"I saw you talking to your dad. You haven't broken our agreement, have you?"

"No." Emma attempted to walk around Bobby, but he continued to block her path. "Can you get out of my way?"

Bobby checked the porch to make sure nobody was watching them. He stepped forward and bent down so that he was eye to eye with Emma.

"I just want to make sure you aren't thinking of talking to

your dad about what you saw. Trust me, Emma, he's not the person you want to confide secrets with."

Emma's pulse quickened. She wasn't consumed by fear. All she felt was anger. Emma didn't know what her aunt had been talking to Bobby about in his truck, but she never forgot the way he kissed her mother after killing Eddie.

"He's my father," Emma hissed. "My dad. The best dad anyone could ask for. You keep coming around this house trying to kiss up to my family. I know the monster you really are. You will never be half the man my father is."

Bobby recoiled slightly, taking a step back. He didn't like Emma's brash attitude and attack on his character or intentions. Bobby grabbed Emma by her shoulders, locking her to the ground.

"Stop worshiping your daddy and thinking he's some saint. Your Uncle Carl didn't die at the beach, Emma. It wasn't some accident. Your father killed him."

Emma let out a gasp. She felt the blood drain from her face. She studied Bobby's eyes, searching for the slightest sign of deception.

"That's not true."

"It's the truth. Ask him yourself. I cleaned up his mess. Just like I cleaned up the mess I made of that punk Eddie."

"No!" Emma lowered her head as tears began to run down her face.

Bobby smiled and gently released the young girl.

"Don't think you can run to him to protect you, OK? I don't know what else you saw that day, but you best keep that mouth of yours shut. Or I will close it. Permanently."

Emma pushed her way past Bobby and ran into the barn.

***

From the outside, the Johnson family barn was an ominous, imposing structure. Inside, the aroma of the cows and golden hay, along with the soft light that came in through the small upper windows, always made it a place of peaceful solitude for Emma.

"I saw her come in here earlier," Susan said.

Sara stepped past her cousin and pulled Susan into the barn. She quickly closed the side door behind them.

"Mom needs us both inside before we can cut the cake," Sara said. She looked around the dim, quiet barn. "Emma!"

All was quiet, save for the muffled giggles of teenagers running around outside. Bands of light cut across the barn, intersected by falling wafts of yellow straw. Becky, Sara's favorite cow, strolled to the edge of her stall to see what the commotion was all about. The cow stared at the two girls, gently waving its tail back and forth. Becky shoved her head over the top railing of her stall, accidentally knocking a pitchfork to the ground. The tool came to rest beneath the ladder that led to the loft.

The silence was broken by the rustle of shifting mounds of hay from overhead. Sara and Susan looked up at the loft above the stalls and watched as dust, soot, and hay fell from the edge. After a few moments, Emma peered her head out through the railings.

"What?" Emma asked flatly.

"Why are you up there?" Susan asked. She walked over to the ladder, gripped the rails, and looked up at her cousin. "Everyone is wondering why you aren't enjoying the party."

"I just want to be alone."

Susan planted her left foot onto the lowest rung and carefully climbed the ladder. Sara followed close behind. Once in the loft, they found Emma leaning against a pile of hay in the back corner. She was holding her legs close to her chest, resting her head on her kneecaps. The earthy scent of hay was everywhere.

"Are you OK," Susan asked. Emma looked up at her cousin, exposing her swollen red eyelids. "Have you been crying? Why?"

"I just want to be alone," Emma repeated.

"What is *with* you?" Sara demanded to know. "You've been so damn moody for months now. I'm sick of it."

"Sara, please," Susan interrupted. "What is it, Emma? You can tell us. Family, remember?"

Susan held her thumb up close to Emma's face. The scar from their blood bond four years prior was nowhere to be found. Emma understood the gesture's significance. She simply turned and looked away.

"I don't get you!" Sara said.

"Sara, don't ...."

"No, Susan. Emma's been in a mood since her crush Eddie ran off this summer. She's been a complete clam. Why?"

Susan held an arm out and pushed Sara to the side. Sara let out a sigh and took a seat against the railing. The floorboards beneath them creaked as the girls shuffled about. Susan sat beside Emma and put her arm around her.

"What is it?" Susan asked.

Emma wiped the tears from her cheeks. She looked deep into her cousin's blue eyes before throwing her arms around her. The potency of the hug startled Susan.

"I wish I could," Emma said softly. She released her cousin and looked over at Sara. Her sister's arms were crossed, and she was pouting. "I wish I could tell you both. This is just something I have to deal with, OK? If I tell you two, well, it ... it's just not safe."

Sara and Susan looked at one another. Susan shook her head and shrugged.

"It's that day," Sara said. "The day your bike broke. You haven't been the same since. Why? Why, Emma?"

Emma's eyes darted back and forth between Sara and Susan. She desperately wanted to tell them everything that she saw, as well as the threats from Bobby. All she could do was imagine Sara or Susan having an unexplained accident at the hands of Bobby. Emma knew she could not let that happen.

"You're right, Sara," Emma said. "It all started that day. I need you both to understand that I have to remain quiet, OK? I know we have a blood bond. I know we are family. But I am doing this for all of us. To protect our family."

Sara sighed and threw her hands up in disgust.

"For how long?" Susan asked, keeping her tone calm and supportive. "You can't stay like this forever."

"I know," Emma replied. "I just need time to sort things through."

"Time?" Sara asked. "It's been months."

"Sara," Susan interrupted. "You aren't helping things. Relax."

"You aren't here all the time like I am, Susan." Sara took a deep breath to try and calm down. "Emma, there are days you are fine. Things are back to normal. But then you get in these moods and shut down. What is it? What?"

"What's different today?" Susan asked. She looked over at Sara. "If Emma has good and bad days, there must be a trigger. Maybe it's someone here at the party?"

Sara crawled forward on her hands and knees and sat next to Susan. The three girls were now sitting in a circle facing one another.

"You're right," Sara said. "All this time I've thought Emma's moods were unpredictable. But are they?"

"I'm sitting right here, Sara," Emma said. "Don't talk about me like I'm not in the room."

"Then talk to us," Sara replied.

Susan and Sara waited, but Emma remained silent.

"Is it Mom?" Sara asked. Emma did not respond. "Dad? Aunty Jen? Bobby? Who else ...."

Emma tensed up when Sara mentioned Bobby. Sara and Susan both noticed it.

"It's Bobby," Susan said with excitement. "What about him?"

"Enough!" Emma cried. "Stop it. Both of you just stop."

Sara glared at her sister, disgusted by Emma's refusal to open up.

"I've had it," Sara hissed back. She stood up and dusted the hay from her jeans. "I'll be in the house, having fun. When Mom asks where you are, I will tell her I don't know. Because honestly, Emma, I don't know where you are anymore."

Susan slid over to be by her cousin's side, wrapping her arm around Emma's shoulder. Sara walked back over to the railing, stopping where it opened to the ladder.

"Sara, wait," Emma said. Sara turned and waited, hoping her sister may have finally come to her senses. "Don't say anything to Mom. About me. Or Bobby. Don't say anything to anyone."

Sara shook her head in disappointment and started to descend the ladder. She stopped when she was low enough so that only her head appeared above the edge of the loft.

"Remember this day, Emma," Sara said sternly. "I'm done reaching out to you. Our blood bond is terminated."

ELEVEN

A New Direction

Tom ran his thumb across his phone's screen, quickly scrolling through the last few months of accumulated photos. He zoomed out so that he could easily scan by date until he reached the pictures from last December's trip to Provincetown. After a few moments, he found the images Julie had taken at the candle store. One of them was of Marc standing behind Tom, resting his chin on the top of Tom's head.

"That was right before Marc found the arrows," Tom said softly. He glanced over at Max, resting by his side. "I still can't believe he's gone."

Tom relocked his cell. The screen showed 11 a.m. He realized his last text from Julie was well over an hour ago. She told Tom she was leaving to run her errands and would need another hour.

"She said she needed to get her stupid cocoa butter," Tom said with frustration. He turned and looked at Max. "That shouldn't take an hour. She could have walked to the store and back by now. She's completely ruining our beach day. Traffic at this hour is going to be brutal. We are just fucked."

Max immediately recoiled and lowered his ears.

"Sorry," Tom said softly. He ran his fingertips across the

dog's head. "Daddy said the F word."

Tom learned early on that foul language upset his rescue dog. He wasn't sure if Max had a bad history with the word, or if it was merely Tom raising his voice in anger. Perhaps it was a combination of the two. All Tom knew was that swearing brought his dog stress. He leaned forward and pulled Max close to his chest.

"At this rate, we will be lucky to reach the beach by one. Maybe even two. I've got to drop you off at Mom's house. Plus we have to stop for lunch. This day is just falling apart."

Tom unlocked his phone and sent Julie another text.

Do I need to come over and get you?

As Tom waited for a reply, he scrolled back through the past five unanswered messages sent to Julie. Tom checked the status below each one.

"Max, I just realized she hasn't read any of these. Not one. I wonder if her phone is off. We might need to go over there."

Both Max and Tom jumped at the pounding on Tom's front door. Max leaped from the couch and began barking and spinning in circles. The dog bolted for the door and continued to bark ferociously. Tom placed his head against the living room window to see who was on the porch.

"Stop, Max," Tom commanded. Max continued to bark as Tom made his way to the front door. "It's just the new neighbors."

Tom curled two fingers under Max's collar to restrain him and then opened his front door. Robin, Tara, and Robin's brother Darryl were standing there.

"Doggie!" Tara cried. She ran into Tom's hallway and flung her arms around Max. The dog stopped barking and started wagging his tail. Tara giggled as Max ran his damp cool nose across her face.

"Hi, Tom," Robin said. "Sorry about Tara."

"It's fine," Tom replied. He looked up at Darryl. "Hey."

"Hey," Darryl replied.

"I'm heading out of town today, and I need a favor," Robin said. She looked down at Tara.

The blood emptied from Tom's face as he suddenly pictured himself being Robin's new babysitter. He shot the young girl a cautious glance. Robin burst out laughing.

"Lord no!" Robin said. "I just need you to keep an eye on the place. I'm expecting a delivery. We're going up to Boston to get the last of my stuff."

"Boston? That's a big switch to come here."

"It is, but you know, I think it was the right move. I know my flight options here won't be as great as Logan. So I may still need to go up there when I travel for work. But with my mom close by, I think it's for the best."

"Hope Street is a great area. I think you'll like it here."

"I'm going to miss Boston, though. Darryl lives up there. That might make dating tough for you two."

"Robin!" Darryl said. "Would you stop already?"

Tom and Darryl grinned as they looked each other up and down.

"I'm heading to the beach today, so I won't be able to keep an eye out for your delivery. Does it need to be signed?"

"No, I just didn't want someone to swipe it."

"It will be safe here. Like I said, you picked a good area."

Robin looked down at Tara and Max. Tara found a rope toy, and the two were engaged in a fierce battle of tug of war. Max was slowly dragging the young child down the hallway and into the kitchen.

"Let's go, Tara We've got a busy day ahead."

Tara released her end of the rope, sending Max tumbling backward. She ran to him and kissed him on the head before returning to her mother.

"Enjoy the beach," Tara said. She put her arm around Tara and led her down the porch stairs.

"Nice to see you again, Tom. Sorry about my sister."

"No worries. Jewels is just as bad."

Darryl smiled and gave Tom a wink before leaving. Tom was surprised to find himself blushing. He closed the door and turned and looked at Max, who was busy in the kitchen chewing on his rope toy.

"What do you think, Max?"

Max dropped his toy and trotted down the hallway to be

by Tom.

"Darryl seems nice, doesn't he? But he's up in Boston. I've never been able to make a relationship work with someone that far away." Tom paused and knelt down beside his dog. "What am I saying? We both know I can never make it work with anyone. Probably best to just start as friends. After all, Jewels was right when she said we both need more friends. Robin is a bit pushy but nice. I know her and Jewels will end up as good friends. And you obviously have a new best friend with Tara. I should probably reach out to Darryl."

Tom patted Max on his head and went over to the sofa to check his phone. He frowned when he saw the blank screen.

"We should walk over and check on Aunty Jewels. Or maybe drive? We could finish packing Ruby and assume she's almost ready to go. Or ...." Tom glanced back at Max. "Or we could be bad. Should we be bad?"

Max stared at Tom, panting from his tiresome playtime with Tara.

"I vote bad. Here, Max."

Tom flopped onto the couch and patted the cushion next to him. Max ran over and jumped up, settling in close to Tom's side. Tom put one arm around Max, and with his free hand opened the GPS tracker app on his phone. There were two devices listed. One was labeled "Max." Tom clicked on it, and the map beneath the list zoomed in on his exact location in Providence, displayed as a blue blinking cursor with a series of concentric pulsating rings around it. He smiled as he palmed the tracking fob on Max's collar.

"You are not to tell Aunty Jewels about this." Tom selected the next device on the list, labeled "Jewels." There was a slight pause before the map image began to zoom out. "If she knew I put a GPS tracker in her bag she would freak out. But she wouldn't let me track her phone and ...."

Tom furrowed his eyebrows as he watched the image zoom and pan east. The map was tracking well beyond Providence.

"What the fuck?"

Max immediately sat up and lowered his ears.

"Sorry. Sorry. It's OK. Where is she, Max? Where's Aunty

Jewels?"

Max instinctively turned and looked at the window. Tom released his dog and Max ran to the front door and waited. Tom leaned forward and studied his phone. The map stopped panning as the blinking cursor settled in on Route 6, near Dennis, Massachusetts.

"This makes no sense. Why is she way out there?"

Tom flipped back to the text messages he exchanged with Julie earlier in the morning, before she went silent.

Where are you? It's 9:30!

I still have to run my errands.

WTF? Can't they wait?

I need my cocoa butter!!!!

Traffic is going to suck the longer we wait.

Don't obsess.

Me? I'm not the one seeing The Ghost of Mrs. Closed! LOL

That's NOT funny. I need at least another hour. I will text when ready.

OK.

Looking forward to a fab beach day!

Ditto on that, Jewels.

A sense of panic began to set in as Tom started to wonder if Julie hadn't imagined things. Tom tapped his knee, signaling Max to sit by his side. He stroked the dog's neck, trying to calm himself down.

"What if that *was* the sister?"

Tom's phone suddenly rang, breaking his concentration. The ringtone was the "Imperial March" from *Star Wars*. He frowned as he answered it.

"Hi Mom," Tom said.

"What time are you dropping Max off?" Dorothy asked. "I can't wait around all morning. I thought you wanted to beat the traffic? Weren't you planning to be here by ten?"

"That was the plan, but, Jewels isn't, um ...." Tom's mind raced as he tried to come up with an excuse to make. "She's not feeling well."

"What's wrong? She seemed fine yesterday. Does she have a fever? Runny nose? Where did you end up going for dinner? I bet she ate something bad. I told you I should have cooked for you. Should I call her?"

"No, Mom. No. I don't think I will be coming by with Max today. The beach trip is canceled."

Tom stood up and shuffled over to his bedroom. He set his phone to Speaker/Mute and began collecting his backpack and archery case.

"Canceled?" Dorothy yelled. "Do you mean to tell me I've been waiting around all morning for nothing? Do you know how much more I have to do to get ready for the cookout on Monday? Are you sure there isn't something else going on? This all seems very last minute."

Tom groaned as he grabbed his phone and unmuted the call.

"She's cramping, OK? It's that time of the month, and she's all cramped up. I think she called it a very heavy flow. Do I need to give you more details?"

There was a slight pause before Mrs. Leblanc spoke. When she did her voice was much calmer in both its tone and pace.

"That won't be necessary. I'm sorry I yelled. Let me know if things change."

"Sure thing."

Tom ended the call and opened his archery case. Everything inside was perfectly arranged. He removed a black plastic bin of bullet tips used for target practice and replaced them with a new set. Tom opened the silver metal box to inspect his recent purchase of rear-deploying broadhead tips. Rick Peterson, Tom's instructor from Ocean State Archery, had recommended them. Rick said they were deadly and extremely effective for hunting.

Max cautiously entered the bedroom, keeping an eye on the two bags now piled on Tom's bed. The dog laid down across the doorway, blocking the exit.

"Not now, Max."

Tom stepped over his dog and went into the kitchen. He grabbed four bottles of water, a few protein bars, a plastic bowl, and a bag of Max's dog treats. Tom returned to the bedroom and tossed everything into his backpack.

"Lose the long face, Max. We're going for a ride."

Max sat up and flipped his ears straight into the air. His tail started wagging back and forth, banging against the bedroom doorway.

"You heard me. Did you want to go for a ride?"

Max jumped onto Tom, almost knocking him to the ground. Tom giggled as he grabbed Max by his front legs and lowered the dog to the ground. He secured his archery case and then zipped up his backpack, tossing it over his shoulder.

"OK, let's go."

***

Tom pulled Ruby up to the curb in front of Julie's apartment. Her street was eerily quiet for a holiday weekend. Max was seated in the back of the Jeep. As soon as Tom shut off the engine, the dog thrust his head between the front seats and looked at Tom.

"No. I need you to stay. OK? Stay, Max."

Max watched as Tom exited his Wrangler and headed down Julie's driveway. Tom looked back and pointed at Max. The dog understood, and with a slight whimper laid down across the rear seat.

Julie's car was the only one in the back lot behind the three-story house. Tom tried the car's door handle, but it was still locked. He bent down searching for anything that might belong to Julie. Tom quickly became frustrated after realizing there was nothing but dirt and leaves scattered beneath his feet. He looked over and scanned the first floor and saw Mr. Fluffy sitting in the back window watching him.

Tom jogged back to the front door and pulled his keys from his pocket. He fumbled through until he found the one for Julie's apartment. He did not bother to knock, and let himself in.

"Jewels?" Tom waited a few seconds. Mr. Fluffy appeared at the end of the hallway. "Jewels? Are you here?"

Tom closed the door and quickly inspected the kitchen, bedroom, and bathroom. He was about to leave when a chilling thought occurred to him. Tom went back into Julie's bedroom and approached the closet. He took a deep breath before flinging the door open. Tom was relieved to find nothing but clothes inside. He looked down and smiled at Julie's Zombunny slippers. Julie's cat emerged from between Tom's legs and pounced on one of the furry mangled rabbits.

"I wish you could talk," Tom said to Mr. Fluffy. "You probably know where she went."

Tom made a brief stop in the kitchen to make sure there were food and water for the cat. He gave one last look around before stepping outside. Tom double checked the lock on the apartment door and ran over to Ruby. He was glad to see that Max was waiting for him and did not go exploring. Tom opened the GPS tracker on his phone and pulled up Julie's device. The map panned past Dennis, moving further out along Cape Cod.

"Please prove me to be wrong." The pulsating cursor finally came to a stop. It now showed her location as east of Harwich, less than twenty miles from Wellfleet. Tom closed his eyes as he recalled Julie's abduction and horrific events that had transpired in Wellfleet two months earlier. He opened his eyes and exhaled. "Not again."

Tom felt his eyes well up as he climbed into his Jeep. Max, always attuned to his master's emotions, immediately thrust his head into the front of the vehicle and slid his snout against Tom's shoulder. Tom pulled his dog closer.

"I know I should call Trevor, Max. But what am I going to tell him? That I put a tracker in her bag and she's off at the

Cape without me? All he'll do is throw a bunch of questions back at me to tell me I'm wrong. He didn't believe me last time. I had to be the one to save her. Me! Not Trevor. Not the cops." Tom wiped the tears from his cheeks and fired up the engine. "I can't rely on them."

Tom buckled his seatbelt and gave Max a gentle push reward. The dog understood the gesture and spun around twice before laying down. Tom fired up the engine and tossed a pair of sunglasses on.

"Time for a road trip, Max. We need to go save Aunty Jewels."

TWELVE

The Plan

Bobby shoved the last chunk of hamburger into his mouth, letting the melted cheddar cheese drip from his lips. He didn't bother to wait to swallow the food before tearing open the second burger on the plate in front of him. Laura frowned as she stared at the greasy chicken sandwich Bobby brought for her. She looked over at the clock hanging on the kitchen wall.

"It's after noon," Laura said. "She should have been back by now."

"Relax," Bobby replied. He snatched the last of the French fries and tossed them into his mouth. "We expected delays."

"The plan was for her to get the girl last night or early this morning. That drive is less than two hours. Something must have gone wrong."

"We both knew the chances of her grabbing Julie last night were a long shot. Today's the day."

Bobby took a sip of his cola and quickly consumed the rest of his cheeseburger. He looked over at Laura and frowned at her uneaten sandwich.

"We told her to be discreet, Laura. That was the plan. The later she left Providence the longer the commute. You know what holiday traffic is like out here."

"You're right. I'm just worried. We're asking a lot of her."

Bobby picked up Laura's chicken sandwich and held it close to her mouth.

"You need to eat. We have a very long journey ahead of us."

Laura nodded and took a small bite of the sandwich. She winced as her ill-fitting dentures resisted the effort needed to chew through the shredded lettuce.

"Is everything set?"

Bobby nodded and was about to reply when the chime of his phone interrupted him. He glanced down at the screen and smiled.

"It's Emma," Bobby said. He held the phone up so Laura could see the message.

Just crossed town line. Bag is full. See you soon.

"That's the signal," Laura said.

"I'm shocked that Emma got her. I didn't think she would go through with it. I always thought I should have been the one to go to Providence."

"We agreed this was the safest way. What if you went out there and got caught? I can't lose you again, Bobby. Trust me, putting Emma at risk was the right thing to do. Imagine her telling the police that I'm still alive? They'd think she was crazy. I've left no evidence anywhere that she could use to pin this on me. Or you. We have our escape plan ready to go. Letting her take the fall was the only way to see this through."

Bobby took a few of the fries from Laura's lunch. The salt and grease on the warm planks of potato brought him little comfort.

"I could have gone and brought them both back here. Not just the girl."

"That would have been too risky. The girl is what matters to me. She's the one that killed my daughter. Once we settle things with Julie, we can escape. Tom will be made to suffer Trust me."

"Honestly, Laura, we should have left town weeks ago and

let it be. Bringing her back here is dangerous enough. As much as I admire your desire for vengeance, we're both taking a big risk with this plan."

"After what she did to my Sara? To me? Never, Bobby. That girl must pay. She must! They both will."

"Angel, I told you we won't have time to make candles. We need to leave later this afternoon, after Julie's dead."

"We need to try, Bobby. If we can't do it today, then we can make the candle after we're gone. All I need is a piece of her to take with us."

Laura's commitment to seeing this through filled Bobby with pride. He leaned over and kissed Laura on the cheek. Her ice-blue eyes reflected the love and history they shared. Decades of a tortured affair were about to come to the conclusion they had both desired for an eternity. They would finally be together.

"You've really thought every step through, haven't you?" Bobby asked.

"Not all of it. I left our escape plan up to you. You're sure Cindy's up for it?"

"Nick told me we could trust her. Cindy's a strong gal. I've spent a lot of time with her. By this time tomorrow, we'll be hundreds of miles away."

Laura felt herself begin to relax. Their weeks of planning were finally coming to an end. She peeled back the top bun of her chicken sandwich and slid the lettuce off before attempting another bite. Laura closed her eyes and began to mentally run through everything that needed to happen once Emma arrived with Julie. She stopped chewing, opened her eyes and looked at Bobby.

"We need to be ready for the unexpected. Specifically, we need to be ready for Emma."

"Emma? Everything's set."

"I mean we need to be ready if Emma turns on us."

"Turns? You just sent her to abduct Julie. Now you're worried she can't be trusted?"

Laura ran her hands across Bobby's square jawline. The silver stubble along his chin nipped and tugged at the soft dewy folds of skin beside her thumbs. She looked deep into his eyes and thought back to the passionate nights they shared so long ago. Time had aged his face, but not the love she felt for him.

"I have her convinced that Julie killed Sara, and tried to kill me. She thinks she's bringing her here for a forced confession. We need to be ready in case she finds out that's not our plan. Or simply changes her mind."

"Did you get into specifics with her? Did you tell her how or where we plan to get the confession?"

"Specifics?" Laura closed her eyes and tried to recall the discussions she'd had with Emma. Her daughter had repeatedly pressed her, trying to get the details on what they had planned for Julie. Laura sighed as she opened her eyes. "No, Bobby. I kept it as vague as possible."

"Good. Once Emma arrives, I'll get Julie from the back of her car. Then you need to send Emma home to Chatham. She can't be here for what we are planning to do with Julie."

"I know." Laura frowned and lowered her head. "I just worry. Do you remember what a rebellious child Emma used to be? Do I have to remind you of the hell we went through with her after that drifter?"

"I remember."

"So don't be surprised if Emma decides to get all righteous on us."

"This is exactly why I didn't want her involved at all. When I found out you weren't killed in that fire, I knew it was so that we could finally be together, Laura. You should have sent Emma away once she found you."

"Don't you see, Bobby? It's better this way. If Emma gets too close, she can take the fall. She's our safety net. Besides, I really wanted to try and make amends with her. She's all I have left."

"What about me? You've got me."

"You've always been there for me, Bobby. No matter what happens with Emma today, I'm yours. We will leave this place and never return. We just need to be ready for the unexpected."

Bobby stood up and wiped his face with a paper napkin. He spent a bit of extra time drying his fingers before he reached behind his waist with his right hand. Laura's eyes widened at the sight of the revolver Bobby presented to her.

"This belonged to my father. I keep it at my place for home defense. I've never killed anyone with it, but it's come in handy from time to time to scare someone off."

Laura stood up and walked over to Bobby. He held the gun out for her. Laura hesitated momentarily before running her fingertips along the worn snubbed barrel of the gun. Bobby lowered his hand, allowing the weapon to slide forward into Laura's hands. The nickel finish on the old Smith & Wesson Model 12 had dulled over time, but the weapon still packed a solid punch.

"Is it loaded?" Laura asked as she wrapped her hand around the handle. "I've never fired one before."

"No. I've got the bullets in my truck. Do you want me to show you how to use it?"

Laura studied the gun with a mix of awe and fear before carefully handing it back to Bobby.

"Do you really think we will need this?"

"You said we needed to be ready, Laura."

"I know. But, well, I could never shoot Emma, Bobby. Never. All I meant was we should have a backup plan in case Emma becomes a problem for us."

"What if you have to choose?"

"Choose?"

"What if Emma does turn on you, and you have to choose between your daughter or me. What will you do?"

Laura shook her head and turned and walked over to the door that led out to the side porch. She stared through the glass, looking at the ashen pile of shadowy debris that used to be the barn. Her head was filled with the cries of ecstasy she and Bobby shared in the loft long ago, as well as the cries of horror as Sara burned to death.

"This family has seen so much death, Bobby. I pray I don't have to make that choice."

THIRTEEN

Christmas

1988 Saturday 24-Dec 6:30 p.m.

Sara waited patiently, watching her aunt fill the Christmas tray with three mugs and a glass decanter. The white ceramic cups were bowl-shaped to mimic the tummies of jolly snowmen, with handles painted to look like a twig-shaped arm. The pitcher was filled with eggnog sprinkled with cinnamon.

"Can you spike it?" Sara asked, eyebrows hopefully raised.

"How old are you now?" Jennifer asked.

"I'm sixteen."

Jennifer opened a cupboard and selected a bright red plastic bowl. She tore open a bag of potato chips and dumped them into the container, placing it onto the tray next to the drinks.

"Maybe in a few years, Sara," Jennifer said as she handed her niece the tray. "Are you girls having fun downstairs?"

"We are. I love your basement. It's so much nicer than ours. This has been a great Christmas, Aunty Jen."

"I'm glad to hear that."

Jennifer looked into her empty wine glass and frowned. The space to the left of the kitchen sink was lined with two used wine bottles and several hollow beer cans. She opened the refrigerator and retrieved a bottle of chardonnay and poured herself a glass, taking care to fill it almost to the top.

"Sara, can you do me a favor and turn that music down? We can hear it pounding through the floor up here."

"But it's Bon Jovi!" Sara rolled her eyes at her aunt.

"I thought you brought movies to watch."

Jennifer opened the door to the basement and guided Sara to the top of the staircase.

"We did. That's what these snacks are for. Did I thank you for making a rosemary turkey?"

"You did, Sara. Several times."

"It's not as good as your rosemary chicken, but it was still yummy."

Sara smiled and descended the stairs to the basement. Jennifer closed the door behind her and let out a long sigh. She sipped her wine and walked over to the side door and glanced out at the garage. Her eyes wandered to the garden in her backyard.

"Everything OK?" Bobby asked as he entered the kitchen.

"I think that was the last of my rosemary," Jennifer replied.

"You can grow more."

"No. No, Bobby, I can't." Jennifer turned to face Bobby. They were alone in the kitchen. "Carl was my partner out there. I thought I could do it without him, but I can't. It's hard doing it alone. Being alone."

Bobby felt a sense of unease wash over him. Jennifer had a look in her eye that he hadn't seen in years. He took a few awkward steps back as Jennifer made her way toward him. She rested her hand on his chest, forcing Bobby to lean back against the door to the basement. Despite outweighing her by fifty pounds, Bobby suddenly felt trapped.

"You aren't alone. You have Susan."

"That's not the kind of companionship I miss." Jennifer ran her hand down Bobby's deep pine colored button-down corduroy shirt and past his brown leather belt. He grabbed her hand just as her fingers slid below the brass buckle. "I remember a time when you wouldn't stop me."

"That was a long time ago, Jennifer. I've told you to let it go. Why are you bringing this up here? Now?"

Bobby flicked his hand, forcing Jennifer to take a slight step back. He folded his arms and replanted his feet securely on the floor, keeping his body firmly against the door behind him.

"It's been years since Carl's death. I've moved on, Bobby. I'm ready. Ready for us to be together. But you continue to resist me."

"I told you, Jennie, people change. You need to let this go."

Jennifer took two gulps from her wine glass, never allowing her gaze to leave Bobby's eyes.

"Answer me one question."

"What?"

"Who is she?"

Bobby paused and furrowed his eyebrows.

"Not this again. I told you, there's nobody."

"Bullshit. I know there's another woman. It's the only reason you've resisted me all these years."

Bobby chuckled and lowered his head. He raised his right hand and tapped the rim of Jennifer's wine glass. She glanced at his finger and then glared at him.

"Don't blame my drinking. You loved me until you got me pregnant. Marilyn should have brought us closer, but instead, you pulled away."

"Lower your voice." Bobby stepped forward, forcing Jennifer to retreat to the counter near the sink. "I don't love you, Jennie. I'm sorry. I don't."

"That's not true. You told me many times that you did. I remember, Bobby. Don't you?"

"I do, Jennie. The truth is that I only told you what you wanted to here."

"What? Why? Why would you say you loved me if you didn't?"

"Because it's what you expected. It's what you needed."

Bobby turned and started to leave the kitchen. Jennifer reached out and grabbed him by the elbow, spinning him around.

"Then tell me the truth now, Bobby. Is there someone else? Was there? I thought I meant something to you."

"We had something special a long time ago, Jennie. It was great sex. But that's all it ever was. My heart is elsewhere. It always has been, and always will be." Bobby ran his fingers across Jennifer's cheek, pushing her hair back. He could see the longing and desperation in her eyes. "If you must know, Jennie, there is someone else. She means everything to me. I'm sorry, but you and I will never be anything other than friends from now on. Please just let this go."

Jennifer felt her eyes well up as Bobby left the room. She tossed her head back, filling her mouth with the last of the chardonnay. The mild burn of the alcohol washing down her throat brought her little comfort. A sense of loneliness came spilling across her. She realized it was quiet. Too quiet. The thumping music from downstairs had stopped.

A loud creak broke the silence. Jennifer glanced over her shoulder and looked at the basement door. With a mix of curiosity and anger, she opened the door. Emma was standing on the other side.

"How long were you standing there?" Jennifer asked. She took Emma by the wrist and pulled her into the kitchen. "How long?"

The music downstairs roared to life again. Jennifer slammed the door shut and dragged Emma across the kitchen.

"Not long," Emma cried. She fought to hold back tears. "I just came up to pee. I didn't hear anything. Honest."

Jennifer studied her niece, looking Emma up and down. It was apparent to her that Emma was lying. At the same time, she realized that Emma also looked scared. Not just scared, but terrified.

Jennifer opened the fridge and snatched the bottle of white wine from the shelf. She poured the last of the chardonnay into her glass and slid the empty bottle next to the others sitting beside the sink.

"What is it?" Jennifer asked. "I know you heard us, Emma."

"It's nothing."

Emma clenched her fists as she desperately tried to keep herself from crying. Her lower lip quivered as a single tear made its way down her cheek.

"Even if you heard everything, Emma, there's no reason for you to be crying. What happened between Bobby and me has nothing to do with you."

Emma dropped her head into her palms and began to sob. Jennifer opened the door to the driveway and pushed Emma outside. The cold air, hovering just above freezing, was a shock to both of them. She marched her niece over to the garage. Jennifer opened the side entry door and pulled Emma inside.

Jennifer's bright blue metallic Chevy Celebrity was parked next to them. She opened the back door and forced Emma to take a seat sideways, with her legs hanging out. Jennifer closed the door to the garage and took another sip of her wine. It was cold and dark inside the garage, but the closed door prevented the icy wind from blowing across them.

"Talk to me, Emma. Why the tears?"

Emma's mind filled with a cacophony of images and words. She mentally ran down the list of people in her life. One by one she marked them as someone she either could not trust or needed to protect. The only person she never thought to confide in was now standing in front of her. Emma wiped her cheeks dry and took a long deep cleansing breath, keeping her eyes focused on her feet.

"I heard what Bobby said to you. Everything."

"Such as?"

"That you two used to ... to be together. And that Mary was his baby, not Uncle Carl's." Emma raised her head and looked into her aunt's eyes. "Is ... is that true, Aunty?"

Jennifer lowered her head and gazed into her wine. Her mind and thoughts were growing cloudy due to the six glasses of chardonnay coursing throughout her system. She nodded as she looked at her niece.

"It's true, Emma. Bobby and I had an affair. It was many years ago. Mary was his baby. When Carl and Mary died, it was just ... just too much. Bobby had ended things long before then. But why would hearing that make you cry?"

"I … I don't like Bobby."

"But that's no reason for you to be crying." Jennifer knelt down resting her goblet on the dusty cement floor. She took Emma by her hands and squeezed them gently. "He hurt me, yes. But don't cry. He's obviously in love with someone else. I just don't know who. At least he finally admitted there was another woman."

Emma pulled her hands away from her aunt's embrace and folded her arms across her chest. The pale look on her niece's face filled Jennifer with dread. She leaned forward and rested her hand on Emma's knee.

"Do you know?" Jennifer asked.

"I … I know a lot of things, Aunty. But I can't tell anyone, or he will hurt them. Or me."

"Who will?"

"Bobby." Emma lowered her head into her hands and began to sob again.

Jennifer stood up and looked through the glass panes of the door back. The view inside the house was obstructed, but the kitchen appeared to be empty. She tapped Emma on her knee and motioned to the other side of the back seat. Emma slid over to the passenger side. Jennifer jumped in next to her and slammed the car door shut.

"You can talk to me, Emma, OK? You can trust me."

"But Bobby told me not to. He said he would hurt me, or Sara, or Susan. I … I don't want anyone else to die."

It was dark and cold inside the garage. The interior of the Chevy was a bit warmer from the body heat they were generating. Jennifer felt a sense of rage begin to bubble from deep within her gut. She took several deep breaths to clear her mind, her warm exhaled breath condensing in the chilly air.

"Anyone else? What do you mean about dying? Did he threaten you? Did he say those exact words to you? When?"

Emma clasped her hands together and began to rub them back and forth. The thin red berry cotton sweater she was wearing was not keeping her warm. Looking at her aunt, however, brought her some relief. For the first time in months, she felt like there was someone she could talk to.

Someone that would defend her.

"Multiple times, Aunty. It started with Eddie."

"Who?"

"The homeless guy my dad found at the park a few months ago."

"Oh right. The one that ran off."

"He didn't run away, Aunty. I ... I saw what happened."

Emma looked out the window beside her. The garage wall was lined with shelves that ran from front to back and top to bottom. They were filled with a wide variety of cardboard boxes and plastic tubs. Emma couldn't help but wonder how much of it belonged to her departed uncle. She looked back at her aunt.

"Bobby killed him."

Jennifer stared at her niece in disbelief. She studied her eyes, looking for any sign of doubt or confusion. Jennifer quickly realized Emma was telling the truth. Or at the very least, believed what she was saying.

"What did you see, Emma? It's OK, you can trust me. We're family."

Emma pulled her fingers close to her lips and blew warm air across her cold hands. She shoved her hands under her legs to try and keep them warm. Her body was shivering, from both the temperature and memories filling the Chevy.

"I got home early because the chain on my bike broke. I saw Bobby and Eddie unloading that big pot that Bobby brought us. The one that's in the barn now. Bobby was in the back of the truck, and he flipped it onto Eddie."

"Well, Emma, isn't it possible that it just slipped off? I mean accidents do happen."

"Aunty, he jumped out of the back and then flipped it over again. I *saw* him kill him!"

Emma began to cry again. Jennifer pulled her niece into her arms and kissed the top of her head, reassuringly running her fingers through Emma's hair.

"It's OK, Emma. I'm here. I believe you." Jennifer gave Emma a long hug and waited for the young girl's trembling body to relax. "What about your mother? Did you tell her what you saw?"

Emma wiped her burning eyes and sighed.

"I saw something else, Aunty. After Bobby killed Eddie, my mom came outside. I was hiding in the bushes and thought my mom would come out screaming. Instead, she ran to Bobby, and they ... they kissed."

"What do you mean they kissed?"

"I mean they *kissed*, Aunty."

Jennifer's heart began to race. She looked around the back seat, frantically searching for her wine. She sighed when she realized she left it on the floor of the garage.

"I assume this wasn't on the cheek?"

"No. They really kissed. Then they walked off into the barn. I freaked out. I mean, Bobby just killed Eddie, and my mom kisses him like nothing happened. Why?"

"And you never told your mother what you saw?"

"Only some of it. I told her I saw Bobby dump the cauldron on Eddie from inside the bed of the truck. She told me it was an accident."

"What about the kiss?"

"I lied. I told Mom I ran off when I saw Eddie get crushed. She doesn't know I saw Bobby flip it over again. Or their kiss."

"I see. But, Emma, that doesn't explain Bobby threatening you. When did that start?"

"It was the day after I told my mom. She told Bobby what I told her. He's threatened me a few times, Aunty. Anytime he thinks I might say something he comes over and warns me. He said Sara or others would get hurt if I told them. And all my mom does is defend Bobby. I've had nobody to turn to."

"Nobody is going to hurt you, Emma. Do you hear me? I won't allow it."

Jennifer took Emma's hand and pulled it to her lips, leaving a gentle kiss on her cold fingertips. Emma smiled due to the weight that was suddenly lifted off her shoulders. For the first time in months, she finally felt safe. Sitting in chilling darkness with her aunt in the Chevy's back seat, hidden away in the garage felt like the safest place on earth to Emma.

"I'm surprised you didn't tell your father. Did Bobby threaten him too?"

Emma's smile faded, and she closed her eyes. She knew there was one more thing she needed to tell her aunt.

"I wanted to, Aunty. Honest, I did. But there's something else you should know. When Bobby threatened me, he told me I couldn't run to my dad. He said that my dad, well, that my dad is ... that ... he ... well ...."

"Spit it out, Emma. What?"

"Bobby said my dad killed Uncle Carl."

"Your father?" Jennifer shook her head in disbelief. "No. No, that's ... that's not possible."

"I think he's lying, Aunty. I think Bobby did it. He killed Eddie. I bet he killed Uncle Carl too."

Jennifer looked back toward her house. Sitting in the car made it impossible to see outside the garage. She suddenly felt very trapped. She grabbed the handle and popped the door open. As she stepped out of the car, she kicked her wine glass against the wall, shattering it into several pieces.

"They told me Carl's death was a suicide."

Emma slid across the bench seat and quickly exited the vehicle. She stepped close to her aunt, gently resting her hand on Jennifer's shoulder to try and bring the trembling woman some comfort. Jennifer, lost in her thoughts, stared at the glass fragments scattered around her feet.

"I don't know what to believe anymore," Emma said.

Jennifer gently closed the Chevy's back door and motioned Emma toward the exit. Emma followed her aunt until they reached the door to the kitchen. Jennifer looked back at her niece. Emma's cheeks were pink from the cold air funneling between the house and garage. Jennifer took her niece by both hands.

"You can believe in me, Emma. You don't have to live in fear anymore. I'm going to take care of everything."

Emma felt her chest tighten as her eyes began to well up again. The relief and trust she felt with her aunt quickly faded from her heart.

"No, Aunty! Don't say anything. Please? Bobby will hurt me. Or you. Please don't."

"That man will never hurt anyone again, Emma. I will defend you as I would my own daughter. That man needs to answer for what he's done."

Jennifer flung the side door open and shoved Emma across the kitchen until they were beside the basement door. Bobby was standing in the dining room, staring at them. Jennifer opened the door, allowing the music from below to come blaring out. Emma started to cry as Jennifer shoved her onto the top stair that descended to the basement.

"Stay down there," Jennifer demanded. "Make sure everyone stays down there."

Jennifer quietly closed the basement door. Bobby took a few steps back as Jennifer approached him. Her cheeks were flush with anger, as well as the frigid temperatures from outside. She thrust her index finger into Bobby's chest.

"Get your ass into the living room," Jennifer stated. "Now."

Fred and Laura were sitting next to one another on the sofa, enjoying coffee spiked with Sambuca. A small stereo system tucked in the corner was playing "It's the Most Wonderful Time of the Year" by Johnny Mathis. The coffee table was filled with assorted homemade cookies baked by Laura, including oatmeal raisin and chocolate chip. A fresh cut Christmas tree was tucked away in the opposite corner, adorned with silver tinsel, a rainbow of lights, and cherished family ornaments. The scent of fresh pine, warm cookies, and coffee filled the air.

Bobby followed Jennifer into the living room, his hands tucked into his pockets. Laura smiled as the two approached the table of sweets. Jennifer ignored Fred and Laura and marched across the room and turned off the stereo.

"Oh, but I love that song," Laura said. "Why did you ... What's that face for? What's wrong?"

Jennifer pointed at the empty seat next to Laura. Bobby took the hint and sat beside her. Fred, Laura, and Bobby stared across the room at Jennifer. All was quiet, save for the muffled thumping from the music in the basement below. Jennifer's eyes settled on the carafe of coffee and bottle of Sambuca. She quickly poured herself a cup of spiked coffee and took a calming sip.

"How did my husband die?" Jennifer asked. "I need to know the truth. Right now."

Laura looked back and forth between her husband to her left, and Bobby to her right. Fred's pleasant demeanor from just minutes ago vanished. Bobby looked, surprisingly to Laura, quite concerned.

"You know how, Jennie," Laura said. "He killed himself on the beach. After the girls ...."

"No, Laura. That's the lie all of you told me four years ago. So which one of you did it? Fred? Bobby? I know it was one of you."

Fred's lips and throat dried up as if a giant sponge had materialized on his tongue. He opened his mouth to speak, but he could not form any words. Laura scratched at her neck, as she searched for the proper response.

"What did Emma say to you?" Bobby said.

"Emma?" Laura said softly as she looked over at Bobby.

"You leave her out of this," Jennifer said threateningly. She took a step closer to the coffee table positioned between her and the sofa. "So help me God, Bobby, if you ever so much as touch that girl I will kill you. Do you hear me?"

"Jennie!" Laura said. "What on earth has gotten into you?"

"You know, this all is starting to make sense now." Jennifer paused and downed another shot of the licorice flavored coffee. "For the life of me, I could never understand how my husband could kill himself. I mean, I bought it at the time. What with his mood swings and those horrible drugs the doctor had him on. But I could never understand that knife. That huge long machete impaling him into the sand dune. I always wondered how he could stab himself like that, locking his body into the side of that cliff."

Jennifer felt her rage and anger beginning to clear. She looked across the room at her sister, brother-in-law, and former lover. Three people that at one time meant the world to her now seemed like strangers sitting in her home. Jennifer finished her coffee and placed the empty cup on the table.

"Because obviously, he couldn't. Even the police said he must have had a huge adrenaline rush to pull that off. But now I know the truth. So, there is only one question I have. Was it Bobby or Fred?"

"Jennie, I don't understand ...."

"Shut up, Laura. I'll deal with you later. My money is on Bobby. Fred, you have a temper, but there is no way ...."

"It was me," Fred said slowly. His body shook as he gasped for air, allowing his next three words to escape him with a roar. "It was me!"

Fred burst into tears. Years of guilt and anguish battled one another to explode from his body. He heaved and rocked back and forth as he wept into his palms.

"It was an accident, Jennie," Fred said. He looked up at his sister-in-law. "I swear to God it was an accident."

"Fred, please," Laura said. She reached out to take Fred by the hand. He pushed it away.

"Enough lies, Laura," Fred continued. "Enough. I'm so sorry, Jennie. Carl and I got in an argument in the barn. It turned into a fight. A real knockdown brawl. He tried to kill me. I ... I was only defending myself. I swear."

Jennifer allowed a single tear to fall down her cheek. She knew Fred to be a sincere man, and that his confession was pure. She closed her eyes and said a small prayer to herself in memory of her husband.

"Thank you," Jennifer said. "Thank you for your honesty, Fred. You're right. This family has too many lies and secrets."

Bobby shifted uncomfortably at the end of the couch. He diverted his attention to the dining room, watching for the girls to arrive. The music was still reverberating through the floor beneath them.

"Then we have one more unanswered mystery to solve tonight," Jennifer said. Although inebriated from far too much alcohol, Jennifer felt confident. Perhaps overconfident. "Tell me, Bobby. Your other lover. Is it Laura?"

Fred wiped the mucus dripping from his nose and turned to look at his wife beside him. Laura was studying the plates of cookies and treats spread out on the table, afraid to look at anyone else.

"What are you talking about?" Fred asked.

Laura awoke from her trance and looked at Bobby. Bobby realized all eyes were on him.

"Other?" Laura said.

"I told you to let this go, Jennie," Bobby replied. "You've obviously had too much to drink. Perhaps we should all call it a night."

"Emma saw you," Jennifer said, with all the air of a prosecutor giving her closing statements to a jury. "The day you killed that drifter."

"What?" Fred cried. His tears, guilt, and regret were now a distant memory, replaced by confusion. "Eddie left. He packed up and left."

"No, Fred," Jennifer continued. "Emma came home early that day. She saw Bobby dump that big cauldron onto Eddie. Twice. Apparently, the first time didn't do the job. Then she saw you, Laura, my *dear* sister, come outside and kiss Bobby. We aren't talking about a peck on the cheek, are we?"

"Is this true?" Fred asked, he turned and stared at his wife.

"Of course not," Bobby said. "Emma doesn't know what she's talking about. It's like we told you, Fred. That punk kid ran off."

Laura kept her head down. Even with her eyes closed, she could feel the piercing stare of her husband. Laura could not bring herself to look at him. Fred stood up and walked to the other side of the room, taking a position next to his sister-in-law.

"The stain," Fred said as he glared at Bobby. "That stain on the driveway. It wasn't goat blood, was it?"

Bobby felt trapped. His thoughts whirled as he tried to come up with a way to spin the story. He looked at Laura for support. Her ice-blue eyes, normally filled with passion for him, appeared lifeless.

"Look, Fred, I don't know what else to say."

"Did you kiss my wife?"

"No."

"Bobby and I were having an affair," Jennifer interjected.

"For many years. I finally figured out there was another woman. I just wasn't sure who."

Laura was lost in thoughts completely unrelated to the drifter. Jennifer just confessed, repeatedly, to having an affair with Bobby. She shook her head and drew a deep breath as she turned to her lover.

"Bobby?" Laura asked.

"Don't look at me like that," Bobby said. "She's obviously drunk."

"Are you denying our affair?" Jennifer asked.

"Did you sleep with my wife?"

"No," Bobby bellowed. "Enough of this bullshit."

"Yes," Laura said quietly. She slid her hand across Bobby's thigh, giving it a gentle pat. "Enough already. It's all true."

"Laura!" Bobby tried to push Laura's hand off his leg, but instead, she took his hand into hers. "What are you doing?"

"They're right, Bobby," Laura said. "This family has seen too many lies. Kept too many secrets."

The room was quiet as the four occupants took their time studying one another. The floor no longer rattled from the music downstairs. Outside, the rain started to fall, and the only sound in the room was the gentle plinking of water droplets as they struck the front window.

"Bobby and I started an affair many years ago. It's ... it's been on and off since then." Laura stood up and walked over to her husband. "Fred, you have to understand that I never meant to hurt you."

"Do not touch me, Laura."

Fred's heart pounded in his chest. He clenched his fists, turned, and walked to the front door, shooting Bobby a hateful glance. A brass standing coat rack stood in the corner of the foyer. The eight hooks were packed with jackets and hats. He rummaged through the clothing until he found his light brown canvas coat.

Laura ran to the front hallway and grabbed Fred by the arm. He jerked it free and hurriedly tossed his coat on.

"Fred, where are you going? We have to talk about this. You can't just ...."

"I can't just what?" Fred bellowed. "I can't just walk away

from a marriage? I can't just cheat on my spouse? I can't just lie to my family? I can't just shit all over my wedding vows? Please, Laura, tell me what I can and cannot do!"

"What's going on?" Sara asked. "Are we leaving?"

All eyes turned toward the dining room. Sara, Emma, and Susan were standing next to the dining room table watching the scene unfold. Sara and Susan were completely confused by what they were seeing and hearing. Emma, pale as a ghost, stayed focused on her aunt.

"I need to leave, Sara," Fred replied. "I can't stay here anymore. I can't. Emma, I ... I ... I don't know what to say. I wish you would have come to me first."

Fred lowered his head, turned and walked out the front door, slamming it hard behind him. Laura looked at her daughters and niece standing bewildered and confused. She realized the family would never be the same again. Her eyes settled on Emma. She thought back to the conversation they had in the kitchen the night Emma had confessed what she saw. Laura's jaw fell open as she realized Emma had lied to her.

"Are you happy, Emma?" Laura asked.

"Me?" Emma replied.

"What did you do?" Sara asked.

Laura entered the dining room, walked up to Emma, and smacked her across her face. Emma screamed and stepped behind her cousin Susan. Susan stood there, paralyzed.

"You've destroyed this family, Emma," Laura cried. "Why didn't' you tell me the truth? Why did you have to run to your aunt?"

"Me?" Emma asked again.

Jennifer quickly made her way across the room to get to Laura. As she passed Bobby, she pointed at him and waved her finger.

"I'm not done with you yet," Jennifer said. She grabbed her sister by the shoulder and pulled her away from Emma. "How dare you hit your daughter. After the lies and secrets that you've been keeping you have the *nerve* to lay blame on her? All she did was tell the truth."

"No, Jennie, all she did was ruin everything."

"All of these years, lying to me," Jennifer said with a heavy sigh. "My own sister. If I can't trust my sister to be honest, who can I trust?"

Sara couldn't help but stare at Emma.

"Look who's talking?" Laura replied. "Did Carl know what you were doing?"

Jennifer shook her head and frowned. She looked over at Bobby. For the first time since meeting Bobby Mason, she felt nothing but guilt and regret. Jennifer shot her sister a dismissive look before returning to the living room.

"If anyone is to blame for what's happened tonight, it's you, Bobby. You're the one that has destroyed this family. The secrets and lies all lead back to you. I want you to leave my house. You're no longer welcome here. Ever."

Bobby stood up and sauntered over to the coat rack. He dug out his black leather jacket and put it on, drawing the zipper closed at the neckline. He pulled a pair of black leather gloves from his pocket and slid them over his hands.

"I'm sorry," Bobby said. He looked at Sara, standing a few feet from Susan and Emma. He wanted to make sure Sara knew he was talking to her, and only her. "I'm sorry Emma didn't listen to me."

Bobby gave one last look at Laura and Jennifer. Laura's face was still covered in shock and disappointment. Jennifer, however, seemed relieved if not borderline happy. Bobby opened the door and stepped out into the cold rainy night.

***

Fred slowed his Cherokee as he made the turn off Route 6. The temperature was a few degrees below freezing and falling fast. A light rainfall currently blanked the outer Cape. The windshield on the Jeep began to fog, and Fred adjusted the defroster to try and keep it clear. The wipers were struggling to prevent the rain from icing up as it hit the glass. Fred leaned forward and used the cuff of his jacket to clear an opening in the fog building up inside the window.

"Goddammit," Fred exclaimed. He gripped the steering wheel to steady his Jeep. "As if this night hasn't been bad enough."

The road ahead was clear of traffic, so Fred turned his high beams on. All that did was illuminate the drizzle falling from the sky, dropping visibility to mere meters. Fred frowned and turned them off, opting for his fog lights. They were an aftermarket set and quickly lit up the roadway in a murky shade of butterscotch. Fred breathed a sigh of relief at the newfound clarify provided by the lights. His SUV continued to shimmy. Even with four-wheel-drive engaged, there was no way to know when black-ice would appear. Especially in these conditions.

"Bobby," Fred said, seething with anger. "That fucking bastard. How could I have missed it? How long did she say this has been going on? Years? Eddie tried to tell me. I think Emma was trying to tell me on her birthday. Dear, sweet, Emma. I should have pressed you harder."

Fred was momentarily blinded by a flash of light reflecting from his rearview mirror. A vehicle was approaching from behind with their high beams on. He squinted and adjusted the mirror's angle, aiming the light toward his chin.

"Moron," Fred said, returning his attention to the road ahead. The lights behind him continued to get closer. "Doesn't this asshole know how bad these roads are?"

The narrow two-lane road Fred was on did not have a breakdown lane. There was no way Fred could pull over to let the other vehicle pass. He considered lowering his window and waving them past him, but the bitterly cold rain and wind killed that idea. Fred looked at his speedometer. He was crawling along at what he felt was a reasonable 25 mph.

"You'll just have to wait in line, buddy."

The Cherokee's rear end wavered as the tires fought to stay on the road. The icy roadway and nearly frozen rain were conspiring to form pockets of black ice. Fred decided to slow his vehicle a bit more. He checked his driver's side mirror. The lights from behind were getting closer.

"What the fuck is wrong with this asshole?" The vehicle started to drift into the opposite lane to pass Fred. Fred eased up on the gas to let them get by. "Good riddance."

A few seconds later Fred's Jeep began to rotate. He looked

over at the lights blaring directly behind his left shoulder. Before Fred could react, his Cherokee went into a 360-degree spin. The vehicle that attempted to pass him slowed and came to a stop on the edge of the road, the high beams blanketing the scene ahead with white light. Fred's Jeep ran off the roadway and slid sideways into an embankment, crashing against two huge pine trees before spinning to a halt.

The driver's side of the Cherokee was banged up quite severely, with both the front and rear doors dented. The driver's window was shattered, with most of the glass now missing. The engine, surprisingly, was still burbling along.

Fred blinked his eyes and looked around the cabin. The dashboard lights were illuminated, casting a faint glow to the interior. He checked his hands and was relieved to see they were both intact and not covered in blood. He attempted to take a breath but instead let out a howl. Fred tried to grab his chest, but the pain was too severe.

How many ribs did I shatter? Fred wondered. He slid his hands up to his face. His eyebrows were wet. Fred wiped his brow and then checked his fingers. *Shit.*

Panic started to consume Fred. He blinked and realized blood was running down his head and across his face. Fred looked over his shoulder and squinted at the high beams coming from the vehicle that was now stopped a dozen yards away. One of the headlights went out, blocked by a figure standing in the road.

Fred coughed and checked his hands. Crimson blood was splattered across his palms. He started to get lightheaded.

I need to get to the hospital. A doctor. I need a doctor.

A shadow unfolded on the Cherokee's door and made its way across the interior of Fred's Jeep. Fred, dazed and confused, spent a few moments staring at his hands. He turned and looked through the shattered opening of the driver's window.

"Hello, Fred," Bobby said.

"Bobby?" Fred said, before coughing up more blood. "You ... you need to help me. I'm in bad shape."

"I can see that."

Bobby checked the window's opening. Several jagged pieces of glass were sticking out from the frame's edges. He leaned his head inside the Jeep, taking care to keep a safe distance from the shrapnel.

"This doesn't look good, Fred."

"I ... I ... I need an ambulance."

"The ambulance won't make it in time."

Fred coughed again and used his sleeve to wipe his hands dry. He squinted and tried to focus on Bobby's face, only inches from his. Between the lighting and loss of blood, Fred found it hard to concentrate on anything.

"What? What do you mean?"

Bobby stood up and looked back and forth along the deserted roadway. He smiled at the privacy surrounding them. Bobby bent back down to the window.

"Remember Susan's birthday party? When she turned thirteen?"

"What?" Fred was losing consciousness. His breathing became shorter and shallower with each inhalation. "I ... I don't understand."

"You thought Laura was having an affair with Carl. That's why you got into the fight with him. That's why he got killed."

"Bobby, why are you telling me this?"

"All because you overheard her on the phone the night before. She told you she was planning Jennie's birthday. You fell for it. I just wanted you to know, Fred, that you were right. Laura was on the phone talking to her lover. But it was me. You just took your anger out on the wrong guy."

Fred felt a rush of adrenaline and used the last of his strength to pull himself upright. He dragged his hands along the inside of the door, frantically trying to find the handle.

"Oh, and one final piece of the puzzle you should know about. Rose was *my* child. Not yours. Laura and I always talked about raising a family together. And with you out of the picture, I can finally have her all to myself. Goodbye, Fred."

Bobby took one more look up and down the empty road to confirm they were alone. He reached into the Cherokee, wrapped his gloved hand around Fred's neck, and began to repeatedly smash his head against the steering wheel.

FOURTEEN

The Basement

The first image that came into view was a wall lined with narrow wooden shelves. The twelve-inch-deep pine planks were painted a cream color, but caked in years of accumulated dust and grime. Julie blinked a few times to get her eyes to focus. The shelves appeared to be at a steep angle. She couldn't understand why the various jars and canisters were not sliding off. As her mind cleared, she realized her head was tilted at an angle. Julie let out a groan as she pulled herself upright.

Where am I? Julie wondered as she glanced around her surroundings.

There were no windows in sight. The small room was damp and smelled of mold. The only light to be found was from a single overhead bulb, screwed into a porcelain mount secured to a beam. The lightbulb flickered and hummed as it struggled to keep from failing.

Julie took a few deep breaths to try and wake herself up. She attempted to check her pockets but realized her hands were bound behind her back.

"Not again," Julie said softly. She shook her head back and forth vigorously, mentally willing herself to wake up. She looked down at her legs and let out a half smile. "At least I'm not in a school chair."

There were two exits from the room. One to the left and the other to the right. The opening through the doorway to the right was pitch black. Julie could hear the faint whistle of a partially open window or perhaps a door coming from the darkness. The other doorway appeared to lead to a larger room with walls covered in the same walnut colored paneling as the room she was in.

No cauldron. No school chair. At least there's that.

Julie tugged at her arms and feet but to no avail. Her limbs were securely locked in place. She couldn't even wiggle her wrists. The gray metal folding chair beneath her was lightweight. She used her body weight to jump up and down a few times, but the ropes would not give way.

Julie looked back at the shelves she first spotted when she regained consciousness. The bottom two shelves were lined with a variety of cans of paints and stains. They all looked quite old, their sides covered with dried drippings. The top shelf was filled with candles.

Julie's throat tightened as she let her eyes take in each glass jar. She counted a total of six candles. The first five were cylindrical with open tops and varied in color. The flickering overhead light made it difficult for Julie to study the candles in detail. Her eyes finally settled on the one sitting furthest away from her. It was a glass mason jar. The lid was closed, but the sage green colored wax was instantly recognizable to Julie.

"Rosemary."

Julie felt her heart begin to pound as she put the puzzle pieces together. She closed her eyes and thought back to the confrontation with Emma back in her driveway. The last thing Julie remembered was their argument and then her trying to get to her phone. Julie opened her eyes.

"She drugged me."

Julie looked around the room as panic set in. A Fellowes thermal bookbinding machine sat on a table in the opposite corner of the room. Sitting next to the device was a children's school chair. Julie immediately recognized it as being identical to the one from the barn. The foldable desktop cutting across the front of the chair was stacked with a dozen copies of the book "Urban Legends of Cape Cod."

Julie was about to scream for help when she heard a door slam. It came from upstairs. Her temples throbbed from her racing heart. Footsteps now made their way across the room above her head.

Where am I?

***

Emma walked over to the kitchen table, carrying Julie's purple leather handbag. She used a white cotton bath towel in her other hand to dry her wet hair.

"How was the shower?" Laura asked. "Feeling refreshed?"

"It was great." Emma flung the bag onto the table. She dragged a chrome stool closer and took a seat, using her fingers to jam the towel into her damp ears. "I was so grimy from sleeping in my car overnight and sitting in hours of traffic. I feel so much better."

"I'm glad. Now that you've cleaned up, you should head home to Chatham."

"Is there anything to eat? I'm starving."

Laura folded her arms and frowned as she studied her daughter. She and Bobby were on a tight timeline, and she needed Emma to leave. Laura gradually let her eyes wander to the table.

"What's that?" Laura asked as she pointed to the purse slumped in the middle of the kitchen table.

"It's Julie's," Emma replied. "I forgot I'd left it in the car."

Laura closed the cupboard she was standing in front of and turned off the burner heating the water for her tea. The faded copper kettle hummed as the heat beneath it died down. She emptied the boiling water into her teacup and walked over to the chrome and turquoise vinyl table.

"Why would you bring this here?"

"Why not? You told me to be discreet, remember? No loose ends."

Laura sighed and nodded in agreement. She peeled back the brass zipper that ran across the top of the purse and shoved her hand inside. After a few seconds, a frown spread across her face. Laura pulled out Julie's phone and waved it at Emma.

"This, Emma. This is a loose end. They can track you with these things."

"Relax." Emma tossed her damp towel on the chair beside her. "It's off. I powered it down before I left Rhode Island."

Laura twisted her hand back and forth, inspecting the device. Julie's phone was covered in a soft rubber case. The pink edging and red, white, and pink hearts along the back were gouged and smeared from years of abuse. Laura tapped the glass screen a few times and then shook it.

"Trust me, Mother, it's fine."

Laura brought the phone over to the counter next to the toaster and opened the closest drawer, retrieving a stainless-steel meat hammer. She spun the handle in her hand, selecting the side with the larger teeth. Laura placed the device on the countertop and smashed the cellphone with one swift blow.

"What else is in that bag?"

Emma flipped Julie's bag over, dumping the contents onto the kitchen table. The metal top rang out as Julie's belongings scattered everywhere. Laura joined her daughter at the table, and the two began to sort through the items – gum, keys, lipstick, a small hairbrush, a compact mirror, and several small oddly shaped items.

Laura picked up a two-ounce, plastic oval bottle. She pulled the top off, revealing a push-top dispenser. She raised the nozzle to her face and inhaled. Laura smiled at the scent of cocoa butter.

"It's just a bunch of junk," Emma said.

"What's that?"

"What's what?"

A piece of black plastic was peeking out from beneath a travel-sized bag of tissues. Laura grabbed it and gave it to Emma. Emma twirled the one by three-inch long block in her hand. The front and back of the item were featureless, with only an odd arrow-shaped symbol on the front.

"I have no idea." Emma used her thumb to flip it

sideways, revealing a sticker along the edge. Emma scanned through the rows of printed information. "Shit. I think this is a GPS tracker."

"A what?"

"I could be wrong. But it looks like a tracking device. Why would she have one in her purse?"

Laura snatched the tracker from Emma and walked over to the counter with Julie's smashed phone. She picked up the meat tenderizer and quickly crushed the device into several fragments. Laura smiled as she surveyed the bits and pieces of mangled technology.

"No loose ends." Laura grabbed her tea, returned to the kitchen table, and sat across from her daughter. "You should have left that bag back in Providence."

"Sorry, but I thought it made sense to take it with me. I couldn't just leave it in her driveway or throw it in the trash. You said not to leave any evidence, right?"

"That's a good point. You're right." Laura sighed as she rubbed her temples. "I'm sorry, Emma. This has been a stressful 24 hours."

"I still can't believe I went through with it."

"I'm proud of you."

"Thanks. I guess."

Laura took a sip of tea and let her eyes inspect Emma's face as her daughter stared at the scattered contents of Julie's purse. Emma looked tired but also concerned. The worried look in Emma's eyes troubled Laura.

"Did she say anything?" Laura asked.

"Who? Julie?"

"When you injected her. You said that drug takes time to kick in."

"I had to guess the dosage based on what I thought she weighed. It took a few minutes, which is normal."

"But did she say anything?"

Emma looked over at her mother's piercing ice-blue eyes and reassuring smile. She looked away and recalled the accusations Julie made in the driveway.

"She rambled on a bit. Just confusion over what was happening."

"Did she see your face?"

"I was wearing a baseball cap and sunglasses and injected her from behind. I'm sure it was all a big blur in her eyes."

"You did good, Emma."

Emma forced a smile, stood up, and walked over to the stove. She ignited the burner under the copper kettle, and grabbed a mug and teabag and set them on the counter.

"Would you like more tea? I decided I could use the caffeine. I'm drained. And hungry."

"I'm fine, Emma. But you need to go home."

Emma leaned against the counter and waited for the water to boil. She took a deep breath as she collected her thoughts. Her head was filled with too many unanswered questions. She needed answers before she could leave. A box of donuts sat open next to the toaster. Emma reached inside and pulled out an apple-cinnamon flavored one.

"Before I go, I need you to tell me the truth about something."

"The truth? About what?"

Emma took a bite of the stale donut. The tangy, gooey filling and powdered cinnamon brought her much needed comfort, as well as a bit of energy.

"The day at the beach. Susan's thirteenth birthday party."

Laura took a sip of tea and ran her fingers along the silver chain around her neck.

"What more is there to tell? I told you the truth last month, Emma. We lied to you as teenagers. Twice. Your Uncle Carl didn't die in the rough waves with the girls. And he didn't commit suicide. The truth was that your father killed him. But it was only in self-defense. Why won't you believe me? I thought we settled this."

"I'm not asking about Uncle Carl. I want to know what happened to the girls."

"Oh." Laura lowered her head, resisting the instinct to look outside for the barn that was no longer there. "The girls had an accident, Emma. A horrible accident."

"It wasn't at the beach, was it?"

"No. No, it wasn't."

Emma waited for her mother to continue. The blare of the

kettle's whistle broke the uncomfortable silence that blanketed the kitchen. Emma poured the boiling water into her mug, dipped the teabag inside, and turned off the burner.

Laura picked up the plastic bag of tissues from Julie's purse. She pulled one out and blew her nose. She pointed at the chair next to her and waved Emma toward it. Emma grabbed her cup of tea and donut and sat beside her mother.

"The girls, God rest their souls, died in the barn. The beach was just a cover story. A way to hide the truth."

"The truth that Bobby did it?"

"Bobby? No! Bobby did no such thing. He's not a killer, Emma."

"Excuse me? What about Eddie?"

"Eddie?"

"Jesus Christ, Mother. The drifter. I saw the entire thing. You can't sit there and lie to my face."

"I'm sorry. I'm sorry, you're right. It was just so long ago." Laura let out a heavy sigh as her mind searched through memories long dormant. "I get confused. The stories can get so jumbled. Yes, Bobby did kill that boy. I like to tell myself it was an accident. I do know that Bobby had nothing to do with the deaths of Marilyn and Rose."

"How can you be sure?"

Laura downed the rest of her tea and dabbed the corners of her mouth with a tissue.

"Because, Emma, I was there. I walked into the barn right after your father killed Carl. You were very young back then, and you don't remember everything about your uncle. He was having a lot of mental issues. He ended up getting in this fight with your father."

"The girls, Mother."

"Oh, right. The girls." Laura paused briefly to collect her thoughts. "The girls fell, Emma. They were in the loft watching the fight. Marilyn fell and hit the table. Rosalyn, my ... my precious Rose, she fell and ... and hit the ladder."

Laura started to cry. Emma pulled the last of the tissues from the plastic wrap and handed them to her mother.

"I'm sorry. I didn't mean to upset you."

"Rosalyn was your sister. It's only fair that you know the

truth."

Emma took a sip of tea and briefly closed her eyes as she desperately tried to piece together decades of conversations and revelations. This morning's phone calls with Jeff and Susan had revealed morbid details about what happened to Mary and Rose after they died. She had to know the truth.

"Can you explain the candles?"

"The candles?" Laura dried her eyes and wiped her nose. "What do you mean?"

"The rosemary candles. You have one. So does Aunty Jen. Well, she did. Susan has it now."

"And?"

"And, well, apparently Aunty Jen told Susan something before she died. She said the rosemary candle had the bones of Rose and Mary inside. Is that true?"

Laura looked away from Emma and closed her eyes, recalling the day Bobby brought her the sage green candle with the oddly pointed wicks.

"No more secrets, Mother."

Laura opened her eyes and drummed her fingers, trying to determine the best response. Emma took another bite of her donut and patiently waited for an answer.

"Yes," Laura replied. "Yes, Emma. It's all true."

Emma slowed her chewing. Given how Jeff and Susan had dismissed the story as the ramblings of an ill woman, Emma wasn't sure what her mother's answer would be. She thought back to the many times she'd come across her aunt blankly staring at the rosemary-scented candle.

"How? Why?"

"Their deaths were such a huge loss to the family. The bones encased in the candles were meant to be a memorial for them."

"Bones. So, is that the family recipe you had mentioned? After I rescued you from the bunker, you told me the rosemary candle was special, and there was a recipe."

Laura groaned as she stood up. She slid her hand around her waist and across her lower back. Laura shuffled across the kitchen and began to rummage through the box of donuts, eventually settling on a chocolate glazed one. She split it in half, leaving the rest behind.

"No, Emma. That's not it."

"Then what's the recipe?"

Laura sighed as she nibbled on the donut. Her daughter was proving to be far too inquisitive, and Laura needed her to leave.

"Do you know who made the rosemary candles?"

"I ... I assumed it was you. Was it Dad?"

Laura smiled and took another bite of her donut.

"Bobby made them."

"Bobby?"

"I was just as shocked as you, Emma. He made one for each of us. To remember the girls by. Wasn't that sweet?" Laura did not wait for a reply. "You paint him out to be such a monster."

Emma felt her shock and confusion pivot to frustration. Her mother was dancing around her question about the recipe. Emma feared her mother was hiding something.

"So, then what about the recipe? This secret family recipe you've mentioned."

"That's for the wax, dear. We use the fat from the cows to make tallow. It's a complicated process. With the barn gone, there's no way to teach it to you."

Laura picked up the donut box and brought it back to the table, holding it at an angle for Emma to study. Her daughter retrieved the uneaten half of chocolate-glazed donut. Laura slowly sat down beside her daughter.

Emma's mind raced as she recalled the accusations Julie had made earlier today. Given her mother's admission about the rosemary candle, Emma couldn't help but wonder if the other candles Julie talked about actually existed. Worse, did her mother and sister try to kill Julie?

"Can I ask you one more thing?" Emma said.

"This is your last question, Emma. Then you need to leave."

"What are you planning to do with Julie? Please be honest."

Laura tore off another chunk of dried donut and slid it into her mouth. The sweet glazing melted as she mashed the meal between her tongue and dentures.

"I told you, Emma, we're going to get her to tell the truth about what she and Tom did in the barn. Bobby will get it recorded on video so we can clear my name."

"Where? How?"

"Why so many questions?"

"I've done everything you've asked! I've gone well beyond my ethical and moral convictions. All because I believed you, and wanted to help you clear your name. I deserve to know everything. The entire plan."

Laura licked her fingers, clearing away the last bits of sugar glazing. She frowned as she studied the scowl spread across Emma's face.

"We'll start as soon as Julie's awake." Laura sighed and folded her arms. She was disappointed to see Emma becoming so rebellious and pushy. "She's in the basement, Emma. Under lock and key. Bobby has it all covered. It's not your concern."

"Where in the basement? That place is a labyrinth."

"No more answers, Emma. You've done your part."

"But, Mother, I think ...."

"We're done!" Laura stood up, picked up the box of donuts, and dumped them into the trash. "We agreed that you get Julie, and then you go home. You've done me proud, Emma. Now it's time for you to return to Chatham."

Laura turned her back toward her daughter and began to wash the dishes that were in the sink. She patiently waited for Emma to take the hint and leave.

"Emma, you've already done so much for me. You've cared for me these past two months. We've renewed our family bond. I can't ask any more from you." Laura turned to face her daughter. "If things fall apart and the police show up, I can't have you involved."

"But I already texted Bobby. I'm already involved. If the police look at the phone records ...."

"Bobby has that covered. You are overthinking this. We've thought this through, Emma. Trust me." Laura took a slow deep breath and adjusted her tone to that of a mother that knows what's best for her daughter. "If something bad happens and the police arrive Bobby and I will be the ones to take the fall. That's been our plan all along. That's why we had you be the one to get Julie. You were the only one that could properly sedate her. We will tell the police that Bobby found me and has been caring for me these past two months. Bobby will tell them he abducted Julie. We stole the drugs from you. Julie never saw you, so there is no way for you to be implicated, right?"

"I guess."

Laura turned off the running water and dried her hands. She walked over to the kitchen table, sat beside her daughter, and gently held her hands.

"I ... we ... *we* lost Sara," Laura said softly. "I can't lose you too. You've done your part. Bobby and I will take it from here. Go upstairs, pack your things, and leave."

Mother and daughter stared at one another, each searching for truth, hope, trust, or belief.

"I remember the last time you made me pack my bags and leave home."

"That was a long time ago, Emma. This time I'm doing what's best for you."

Emma stood up, grabbed her damp cotton towel, and tossed it over her shoulder. She gave her mother a quiet nod as she exited the kitchen. Emma walked to the hallway and stopped at the bottom of the staircase.

"Are you?" Emma whispered under her breath.

FIFTEEN

Saying Goodbye

1989 Sunday 1-Jan 2:00 p.m.

The crystal clear skies allowed for visibility beyond ten miles. The view from the hilltop was breathtaking. Wellfleet Harbor was visible through the tops of the maple, oak, and pine trees that dotted the landscape. It was easy to see the curve of the Massachusetts coastline, stretching back toward Brewster and Dennis. On clearer days you could see all the way across Cape Cod Bay to Sagamore and Plymouth.

On this day, however, no one was taking in the scenery. All eyes were focused on Fred Johnson's casket. Laura and Sara had selected one made of a simple wood veneer, finished with a cherry gloss stain. The sheen and color matched the twin tables Fred made for Laura and Jennifer. The gravesite was surrounded by three separate sprays of flowers. The National Park Service sent an arrangement filled with white Asiatic lilies. Jennifer contributed another with long stemmed red roses. A mixture of blue and white hydrangeas made up the arrangement from Laura. Sara insisted the blue match the turquoise inlays her father used in his woodwork, but the florist was unable to get an exact match. A long spray of blue hydrangeas was draped across the top of the casket.

The Saints of Christ Cemetery was one of the few privately owned burial grounds on the outer Cape. Established in the late 1800s, the site belonged to the Engel family. Part of that family's genealogy was tied to Laura's forbearer's, the Brandt family. Laura, her husband, and her children were all destined to be laid to rest here. The same was true of her sister, Jennifer.

The black lace veil shrouding Laura's face rippled in the breeze shooting in from the bay. She slid a hand beneath her veil and dabbed her nose with a damp white cotton kerchief. Laura shivered and adjusted her black wool coat, pulling it close to her neck. The sun did little to mask the 37 degree temperature that engulfed the outer Cape. She watched in silence as Emma approached the casket.

Emma paused, staring at the blue flowers covering the wooden box that held her father's lifeless body. She let the tears flow freely down her cheeks. Her nostrils burned as the wind cut across her wet nose. Emma knelt down before the casket and wiped the cold tears from her face.

"I ... I wish you were here," Emma said. "I don't know if Bobby was being honest about you killing Uncle Carl. You always had a temper, but I can't imagine you would do something like that. It had to be an accident. Or Bobby did it. Everything's different now, Dad. Mom and Sara don't talk to me. I feel like this is all my fault. I should have told you sooner. I should have told you when we were on the porch at my birthday party. But I was so scared. I'm sorry. I'm so sorry I didn't ...."

Emma burst into tears again, her body ravaged with guilt and loss. She kissed her gloved fingertips and placed them on the side of the casket. Emma stood up and took a deep breath. Her hair blew across her face, blocking her vision. With a heavy sigh, she made the sign of the cross and lowered her head.

"I know it's only a matter of time before Bobby kills me. I wish you were here to protect me. Goodbye, Dad."

Emma closed her eyes, turned, and walked away. After a few steps, she wiped her face dry and opened her eyes. Sara was walking toward her. Emma held her hand out with her palm open. Sara kept her focus straight ahead and walked past Emma without acknowledging her. Emma lowered her head, slid her hands into her coat pockets, and walked over to be with Susan and her aunt.

Sara fell to her knees in front of her father's grave. She lowered her head but did not cry. After days and nights of crying, Sara felt empty. Hollow. All that remained were anger and confusion.

"I can't believe you're gone," Sara said tenderly. "I will never believe the lies that Emma told Aunty Jen. If she hadn't said those things, you never would have driven out into that storm, and you would still be here today. I will never trust her or believe in her again. I keep playing the events of last year over and over in my mind. It's all connected. It all goes back to Eddie. Once that drifter showed up, it was the beginning of the end. Emma changed after that, and her lies and secrets destroyed this family."

Sara stood up and ran her hands along the hydrangeas draped across the casket. Most were sized between four and six inches across. She noticed one that was much smaller than the others. Sara slid her fingers beneath it and pried it from the arrangement. She held it to her nose, took a deep breath, and frowned at the lack of scent.

"You were the best dad," Sara said. "I'll take care of Mom for you. I promise to make you proud."

Sara tucked the flower into her coat pocket, turned, and walked away. The brittle grass snapped beneath her boots as she strolled back to be with her mother. Susan passed Sara on her way to pay her respects. She smiled as she approached her cousin, but Sara lowered her head, refusing to make eye contact with Susan.

Laura held her open arms out for her daughter. Sara buried her head on her mother's shoulder and wept once more. Laura ran her hand down Sara's head, gently stroking her hair.

Fifty feet away stood Jennifer and Emma. The wind drove a brutal, bitter gust between the two estranged sisters. Jennifer patted her niece on the shoulder and began what felt like a long heavy march across the cemetery. Laura kissed Sara on the top of her head and gently moved her aside. She took aim at her sister and began to walk across the dormant brown grass.

Laura and Jennifer, sisters for over thirty-five years, approached one another with caution as if coming upon a stranger. They paused three feet apart. Sara and Emma stayed far away, watching their mother and aunt, while Susan remained at the casket, kneeling in prayer.

"We've barely spoken since Christmas," Jennifer said. "How are you?"

"How do you think I am? What kind of question is that to ask? My husband left in a rage after the show you and Emma put on. And now he's dead."

"Laura, you have to believe I'm truly sorry. The roads were so icy that night. I'm so sorry."

"You're sorry?" Laura shook her head in disgust and turned away. "Your apology is not accepted."

Jennifer lowered her head, closed her eyes, and reminded herself of what she needed to say.

"Emma wants to know when she can come back home. I told her it's up to you, but I don't trust Bobby. Not after the threats he made. I worry you won't keep her safe."

Laura turned to face her sister once more, but let her eyes wander over Jennifer's shoulder toward Emma standing in the distance.

"Emma told you things she shouldn't have, and now my husband is dead. Bobby won't hurt her. If you must know, I'm not even speaking to him right now. As far as I'm concerned, Emma's destroyed our family. She should have confided in me, not you. She lied to me. I've lost Rose and now Fred. I'm sorry, Jennie, but I'm just not ready to have her back. Not just yet."

"Laura, there's something you should know about Bobby. About us."

A gust of wind slammed against Laura's face. She reached into her pocket and pulled out her white kerchief and used it to tab her eyes dry. Laura turned and started to walk back to Sara.

"Stop, Laura. Please."

Laura reluctantly paused but did not turn around.

"There was a reason I was so outraged about Bobby's affair with you. Bobby was much more than just my lover, Laura. You see, Bobby was ... he was also Marilyn's father."

Jennifer waited several seconds for her sister to turn around. Laura stood motionless, her back toward Jennifer. Sitting at the bottom of the hill was Bobby's Ford F-150, the worn out engine lightly clattering away. She couldn't see him from this distance, but she felt his presence. Laura replayed Jennifer's last words over and over in her head before continuing her walk back to Sara.

***

The half-eaten plate of scrambled eggs and sausage lay cool and soggy. Sara looked at the breakfast sitting on her mother's dish and frowned. It was evident to her that her mother did not have the slightest appetite. Yesterday's funeral services left them both drained.

"I can clean up, Mom," Sara said. "Why don't you go get some rest?"

Laura smiled and pulled herself upright. She stood up and took her plate over to the sink.

"I'm fine, Sara. You did the cooking. Let me do the cleaning."

"Are you sure? You barely ate anything. Was it OK?"

"It was lovely. I'm just not very hungry. Do me a favor and go upstairs to your room. I will get this cleaned up. I also have some calls to make. I need some privacy."

"Sure, Mom."

Sara gave her mother a kiss on the cheek, followed by a long tight embrace. Laura kissed Sara on her head and gently motioned her toward the hallway. The stairs creaked and groaned as Sara bounded her way up to her bedroom. Once Laura heard the bedroom door close, she picked up the phone and dialed Bobby.

"Laura?" Bobby asked as he answered the phone. "It's so nice to hear your voice. You've been ignoring my calls. I can understand why. Jennie's revelation Christmas eve was, well, it was a lot. I know you must be mad at me. I've kept my distance, as you asked. How ... how are you?"

"Honestly, Bobby, I'm tired. I barely got any sleep last night."

"This will all take time to heal. That was a horrible car accident. I so wanted to be there for you. But, well, that news about Jennie and me. I'm glad you called. We have a lot to discuss."

"I need to ask you something, Bobby. And I will need the truth from you."

"Of course, Laura. Anything for you."

Laura paced back and forth across the kitchen, scuffing her slippers beneath her feet. She took a deep breath and closed her eyes.

"Was Marilyn your daughter?" Laura let out a long exhale, relieved to finally ask Bobby the question that's weighed on her since yesterday's funeral. The silence on the other end of the line grew longer. Laura felt her heart sink. "Bobby?"

"I'm here."

"Answer the question."

"Laura, look, Angel, you have to understand ...."

"So it's true. My God she ... she was telling me the truth."

"When did she tell you? How long have you known?"

Laura lowered the phone and covered the end with the microphone before releasing a muffled cry. Her body began to shake as she fought back the tears. Bobby's voice crackled through the earpiece as he continued to talk to her, but Laura was not listening.

"Laura? Laura are you there?"

Laura grabbed a napkin from the counter and wiped the tears that were rolling down her face.

"I'm here. I ... I just don't know what to say to you."

"Trust me, Laura, the affair with Jennie was just that. An affair. It was very brief."

"It was long enough to get her pregnant."

"Marilyn was an accident."

"An accident?" Laura exclaimed. She lowered her voice so as not alert Sara upstairs. "Let me guess, Bobby, you didn't

pull out when you should have. Is that right? My God, did ....
Does Jennie know about Rose?"

"No. I never told her about our daughter. Laura, I ended
things with Jennie before Mary was born. I was never with
her after that. I never loved her. You, Laura. You are the one
that I love. That I've always loved."

Laura walked across the kitchen and grabbed the chair
closest to her. She dragged it across the scuffed and faded
peanut-colored linoleum floor and took a seat on the stiff
turquoise vinyl chair. Laura briefly lowered the phone into
her lap and stared aimlessly out the window, looking at the
barn.

"Laura?"

Laura lifted the phone to her face. The weight of the
handset felt like a lead brick in her hand as she fought to
summon the will to continue speaking with him.

"I ... I don't know what to say, Bobby. Nine years since
Rose and Mary were born. Nine. You've lied to me this entire
time. It's bad enough that you had an affair with my sister.
But to keep the fact that you fathered a child with her?"

"I should have been honest with you. I'm sorry, Laura.
Truly I am. Let me come by. We shouldn't do this on the
phone."

"No, Bobby. I don't think you should come here."

"Sure. You need more time. I understand."

"No, Bobby, you don't understand. I don't think you
should come here. Ever."

There was a pause before Bobby spoke. When he did, his
voice sounded frail.

"Laura. Please. You ... you have to hear me out."

"I've trusted you, Bobby. For over a decade, you have been
my true love. But not anymore. This is all too much for me. A
secret affair with my sister? An affair that gave birth to
Marilyn? We lost her. We lost our precious Rose. And now
my husband is dead. Too many accidents, Bobby. Too much
death."

"Laura, please don't do this."

"I once thought you were my savior. My soulmate. But
now I don't know what to believe. Who are you? Really? I ... I

can't trust you, Bobby. Not now. Not after everything that's happened. Not after these lies."

Laura stood up and carried the phone back to the base hanging on the wall. She poked her head into the hallway and looked at the top of the staircase. The door to Sara's bedroom was still closed. She raised the phone to her face and closed her eyes.

"Laura, I ... I understand. I do. Before you hang up, I want you to know that it's always been you. I've always loved you."

"Goodbye, Bobby."

Laura ended the call, walked back to the kitchen table, and opened the door to the porch. The main barn door was ajar and creaking back and forth in the morning breeze. The ice-cold wind seared the tears that ran down her cheeks. The shock to her system strengthened her.

Laura took a few deep breaths of bitterly cold air before stepping back inside. She slammed the door shut and went back to the phone and dialed her sister. Her hands and fingers trembled as she fought to keep herself from falling apart. Laura waited patiently for the call to go through.

"Hello?" Jennifer asked.

"It's me."

"I'm so glad you called, Laura. We need to talk."

"No, Jennie. You need to listen. My life, my ... my world, has been destroyed. And I can't help but blame you and Emma for this."

"Laura, I don't think that's fair."

"She lied to me and then had to run to you. Emma couldn't keep her mouth shut. If she had only confided in me instead of you, my husband would still be alive."

"Laura, that's not true."

"Now I've lost everything and everyone. I can never forgive you, or Emma, or even Bobby. This is goodbye, Jennie."

"Laura, stop! There is too much unresolved. You can't just end this. We're family."

"We were."

There was a long pause as Jennifer absorbed the tenacity and finality of her sister's words.

"I need you to tell me the truth," Jennifer said. "About the girls. How did they die? Did they drown? Was it Bobby? Fred? I need to know."

"I think it's best Emma stay with you. Permanently. Take good care of her. And please, do a better job with her than you did with Marilyn."

"Wait! Laura, I need to know. Please!"

Laura ended the call. Within seconds, the phone rang again, as Jennifer attempted to continue their conversation. Laura ignored the ringing, returned to her chair and wept. The sound of her tears and the ringing of the phone masked the creak of the staircase as Sara slowly made her way back up to her bedroom and closed the door.

SIXTEEN

Road Rage

Traffic on Route 25 eastbound was at a complete halt. Tom and Max were now two miles from the Bourne bridge. The trip to the Cape was taking forever, the result of never-ending delays due to construction, accidents, and too many people trying to get to Cape Cod for the holiday weekend. The beautiful weather – sunny clear skies and temperatures in the low eighties – brought many last minute vacationers out seeking fun.

Tom glanced at his phone. The screen showed it was just after one o'clock, and there were no new notification messages. Tom gripped the steering wheel and looked up at the open sky above. He was thankful it was a windy day, as the steady breeze kept him from feeling like he was baking in the sun.

Max stuck his head between the front seats and looked at Tom. He let out a slight whimper.

"I know," Tom said. "This traffic sucks. Massachusetts drivers are the worst. Let's see where your aunt is at."

Tom pulled up his GPS app and refreshed the location for Julie's tracker. The tiny red search arrow spun clockwise as the system searched for the signal. The longer the arrow turned, the more concerned Tom became.

"Why is it taking so long?"

After sixty seconds a message appeared on Tom's screen indicating the GPS tracker was offline.

"Fuck."

Max retreated to the back seat.

"Sorry. Sorry, buddy. Why would the signal go dead? Unless ...."

Tom tried the tracker for Max's collar. In less than ten seconds the map began to pan, pulling up their current position. Tom closed the app before the search completed.

"Yours works fine. The battery on hers can't be dead, Max. That's supposed to last weeks. It was fully charged when I slipped it in there the other night."

Tom removed his seatbelt and stood up to get a better look at the roadway conditions. The traffic was starting to crawl about a half mile ahead. He sat back down, secured his seatbelt, and put his Jeep into drive. He glanced over his shoulder to check on his dog and was happy to see that Max was on his side, sleeping.

"That tracker doesn't have an on/off switch. This isn't good. Shit." Tom let out a long sigh before he picked up his phone. "I know I'm going to regret this."

Tom went to his list of contacts and scrolled through, keeping one eye on the traffic and another on his phone. He eased off the brake pedal as the traffic began to move. Tom waited patiently as the call connected and rang five times before going to voicemail.

"Officer Stevens, hey, this is Tom. Tom Leblanc. Listen, I wanted to give you a heads up on something with Jewels. She's sort of, well, disappeared. It's a long story. She went silent, and I tracked her on ... on her phone. It shows her as being out on Cape Cod, which is weird because her car is at her apartment. We planned to spend the day together. The reason I'm calling you is that, well, she thought she saw Emma Johnson this morning. Sara's sister. The one that tried to kill us? Anyway, I told her she was imagining things. But now that she's gone and apparently out on the Cape I think maybe she really did see her. She won't return calls or text messages. So, I thought maybe you could ...."

"I'm sorry, but you've reached the maximum amount of time allowed to record a message."

"Fuck," Tom yelled. He glanced over his shoulder to see Max yank himself upright on his front legs, looking worried with his ears lowered.

"To rerecord this message, press one. If you would like to keep ...."

Tom ended the call and tossed his phone on the passenger's seat.

"I keep telling you, Max, the cops are useless."

Tom shook his head in frustration as the speed of the traffic finally climbed above 25 mph. The spaces separating the cars and trucks around his Jeep began to widen as everyone on the roadway accelerated ahead. After a few minutes, Tom found himself cresting the Bourne bridge. Traffic slowed as he approached the top. Max shoved his head in between the front seats and ran his damp, wet nose against the side of Tom's face.

"How about some music?"

Just as Tom was about to power up the stereo, his phone rang. The "Imperial March" ringtone was the last thing Tom wanted to hear.

"If you weren't here," Tom said to Max, "I would be dropping so many F-bombs right now. Go lay down."

Max spun around twice in the back seat and settled on his side and closed his eyes. Tom reluctantly accepted the call.

"Hi Mom," Tom said.

"I wanted to check on Julie," Dorothy said. "Have you heard from her?"

"Heard from ... oh, no I haven't. Why?"

"I wanted to make sure you were both still coming to the cookout on Monday."

"Monday? Of course."

"Good. Is she feeling any better yet? Is she still planning to bring that Mexican dish?"

"Mexican dish?"

Tom frowned as the traffic came to a halt again. He was almost at the rotary that would connect him to Route 6A that ran along the Cape Cod Canal.

"I don't remember the name. Something native. I'm just trying to plan out how much food I will need." Dorothy paused for a few seconds before continuing. "What's that noise? Where are you?"

Tom closed his eyes and let out a groan. His mind raced as he tried to come up with a convincing lie to tell his mother.

"I'm out with Max taking a ride in Ruby. It's a beautiful day."

"I suppose. But why is it so noisy? Where are you?"

"It's just the wind, Mom. Remember I took the doors off yesterday? I have the roof off too."

The wind blasting across the bridge was gusting at over 30 mph. Tom disconnected his Bluetooth and held the handset to his face.

"Is that better?" Tom asked.

"Yes. Where are you?"

Tom shook his head and glanced back at Max, mouthing "F-bombs coming" to the sleeping dog.

"No place special. Just out for a drive around the city. Max loves taking rides in the Jeep."

Tom waited patiently for his mother to respond. The rotary connecting Routes 25, 28 and 6A were packed with cars. After several seconds he heard a long sigh come through the earpiece.

"Well just stay off the highway," Dorothy said. "You know I worry about you."

"I'm well aware, Mom."

"I know you and Julie have been through hell these past few months. And I know you've tried to keep a lot of it a secret from me."

"A secret?"

"Don't play coy with me, Thomas. I may not know everything that happened out there, but I do know that I know much more than you think I do. Never question a mother's intuition."

Tom kept his focus on the road ahead as he made the final turn through the roundabout and exited onto Route 6A. The trees lining the roadway brought much-needed shade, as well as a considerable drop in the wind speed.

"After your father died you retreated into this little shell," Dorothy continued. "I never knew how much you were obsessing over finding his killer until months later. I know you had a similar reaction after what happened to Marc and Chris. I just want you to know that you can always confide in me, Son. OK?"

Tom cradled the phone against his face, silently pondering his mother's words. The cars in front of him slowed to a halt, forcing Tom to stop his Jeep. A gentle breeze wafted around him. A horn blared from a tugboat chugging through the canal.

"Is there anything you need to tell me?" Dorothy said, gently prodding her son. "Anything you need to ask me?"

"No, Mom. I'm OK. Really. I mean, well, yes, I didn't tell you everything that happened. You do worry a lot, so, you know, I just don't want to burden you with stuff."

"Please, Thomas, your mother is a tough old broad. I can handle quite a bit."

"I know. I know you can." Tom paused as he thought back to the months following his dad's murder. It may have been over fifteen years ago, but there were many moments that remained seared into his memory. "Can I ask you something?"

"Of course."

"After dad died, you were so strong. I remember being amazed at how you just moved us forward. As a family. It's like things didn't skip a beat. I mean, there were many changes. But not you. You were such a rock. How'd you do it? How'd you stay so strong?"

"I had to be strong. For you. For us. I always kept a brave face on the outside."

"But inside you were ... what?"

"I wasn't alone, Tom. I didn't keep it bottled up waiting for the hurt and loss to consume me. There were others I confided in. Mostly your aunt."

"Aunt Judy?"

"I was with her for that long weekend vacation down in Florida. That dreadful snowstorm prevented me from flying home. Trust me, Thomas, I was guilt-ridden about your father's murder."

"Guilty? Why?"

"If I hadn't taken that vacation I would have been home. It's possible my presence could have somehow changed the events that happened that night."

"Mom, there is no way you could know that."

"I know. I know. Well, I know that now. I spent countless hours talking to your aunt. Judy was so supportive. She lost her favorite brother that night, so it was just as big of a loss for her. There were many times that Judy offered to fly in from Philly. At one point she went so far as to tell me she was going to try and take a leave of absence to come to stay with us. I told her I would be fine. Her phone calls were what helped me get through it all. She was my rock."

"I had no idea."

"I guess I held some secrets from you as well."

The traffic began to move. Tom was surprised to notice his stress level had plummeted. Usually, conversations with his mother would have the opposite effect.

"I hope you and Julie talk," Dorothy continued. "About what happened. I don't want you to keep things bottled up inside. If you are still haunted by what happened out on the Cape, you need to find someone to confide in. Someone you can trust."

"Jewels and I talk all the time, Mom."

"Good. Good, I'm happy to hear that. It's important to surround yourself with others you can trust. When I was your age, family was always important to me. I too was an only child, Tom, and I relied on my cousins to be the brothers and sisters I never had. We always had the most wonderful family holidays together. But then over time, the cousins moved away. I wish you had more family that you could confide in."

"I've got Jewels, Mom. She's like family to me."

"I know that, Tom. But you still keep so many secrets. You need to learn to trust others. She won't always be there for you."

SEVENTEEN

The Bunker

The bunker buried beneath the Johnson family property smelled of dust and mold. The dirt floor was littered with dried out empty cans of beans. Roaches roamed the floors and walls, scavenging whatever bits of nourishment they could find. All was quiet, except for a low resonating hum reverberating from the air vent in the back corner.

Emma placed a battery-powered LED lantern onto the round wood coffee table. The harsh white light cast an eerie glow across the room's belongings. She and her mother never bothered to clean up after her mother's prolonged stay here. A soup spoon, caked with dried food, lay resting on the table.

Emma flicked on her phone's flashlight feature and swept the beam along the wall closest to her. Knives and daggers filled the lower shelves. The wooden handles were expertly hand-crafted with a nickel metal and turquoise inlay. Emma allowed the light to pause briefly in front of each weapon. She stopped when she got to the last two items. The first was a machete, and the second a jagged tooth saw. The handles on both were harshly charred.

Emma cast her light higher. A row of mason jars took up the top shelf. She walked over to the far end of the ledge. There was a space missing where the rosemary-scented candle used to be. Emma counted seven other candles, each with a unique color – brown, red, yellow, white, two tan ones, and finally a blue one.

The lids on all seven jars were sealed shut. Emma extinguished her flashlight and slid her phone into her pocket. The lantern provided enough illumination for what she intended to do next. She picked up the first candle and popped the lid open. The candle looked new inside, without even so much as a coat of dust covering the wax. The oddly shaped wick had never been lit. Out of curiosity, Emma held the jar just beneath her nose, closed her eyes, and inhaled. The scent surprised her. She studied the dark chocolate colored wax and inhaled a second time. The aroma of cedarwood and seaweed reminded her of the random pieces of driftwood that would often wash up on the beach. She closed the top and put the candle back on the shelf.

Emma opened the top covering the red candle. Again, she found the pine scent to be somewhat unanticipated. The berry colored wax led her to expect an aroma more along the lines of cherry or apple. Unlike the dark brown candle, this one had seen many hours of use. Multiple layers of wax were melted away, resulting in a terraced topography similar to that of a drained lake. She was about to reach for the yellow candle when she noticed a piece of paper on top of one of the two tan candles.

Emma pulled her phone out and turned the flashlight on. She held the light above the last three candles on the shelf. Each had a white rectangular sticker on the lid. The label on one of the beige-colored jars had loosened from the ever-changing climate in the bunker. Emma turned her light off and removed the candle from the shelf. She placed it on the coffee table next to the lantern and spread the sticker flat with her finger.

"Sesame?"

Emma popped the top open and inhaled the earthy nutty scent of sesame. She furrowed her brow and retrieved the last two jars from the shelf, placing them on the table.

"Ginger?" A quick test confirmed the scent matched the sticker. Emma glanced at the label on the last jar.

"Seabreeze?"

The rubber seal let out a muffled pop as Emma opened the sky-blue colored candle. The scent of the ocean came wafting out beneath Emma's nose. The aroma brought back memories of running along the golden sands of the National Seashore with her sister. The smile on her face faded as she sealed the jar and studied the soot-covered sticker.

"Seabreeze. How do I know that name?" Emma placed the jar back on the table next to the other two candles. "Sesame, Ginger, and Seabreeze."

The air vent in the ceiling moaned as a wind came swirling through from outside. The fresh air brought little relief to Emma. Her hands began to shake as she pulled her phone from her pocket. She looked over at the filthy couch on the opposite side of the table and began to pace back and forth. Emma went to her list of recent calls and dialed.

"Please be there," Emma whispered. She did not have to wait long. After two brief rings, the call connected.

"Well hello there, Aunty Em," Jeff said cheerily. "How's it going?"

"Hi, Jeff. I have some questions for you."

"Sure thing. Hey, are you OK? You sound stressed."

"I'm fine. The candle store owners that were killed. What were their names?"

"What? Why do you want to know that?"

"Please. Just answer me." Emma tried her best to mask the dread that was bubbling up inside her.

"Hamasaki."

Hamasaki? Emma thought to herself. *So, they were Asian.*

"They were such a sweet couple," Jeff continued. "It was sad because they moved here to start that business."

"What about the condo?"

"Condo? What condo? What's going on, Em?"

"What was the name of the condo where Sara supposedly attacked those people?"

"The condo? Oh, the one out in Provincetown. That was .... What was that? Something breezy. Oh. Seabreeze. Seabreeze Village. It was owned by Marc Sirola. His body was one of the ones discovered at Little Pleasant Bay. Why?"

Emma stopped pacing and looked down at the grimy table in front of her. The harsh white light of the lantern illuminated the three mason jars from the side, casting exaggerated shadows across the dusty surface. Emma picked up the Seabreeze candle and ran her thumb along the edge, rubbing the dirt and sediment from the glass.

"Em?" Jeff asked. "Do you want to tell me what's going on?"

Emma rotated her hand, exposing the bottom of the mason jar. There was another sticker underneath the candle. Emma turned her hand so that the light from the lantern would reveal what was written on the label.

"FlickerWood," Emma said softly and began to cry.

EIGHTEEN

Choice

The broken mirror hung in darkness above the sink. The chrome bezel remained intact, surrounding jagged blades of glass. Only one of the two bathroom lights was working. Laura never had the time to replace the mirror after Sara destroyed it two months ago.

Emma closed the bathroom door and flicked the old metal switch on the wall. The lever emitted a loud snap as it connected. The 35-watt frosted bulb in the antique bronze fixture on the left side of the shattered mirror fired to life, providing the only light in the windowless room.

Emma turned the hot water faucet and stared into the bowl. Her nails were filthy from her visit to the bunker. She grabbed the bar of soap and began to scrub her hands. Emma looked up at the mirror, her broken reflection staring back at her in bits and pieces. She placed her hand on the right side of the mirror and recalled the childhood poem she once held so dear.

If I'm unsure and feeling blue.

"Oh, Sara, what have I gotten myself into?"
Emma rinsed her hands and pulled the towel from the

brass ring hanging next to the door. She dabbed the corner of the pink cotton cloth under the running water and proceeded to clean the dirty streaks from her face. The fragmented mirror and poor lighting made this an almost impossible task. Emma did her best and then turned off the water, leaving the towel bunched up in the basin. She stared at her reflection in the largest remaining piece of the mirror and sighed.

"We made some pretty bad choices in our youth. I can't change the past, but maybe I can change the future."

Emma snapped the light switch off and exited to the kitchen. Her mother was seated at the rectangular metal table with her back to the hallway. Emma realized she was fixated on the remnants of the family barn.

"Hard to believe it's gone, isn't it?" Emma asked. She pulled out the chair next to her mother and sat beside her. "I still can't get used to the yard being so open."

"Maybe it's for the best." Laura took a sip of tea from her mug and rested her hand on top of her daughter's hand. "That barn held a lot of memories. Not all of them were pleasant."

Laura placed her empty mug on the table, keeping her focus on the gray and black pile of rubble outside. Emma stood up and took her mother's cup over to the stove and set about making them some more tea.

"What are you doing?" Laura asked. "You need to get back home to Chatham."

"I know," Emma said. "But first, I want to ask you about the candles. The ones in the bunker."

"What about them?"

The igniter beneath the front burner cracked three times before the propane fired to life, shooting blue-tipped flames through the iron grate. Emma placed the pot on the stove and walked over to the corner of the counter, next to the doorway that connected to the hall. Laura, sitting a few feet away, spun her chair around to face her daughter.

"I looked at them. The ones on the shelf."

"When?" Laura asked with surprise. "Did you go back down there?"

"I did."

"I told you to stay out of the basement! Did you go looking for Julie?"

"I found a locked door in the cellar, Mother. Is that where you have her?"

"I don't want you talking to her, Emma. You can't be any more involved than you are. You need to go home!" Laura glared at her daughter, casting a look of disgust and disapproval. "Why did you go back into the bunker? Did you think we put Julie there?"

"No. The bunker is where you kept your rosemary candle. You told me Bobby made that candle using the bones of Rose and Mary."

"The rosemary candle was meant to be a memorial to the girls."

Mother and daughter stared solemnly at one another as each waited and searched for a hint of emotion or reaction. Emma frowned and grabbed a mug from the cupboard for herself. She took two teabags from an open tin sitting next to the stove and placed them into the cups.

"Tell me about the other candles in the bunker. You said there was a family recipe for the wax. Tallow from the cows. I assume there's more to it than just that, or you wouldn't keep brushing it off every time I bring it up."

Laura looked back out at the debris that used to be the barn. The image of Rose pierced atop the pitchfork came rushing into her mind. She closed her eyes and tried to recall more joyful memories, such as her and Bobby making love in the loft. That memory was quickly replaced by Sara screaming as she burned to death beneath the cauldron. Laura opened her eyes as they began to well up with tears. Her gaze settled on the white propane tank in the middle of the blackened waste, standing silently as a tombstone honoring those that had perished in the barn.

"It doesn't matter anymore, Emma. We made the candles in the barn. It's destroyed now. And that's probably for the best. It was a dark place with darker memories."

"You don't need the barn to tell me the recipe."

"It's not important anymore. Please go home."

The kettle whistle started to sing. Emma walked over to the stove, turned off the burner, and filled the two cups with boiling water. She brought them over to the table and sat next to her mother. Laura did not bother to spin her chair back to face the table. Emma took the cue and pushed her chair backward closer to the hallway.

"Then explain the candles with the stickers." Emma blew on the rim of her mug, sending the floral scent of jasmine tea toward her mother. Laura watched the steam evaporate and waft into the air, but did not respond. "Did you know that 'Flicker Wood' was the name that Sara gave to the pond out back?"

Laura twirled the string of her teabag around her index finger and dipped the bag up and down into her mug. She smiled and raised the cup to her face. The moist steam felt good against her nose.

"Sara never told me," Laura responded. "She only told me the name was special to her. I always wondered what it meant. But I don't see how that matters."

"What about the other stickers? The names?"

"What about them?"

"Sesame? Ginger? Seabreeze?"

Laura raised her eyebrows as if she didn't understand what her daughter was asking her. Yet her grip on her teacup tightened as fear and frustration rose within her.

"I know the couple from the candle store was Asian," Emma continued, her confidence growing with each word she spoke. "And the couple that disappeared in December were from the Seabreeze Village condos. That's also where Sara attacked Tom and Julie."

Laura allowed her eyes to drift past Emma. A smile spread across her face as Bobby peered around the edge of the doorway that connected to the front hall. He raised his finger to his lips so that Laura would know not to acknowledge his presence to Emma.

"Emma, I really don't see where this is going. Those labels are just the candle scents. What else could it be?"

"Those candles must be made like the rosemary scented one. Can you just drop it and be honest with me?"

"I've been nothing *but* honest with you."

"Bullshit. She told me what you did. Before I drugged her."

Laura turned and placed her mug on the table behind her. She scowled as she looked at Emma.

"She? Julie? You told me you didn't talk to her."

"I lied. Julie told me about this book of urban legends and that she was convinced you and Sara had made the store owners into candles and planned to do the same to her. And that you did it to her friends. I didn't believe her. But then I found the candles hidden in the bunker, with the labels attached to them. Her story is true, isn't it?"

Laura lowered her head and let out a long exhale. Emma felt an odd mix of disgust and joy at seeing her mother seemingly admit defeat.

"Why did you have to go snooping around?" Laura placed her hands by her sides and pushed herself up off the chair. She groaned as she stood up. "I should have known you were nothing like your sister and couldn't be trusted. You lied to me again, Emma. I had such high hopes for you. Now."

Now?" Emma asked with confusion.

Bobby lunged into the kitchen and jammed a syringe into Emma's neck. Emma threw her hands back, sending her mug crashing to the floor. The white porcelain cup shattered, spraying amber liquid in all directions. She screamed as she fought to pull the needle from her flesh. Bobby kept his arms clamped around her until he finished emptying the injection.

"What the hell?" Emma cried. "What did you do?"

"Relax, Emma," Laura said calmly. She slid her slippers across the floor, brushing the broken bits of ceramic aside and smearing streaks of jasmine tea beneath her feet. "We gave you what you gave Julie. Time to sleep."

"It has to be measured," Emma replied. "You don't want to do the wrong dose."

"I guessed," Bobby said.

Emma tried to wrestle herself free, but Bobby was too strong. Her heart raced as she stared at her mother's watchful glare. Emma fought to hold back the tears that were welling from within. She closed her eyes as she realized the past several weeks were nothing but lies and deceit.

"Stop fighting," Bobby said. "It will all be over soon."

Emma opened her eyes and looked at her mother. The Midazolam was not kicking in. She suspected when it did it most likely would not make her unconscious. The drug needed to be injected into a large muscle for it to be delivered into her bloodstream correctly. Emma realized she could play this knowledge gap to her advantage.

"I trusted you, Mother," Emma said. She let her eyelids droop and began to slur her words. "I trusted you."

"And I trusted you, Emma."

Bobby eased his grip on Emma as her body slowly uncoiled. He felt her begin to slump toward the floor. Bobby released her and let her slide down the front of his body. He caught Emma by her armpits, halting her descent.

"Are you OK?" Bobby asked Laura.

Laura nodded as she stepped forward and ran her fingers across Emma's forehead. She shook her head in disappointment.

"It's too bad it had to come to this," Laura said. "What now?"

"We proceed as planned. I'm going to tie her up first. I have no idea how long she will stay knocked out. I didn't give her too much. Where's the rope?"

Emma opened her eyes and shoved her elbow backward into Bobby's stomach, causing him to release her. She grabbed her mother by her shoulders and flung her to the side, sending her crashing to the ground.

"Emma!" Laura cried as she grabbed a chair and tried to pull herself up. The stool screeched as the metal feet skidded across the floor.

Emma bolted to the door that led to the porch. She cranked the handle and flung the door open. Just as she was about to step outside, Bobby grabbed her by the back of her neck and dug his fingers into her skull. Emma screamed as Bobby threw her face against the frame of the door. Emma collapsed, falling unconscious before her body hit the wooden planks of the porch floor.

Bobby ran to Laura and helped her to her feet.

"Are you hurt?" Bobby asked.

Laura slid an arm around Bobby's waist. He cradled her in his arm as the two walked over to the side door. Emma laid there motionless, her forehead bruised but not bleeding.

"Such a disappointment," Laura said. "I really wanted to trust her. But she lied. She lied again."

"Don't blame yourself. This was her own fault for not doing what she was told."

Laura stepped outside and knelt beside her daughter. Emma's breathing was shallow. Laura frowned as she ran her fingers through Emma's hair. "Such a waste."

"We can't have any loose ends, Laura."

Laura stood up and leaned against Bobby as she stared at Emma. He kissed her on the head and rocked her back and forth. Laura pressed her face deep into Bobby's chest and inhaled his musky scent.

"I need to get a few things before we get started," Laura said.

"Pack what you need. We leave town as soon as this is over."

Laura squeezed Bobby tightly before tilting her head back. He kissed her gently on her lips and lovingly released her. Bobby watched Laura exit the hallway. Her footsteps soon echoed throughout the walls of the old Victorian home as she made her way upstairs. Bobby knelt down beside Emma and turned her face upwards.

"I should have taken care of you a long time ago, Emma. But I loved your mother too much to hurt you. That was then. But now? Now, you will finally pay."

NINETEEN

Fred

1989 Saturday 4-Feb 10:00 a.m.

Laura gently slid her fingertips across the smooth sheet of plastic covering the page within the photo album. She paused her hand below a picture of Sara and Emma building a sandcastle. Several binders were spread out on the coffee table in her living room. The catalogs spanned close to a decade, starting with Rose's birth. Laura was admiring pictures taken at the beach at the edge of the property. She couldn't recall the exact date, only that it was during the summer of 1982.

"Such happier times," Laura said with a heavy sigh.

Three loud knocks at the front door reverberated throughout the expansive living room. Laura folded the heavy ringed binder closed and placed it on the table with the others. She walked over to the door and pressed her face against the glass panel that ran down the side of the frame. The mix of amber, rose, and olive-colored squares, intersected by dark blue roundels, made it difficult for Laura to see who was standing on the other side. She rested her hand on the deadbolt latch.

"Who's there?" Laura asked nervously.

"It's me. It's Bobby."

Laura stroked the brass lock's thumbturn with the tip of her index finger before slowly pulling her hand away.

"Why are you here?"

"Please, Laura. I know you told me to stay away. But I have something for you. I promise not to stay long. Please."

Laura turned and faced the staircase, leaning her backside up against the door. She closed her eyes and took a deep breath. Part of her wanted to fling the door open and throw herself into Bobby's arms. Another part of her wanted to flee upstairs and hide in her bedroom.

"Why couldn't you just stay away," Laura said softly.

With a heavy heart, she took a few steps away from the door to check herself in the mirror in the hallway. She frowned at how tired her face appeared, the messy state her hair was in, and the wrinkled old clothes she was wearing.

Bobby let out a sigh of relief at hearing the sound of the deadbolt snapping open. The wind this morning was brutally uncaring, conspiring with the 24 degree temperature to make for a bitterly cold day. He felt his knees quiver and wasn't sure if it was due to the weather or having to face Laura. Bobby smiled as the door opened.

"What?" Laura asked flatly. She kept her foot and shoulder planted firmly against the back of the door, allowing only her face to protrude from inside.

"Can I come in? Please?"

The wind blasted ice cold air around Bobby and past Laura. She nodded and motioned for him to come inside. Bobby entered the home and closed the door behind him, keeping his right arm behind his back.

"Thank you for letting me in. It's a bitter day out there."

Laura stood motionless and kept her eyes focused on the dormant fireplace on the far side of the living room. She couldn't think of any words to share with Bobby and hoped his stay would be brief.

"Are the girls here?" Bobby asked.

"Sara's in the barn."

"What about Emma?"

"Why? Are you going to threaten her again?"

"I was only doing what I thought was best. Would you like me to speak to her to smooth things over?"

"No," Laura retorted. "Your verbal assaults on her are what drove her to my sister. She's ruined everything. You've ruined everything. As angry as I am at Emma, Bobby, you are to keep your distance from her. Am I clear?"

"Completely." Bobby pulled his arm out from behind his back. In his hand was a cardboard box, roughly six inches square. "I brought you something. A gift."

Laura shook her head in displeasure.

"Bobby, if you think you can win me back with a simple present, you are going to be very disappointed."

"I have no such expectation, Laura. I'm well aware of the pain I've caused you. Can we sit? Please?"

Bobby did not wait for a response and headed to the sofa. The hickory leather of the Chesterfield couch was brittle and worn. Three buttons were missing from the tufts on the back cushion. Bobby took a strategic position in the middle seat and waited for Laura to join him.

Laura felt her chest tighten as she entered the living room. She was about to sit in the chair opposite the couch, but found the gift sitting on Bobby's lap too intriguing. Laura decided it was best to sit down beside him.

The leather on the old sofa moaned as the cushions rubbed together. Across the room, the cream linen sheers covering the windows rustled as the wind pounded the side of the house, creeping in through the drafty old window casings.

Bobby passed the cardboard box to Laura. A strip of clear adhesive tape secured the edge closest to her. Laura ran her fingernail along the seam, slicing the tape in half. The lid gently sprang up. Laura flipped it open and looked inside, admiring the domed glass lid.

"A jar?" Laura asked.

"No," Bobby replied.

Laura reached into the box and retrieved the contents. As she lifted it, the weight and shape immediately felt familiar to her. Laura held the candle up and away from her face so she could inspect it. The deep cherry-colored wax filled roughly three-quarters of the jar.

"Another candle?" Laura wrapped her thumb around the metal latch and flicked it back, freeing the lid. "Why? I don't understand."

Laura raised the jar to her nose, closed her eyes, and inhaled.

"It smells like pine," Laura said. She opened her eyes and studied the half-inch wide flat wick resting in the center of the candle. She turned and looked at Bobby. "What's this for?"

"This candle is for Fred, Laura. It's similar to the rosemary one I made you."

Laura recoiled slightly and allowed her eyes to momentarily glance into the mason jar. She inhaled the sweet pine aroma once more.

"Is this *for* Fred or *is* it Fred? That wick? Is that .... Bobby, is Fred in here?"

"The wick is wood, Laura. You can burn this candle. The pine that you smell in there. That's from the tree that took his life."

Laura gave the candle a suspicious look.

"And? Anything else?"

Bobby slid closer toward Laura. Her body immediately tensed up, but she did not move away. Laura was surprised by how uneasy she felt being so close to Bobby.

"Before the ambulance arrived at the accident, I was able to take some of Fred. It was, well, it was pretty messy in there Laura. It's really just bits of blood and clothing that I was able to boil down into the wax. I couldn't get any fat or bones like I did for the girls, but I wanted you to have something. There's been so much death and loss. That night was devasting, in so many ways. I thought you would want something to remember Fred by."

Laura caressed the side of the jar before sealing the lid shut. She leaned forward and slid the candle across the coffee table. The jar came to a halt directly in the middle of the pile of photo albums. Although the skies were clear and the sun was shining overhead, the sheer cream curtains dimmed the light in the living room. Resting a few feet away, the dark burgundy wax inside the candle jar looked black and lifeless.

"You didn't tell me much about that night," Laura said as she stared at the tiny glass coffin sitting a few feet away. "Was he alive when you found him?"

"No. Like I said, it was a bad accident."

"Was it?"

Bobby stared at Laura, somewhat confused by her question.

"An accident?" Laura continued. "You chased after him that night, Bobby. I have to ask. Was it an accident?"

"I can't believe you would ask me that. Of course it was. All I wanted to do was calm him down and get him to come back to Jennie's so we could all talk this through. His Jeep was already off the road when I got there. There was nothing I could do to save him."

Bobby felt the glare of Laura's ice-blue eyes as she studied his face. He slid his hand across the couch and reached for her hand, but Laura stood up and walked to the hallway. Bobby sighed, gave the mason jar one last look, and headed toward the front door.

"I've got a guy working to repair Fred's Cherokee for you," Bobby added. "I told him to send me the bill."

Laura opened the front door, catching it as the wind attempted to blast its way into her home. She stopped it before it could swing against the backstop. Laura refused to look at Bobby, and kept her head down, waiting for him to leave.

Bobby stepped outside and immediately turned to face Laura. He was surprised to see she was already closing the door. Bobby flung his arm up and stopped the door's progress.

"It was wrong of me to lie to you, Laura. I should have been honest with you about Jennie and Mary. For that I am sorry. Just know that I will always be here for you. You can reach out whenever you need me. A month. A year. A decade. I will always be here, Laura. Always."

Bobby lowered his arm and shoved his hands into his coat pockets. The wind slammed against his back, causing his jacket to ripple loudly. Laura locked eyes with Bobby one last time before closing the door and securing the deadbolt.

TWENTY

Rebel

Tom turned off his stereo and eased up on his vehicle's throttle. The two-lane road gradually transitioned from blacktop to a path of golden sand. He felt a newfound sense of energy as he and Max approached the small lot that connected to the National Seashore. The last time Tom was here with Julie was off-season, and the parking lot was empty. Today, on Memorial Day weekend, both sides were filled with vehicles. Tom frowned as he slowed Ruby to a halt.

"Well this sucks," Tom said quietly.

The narrow opening on the left side of the entrance to the parking lot was still heavily obscured by shrubs and pine trees. A large 42-gallon commercial garbage bin sat at the end of the space. It was also one of only three empty parking slots in the entire lot. Tom pulled his Jeep into the opening and killed the engine. Max immediately woke up from his nap and shoved his head between the front seats.

"Now what?" Tom wrapped his arm around Max's neck and pulled the dog's head against his face. Max tried to nibble on Tom's nose. "You must need a walk."

Hearing the word "walk" sent Max into a state of joy. He ripped his head from Tom's grip and started to spin around in circles. Tom laughed and grabbed his phone and Max's leash. He exited the Jeep and met his dog at the back tailgate. Once he secured the tether, Tom opened the back and Max jumped to the ground. The two headed back out to the main road.

Tom opened his GPS app and made another attempt to locate Julie. The device still showed as offline. He pulled up a history report. It showed the last known location as being approximately a mile up the coast from his current position. Tom zoomed in and recognized the area as being very close to the barn and Victorian home they had visited two months ago.

Max was busy pulling on his leash, stopping to give each and every tree trunk and bush a good dousing of his scent. Tom closed his GPS app and switched over to his phone app.

"I'm giving him one more shot," Tom said to his dog. He waited patiently for the call to connect. After five rings it went to the voicemail box for Officer Trevor Stevens. Tom ended the call without leaving a message. Tom angrily jammed the phone into his pocket. "What's the point, Max? How can I learn to trust in others when they are never there for me?"

Max stopped and briefly looked up at his master, before returning to his mission to mark this entire section of Wellfleet with his scent. On the walk back, Tom copied the last known location of Julie's tracker and dropped it as a pin on his map. Tom led his dog across the street and turned to head back to the parking lot. Once they were back at the Jeep, Tom opened the back hatch so that Max could jump inside. Tom slammed the tailgate closed and walked out into the middle of the parking lot.

Several people were wandering around the far end near the boulders that blocked the entrance to the cliffside trail that descended to the beach. The vehicles around him all appeared to be empty. Tom took one final glance at the main road to confirm he and Max were alone.

Tom went to the front of the Jeep and dragged the garbage bin off to the side, giving him enough room to maneuver his vehicle past it. He stepped through the shrubs to inspect the hidden trail that led north to the beach. He was relieved to discover it looked the same. Tom returned to Ruby, fired up her engine, shifted four-wheel-drive into low gear, and entered the path.

The journey along the cliffside was just as Tom remembered it, including the two challenging areas that resulted in the skid plates beneath his vehicle getting hit. His trip down to the beach was somewhat uneventful, other than coming across a pair of hikers along the way, one of whom seemed quite upset to find a bright red Jeep crawling along the rocky trail. When Tom and Max emerged onto the beach, they were alone.

Tom aimed his vehicle north, keeping close to the sand dunes. He checked his rearview mirror. Dozens of people were running along the beach far away back near the parking area. Thankfully the coastline ahead was clear. Tom monitored his map, keeping a watchful eye on the ever approaching pin, set far inland from the beach. After a few minutes, Tom came to a halt and looked to his left. Weeks of wind and rain had changed the landscape of the ivory-speckled sand dune, but Tom immediately recognized it as the area that led back to the old Victorian house. His map confirmed his location, showing the pin as directly due west – the last known location of Julie's GPS tracker.

Max paced back and forth with excitement as Tom brought Ruby to a halt. The smells of the beach and ocean and the crashing of the waves were unfamiliar to the dog. Max whimpered in anticipation as he watched Tom gather up his backpack and archery case. Tom barely had the tailgate open when Max jumped from the back, landing with excitement on the sandy beach.

"Wait, Max," Tom said.

Max ignored his master and set his sights on two seagulls walking along the shoreline. Just as Tom was about to clip his leash to Max's collar, the dog bolted into a full-blown sprint toward the ocean. The tags on his collar chimed as they banged against one another, holding on for dear life as Max zeroed in on the bright white birds.

"Max!"

The seagulls took one look at the bounding black and tan 55-pound animal and swiftly took flight into the crystal blue sky. Max barked as he slowed to a halt just ahead of the crashing waves. Horseflies buzzed around his ears, causing him to whip his head back and forth. His nostrils flared from the onslaught of amazing aromas surrounding him. As Max watched the birds soaring overhead, Tom quickly connected the dog's leash to his collar.

"Don't make me F-bomb you," Tom said as he struggled to catch his breath. "We still have a long walk ahead."

Once back at Ruby, Tom grabbed his backpack and archery case. Together, he and Max ascended the steep monolithic dune that obscured the path that connected the beach to the Johnson family home. Tom's feet melted into the sunbaked sands, filling his sneakers with grains of rocks and minerals. The tiny particles quickly made their way through the woven strands of his white cotton socks, embedding themselves against his skin and toenails.

Tom looked over to check on Max. His narrow paws and legs sank deep within the dune, but the dog easily tugged them out and clawed his way up the hillside. Max quickly pulled ahead of his master and effortlessly made it to the top. The dog waited patiently for his 25-foot retractable leash to rewind itself into the handle Tom was holding.

"Show off," Tom said as he finally caught up with Max. "I'd like to see you do that with sneakers on."

Tom's phone rang. He checked his screen – it was Officer Stevens. Tom looked over at Max and then at the dense forest off to the west. For a brief moment, he considered declining the call. He let out a long sigh as he answered the phone.

"Hello?" Tom said.

"Tom, it's Trevor. I got your message from earlier and saw that you called again. Sorry for the delay, I've been swamped today. I'm about to grab a very late lunch, so forgive me if I have to put you on hold. Do you want to tell me what's going on?"

"Do I have to tell you the entire thing again? I thought my message was pretty clear."

Tom tugged on Max's leash, and the pair began the descent down the dune. The seagrasses along this side made the ground much firmer, allowing for a fast and easy walk down the sandy slope. The wind coming in from the east subsided as they descended below the view of the Atlantic Ocean.

"Where are you?" Trevor asked.

"Why didn't you tell us about Emma?"

"Emma? Johnson?"

"I read about her in the obituaries. You never told us that Sara had a twin sister. Why not?"

Trevor's concerned tone quickly turned into a defensive one.

"Why would I? It wasn't relevant to the case."

"If we'd known maybe we would have been able to keep an eye out for her. Now she's got Jewels."

Trevor paused to enjoy the aroma of the meats and cheeses spread throughout the deli case in front of him. He smiled as he watched the young man behind the counter build his sandwich.

"Slow it down, Tom. We talked with Emma shortly after Laura and Sara Johnson died. She's been estranged from that family since she was sixteen, OK? We confirmed that with Susan Jones. Emma had no contact with either Laura or Sara for decades. Phone records verified this. Correction. Laura called Emma the day of the barn fire. It was the only call between them for years."

"What was the call about?"

"About?" Trevor lowered his phone and took a deep breath. Tom had a way of pushing him that drove his temper up far too quickly. "Not that it's any of your business, but if I remember correctly, Laura called Emma to apologize for the years they had lost. I don't know why Emma left home, but I can tell you she has nothing to do with any of this. We have her sworn statement on record."

Tom's hand throbbed from how tightly he was holding his phone. He stopped just as he and Max were about to enter the forest. Max took full advantage of his retractable leash and began to explore the woods around him. Tom closed his eyes and tried to recall what Julie told him about seeing the woman outside her window.

"You said you tracked Julie to the Cape," Trevor continued, changing the discussion. "Are you positive she's out there? You mentioned her car was still at her apartment, correct?"

"Right. Yes. I even have a key to her place and checked inside."

"Did you ask her friends or family?"

"I checked social media a few times today and didn't find anything. We were supposed to spend the day at the beach. We talked about it earlier this morning. She told me she had errands to run and would let me know when she was ready. I never heard from her again."

"I'm sorry, Tom, but can you tell me why you think Emma is involved in this?"

"Jewels thought she saw her looking in her bedroom window earlier this morning."

"Julie saw Emma Johnson? She was absolutely clear on that?"

"Well, no, not really. She woke up and saw someone looking in her window watching her. The woman was wearing a hat and sunglasses, but Jewels thought the rest of her face looked like Sara."

"Did she confront her?"

"No. By the time she got outside the intruder was gone."

"You two are a truly paranoid pair, Mr. Leblanc."

"Believe it or not, I convinced Julie it was her imagination. That there was no way Sara's sister was in Providence stalking her."

"But now you think that's exactly what happened?"

"Do you have a better explanation?"

"Hold on."

Trevor muted the phone and placed it on the counter in front of him. The store clerk waited patiently for Trevor to pay for his purchase. Trevor slid a twenty dollar bill across the countertop and grabbed his deli sandwich. Once he got his change, he unmuted the call and left the store.

"You mentioned you tracked her out to the Cape," Trevor

said.

"Well, I *was* tracking her. The signal went offline about an hour ago."

"So that means her phone is off."

Tom tugged on Max's leash to signal him to return. Max was deep into investigating a cluster of Swamp azalea shrubs and resisted the pull from his master. Tom locked the retractor and began to reel his dog in like a fishing line. Eventually, Max obeyed and came bounding back to Tom's side. The pair continued their journey west.

"Not necessarily. I'm not exactly tracking her phone."

"Then what are you following?"

Tom pulled the phone from his mouth and let out a sigh, unsure of how Trevor would respond.

"I slipped a GPS tracking device into her purse the other day."

"You what?"

"I did it as a joke. Sort of. I have a tracker on my dog, and after everything that happened out on the Cape I thought, well, it might be a good way to keep tabs on Jewels."

"You're some kind of friend, Tom."

"She wouldn't let me track her by her phone," Tom said defensively. "What other choice did I have?"

Tom was surprised when Trevor started to laugh.

"No, seriously Tom, the extremity of your concern is rather sweet. Only someone like you would think to GPS tag your best friend like your dog."

"You aren't making it sound very sweet."

Trevor let out a hearty laugh as he climbed into his Ford Police Interceptor and slammed the door shut. He proceeded to peel back the wrapping on his Italian sub.

"Look, Tom, I seriously doubt that Emma Johnson drove to Rhode Island and abducted Julie. I do find it very odd, however, that her GPS tracking device somehow flew off to the Cape, and that she has gone missing. I'm going to look into this for you, OK?"

"Thanks, Trevor. I really appreciate it."

Max's retractable leash was fully uncoiled. Tom could no longer see his dog in the deep brush. He tugged on the tether a few times but could not get a response.

"Sure thing. Oh, you never told me where you were. Please tell me you are not out trying to be the hero."

Tom groaned and started trudging through the low lying shrubs. He let the leash retract into the holster as he made his way closer to a thicket of bayberry bushes.

"I'm out walking my dog, and he's being a pain in the ass." Tom came to the end of the leash to find Max wrapped around a thin white spruce tree. "And he's also completely tangled himself up. I need to go. Keep me posted, OK?"

"Enjoy your walk."

Tom ended the call and strolled up to his dog. Max was laying on the ground hastily devouring a thick stick. He glanced up at Tom and spit several pieces of wood fibers onto the ground.

"Look at this mess, Max." Tom snapped the chrome latch on the leash back and freed it from the dog's collar. "Don't you dare move."

Tom shook his head as he studied the path the leash made through the shrubs and trees. He could not figure out how Max managed to get the tether through so many narrow sections of foliage. It took a bit of effort for Tom to feed the leash backward through the maze of twigs and branches. He gave it one final tug, and the band recoiled quickly, ending in a loud snap as the chrome latch slammed against the red plastic handle.

Max jumped to all fours and started to growl. The hackles across his neck were fully erect. He rotated his ears forward and flared his nostrils. The dog's baritone snarl grew louder and deeper.

"Calm down, buddy. It was just the leash."

Ten feet away, Zeus, the Johnson family Doberman, emerged from behind several pine trees. His lips rippled up and down, dripping with saliva. The old dog's approach was that of a hunter. His prey was in sight, but he was taking his time to assess the situation.

Tom cautiously made his way to be by Max's side, letting his hand come to rest between his dog's ears. Tom ran his fingers gently across the top of Max's head, hoping to calm him down. Max began to growl louder and leaned forward. Tom let his fingers slide around the dog's neck along his collar.

"No, Max. I need you to stay. Sit."

Zeus let out a deep, menacing bark. Max returned the call to action. Just as Tom was about to slip his thumb under the bottom of his collar, Max exploded into a full sprint. Tom desperately tried to restrain his dog, grabbing his collar by the GPS tracker. Max paused briefly before yanking himself free. His bark was now a full-blown battle cry. Zeus lunged forward.

"No!" Tom glanced at the GPS tracker and dog tags resting in the palm of his hand before shoving them into his pocket. "Max! Stop!"

Zeus, outweighing Max by 15 pounds, quickly knocked him to the ground. Although Zeus was bigger than Max, Tom's dog was younger, with much more energy and speed. Max rolled onto his back and used his hind legs to kick Zeus away. Both dogs fought desperately to bite the other's neck, their jaws, and teeth gnashing ferociously.

Tom threw himself into the fight and grabbed Max by the collar to pull him away from the other dog. Zeus took this opportunity to jump into the air and knock both Max and Tom to the ground. Tom lost his grip on Max, sending him tumbling against a tree. Tom stumbled and crashed face first onto the ground. Zeus ignored Max and set his sights on Tom. Before Tom could stand up Zeus dove for his leg. Tom recoiled just enough so that the dog ended up biting his foot instead of his calf.

Zeus clamped his jaw into Tom's sneaker. A Doberman's bite force could exceed 240 pounds per square inch. Zeus' upper canines cut through Tom's shoe and deep into the top of his foot. Tom cried out in pain.

Zeus was not letting go. He began to whip his head back and forth as if he was trying to rip Tom's foot from his body. Tom raised his other leg and was about to kick Zeus when Max attacked, diving straight into the Doberman's neck. Zeus immediately released Tom, and he and Max rolled for several feet.

Max took a protective position between Tom and Zeus. The Doberman jumped up and growled. Blood was running down his neck. He lunged at Max, grabbing him by his front leg. Max yelped in pain. Tom looked around in a panic, finally spotting his archery case resting several feet away. He knew there was no way he could reach it in time. Lying next to him was a three-foot-long branch from a pine tree. The wood was old and brittle.

Tom grabbed the branch, stood up, and smashed the stick across Zeus' back. The rotted wood shattered upon impact. But the blow was enough to startle the old dog. Zeus let out a howl and released Max from his jaws.

Tom ran to Max's side. The dog's right leg was bleeding badly from his forearm. Tom's heart was pounding rapidly, but he no longer feared for his life. Instead, he now feared for his dog's survival. He turned and pointed the shattered stick at Zeus. The Doberman lowered his head in trepidation, and slowly limped off into the woods.

"Are you OK, buddy?" Tom asked. Max stood up and began to growl. "No, it's OK. He's gone now."

Max's leg quivered as he took several steps away from his master. His nostrils flared, and his eyes scanned the forest for any sign of the Doberman. All was quiet. Max's ear twitched at the sound of Tom approaching him from behind. He turned back to see Tom stretching out to secure the leash to his collar. Max growled, turned back toward the direction Zeus went and ran off into the forest.

"No!" Tom cried.

Tom dropped to the ground to gather up his backpack and archery case. He scrambled to find them. Once the sack was secure on his shoulders, he turned and looked into the forest. The hulking pine trees blanketed the underlying bushes and shrubs into shadows, their branches creaking from the gusts of wind blowing in from the ocean. Tom looked back and forth, desperately hoping to hear any sign of his dog, but all was quiet.

Tom pulled the GPS tracker from his pocket. It was still attached to the mangled metal ring that also contained Max's dog tags. The top tag was bright red and shaped like a bone, with the dog's name laser etched into it. Tom returned the items to his pocket.

"I can't lose you too."

Tom lowered his head, grabbed his gear, and continued onward into the dense vegetation.

TWENTY ONE

Urban Legends

Julie, now fully awake, struggled to loosen the ropes that bound her wrists behind her back. She was strapped down in her chair, a captor in this small moldy room. The overhead light continued to flicker every several seconds. Julie thrashed her body back and forth but to no avail. She turned her attention to the unconscious person bound to the school chair on the opposite side of the room.

Emma groaned and opened her eyes. She found herself slumped over, staring at her feet. The blow that Bobby delivered created a large lump on her forehead above her right eye. The throbbing pain reverberated in her head, blurring her vision.

"It's about time you woke up," Julie said.

Emma raised her head and looked across the room. It took a few moments for her eyes to focus. The buzzing of the ceiling-mounted lightbulb sent waves of pain through her eyes. Her jaw fell open when she realized who was sitting across from her.

"Julie?" Emma said with surprise and confusion.

"Were you expecting someone else?"

Emma sat upright and attempted to raise her arms. She looked back over her shoulder and started to tug on her wrists.

"It's no use," Julie said. "That old guy that brought you down here seems to be an expert at making knots. I can barely move my hands."

"Old guy?"

"He wouldn't tell me his name."

"Bobby. That had to be Bobby. Shit."

Emma took a few deep breaths to clear her mind and collect her thoughts. She glanced around the room, opening and closing her eyelids in an alternating pattern to test her vision. Her right eye was having trouble focusing. She could only imagine how bad of a bruise came from being slammed into that doorframe. Emma squinted as she focused on the paneled wall behind Julie.

"Where are we?" Emma said.

"I'm assuming it's your basement."

"*My* basement?"

"OK, your mother's basement. Back at my apartment, you made it sound like she was alive. Is she? Is this her house next to the barn? The books are here."

"Books?"

Julie flicked her head up and aimed her eyes to the side of Emma. Emma turned and studied the bookbinding machine up against the wall. Her gaze settled on the stacked paperback books beside it. The unsteady flashes of light made it even more difficult for Emma to read the binding. She leaned closer and squinted.

"Is that the book you were telling me about?" Emma asked. "In your driveway, you said something about a book of urban legends."

"Why are you acting so surprised?" Julie couldn't help but glare at Emma in disgust. "As if this is all new to you."

"Because it is, Julie. I don't recognize any of this. I left home when I was sixteen. My mother and sister basically disowned me. I went to live with my aunt and cousin. You met my cousin Susan in Eastham two months ago. I came home to this house after the fire. I hadn't been in this basement in decades. I don't even recognize half of it." Emma spent a few moments studying the shelves, walls, and two open doorways. "I was looking for you earlier. I should have tried harder."

"Looking for me?"

"Didn't you hear me? Maybe you were still knocked out. I was trying to open the door, but it was locked. I couldn't make a lot of noise. Not with my mother upstairs."

"Your mother?" Julie asked with complete astonishment. "She's alive?"

Emma nodded slowly. Julie shook her head in shock and disbelief as tears once again welled up in her eyes.

"Legends never die," Julie said softly.

"What?"

The frosted bulb in the ceiling finally stopped buzzing and wavering. It settled into a steady hum as it cast a dim yellow light throughout the small, dank room. A faint whistle of wind emanated from one of the doorways.

"None of this is making any sense to me," Julie said as she regained her focus. She took a few moments to look Emma up and down. "Back this up. The last time I saw you, I was in my driveway in Providence. We argued. And then ... then you drugged me, didn't you? Why?"

"I ... I did. I did, indeed." Emma closed her eyes and shook her head in disappointment as she recalled her confrontation with Julie earlier this morning. "You weren't supposed to see me. I wasn't supposed to talk to you. But, there were so many doubts and questions. I decided I should try to get some answers. You were so angry. It was obvious you weren't interested in talking. Once you knocked me down to call the police, I assumed maybe my mother was right and that you were indeed the bad guy."

"The bad guy?"

"I panicked."

"But you still dragged me out here. Why?"

"I've been asking myself that same question all day. All these weeks of reconnecting with her, and now I can't help but wonder if she was just using me the entire time. Did she mean any of it? Was she *ever* being truthful?" Emma kept her focus on the floor, squinting her eyes as she replayed the past two months of conversations between her and her mother. "My mother painted herself as the victim. She claimed you and your friend Tom willfully killed my sister and burned the barn down."

Julie chuckled and rolled her eyes, letting them wander to the cream-colored shelves covered in candles.

"*I'm* the bad guy? That's just rich."

"That's the story she fed me. Look, Julie, you have to understand I thought my mother was dead. I was shocked to find out she was alive. We've spent the past several weeks reconnecting. She desperately wanted to make amends for the decades that we lost."

"So, you just took her word and agreed to bring me back here so she could kill me?"

"No! No, that's not it. She told me the plan was to simply get you to confess to killing Sara and trying to kill her. All she wanted was her name to be cleared so that she could come out of the shadows. The world thought she was dead."

"So did I. Why would you believe her?"

Emma paused, believing the answer to that question was obvious.

"She's my mother."

The two women stared at each other, eyes locked. Julie could not summon the slightest ounce of sympathy for Emma.

"I guess deep down I hoped the reports about my mother and sister were wrong," Emma continued. "Imagine having no contact with your mother for close to thirty years and then reading that she was involved in assault and attempted murder. And not just my mother, but my sister too. The Sara I knew as a child could never do those things. She was my twin. We were so close back then."

"Well, I'm sorry to disappoint you, Emma. But everything you heard was true. Your sister tried to kill me. Twice. Your mother even tried to saw my legs off in the barn."

"A saw? What?"

Emma closed her eyes and tried to recall the conversations with Julie, Jeff, and Susan over the past two days. Her mother had spent the past several weeks trying to fill in the decades they'd missed. She'd also done her best to answer many of the questions that had haunted Emma. Despite her mother's best intentions, Emma couldn't help but feel a sense of unease with her explanations and justifications. Her mind was a jumble of stories and contradictions.

Who do I trust? Emma wondered. *Who can I believe in?*

The throbbing above her eye clouded her memories as she tried to make the different tales from her mother, Julie, Jeff, and Susan all come into alignment. Emma realized it was a futile effort. As much as she wanted to trust her mother, it was the pounding in her head, from Bobby's assault, that swung the pendulum away from the liars and deceivers. Emma opened her eyes and looked over at Julie.

"I'm so sorry, Julie. For everything. To be honest, I had many reservations about my mother's explanations of what happened. When I approached you in your driveway, I was having doubts and second guessing myself. That's why I tried to talk to you. I wanted to hear your side of things."

Julie took a few moments to study Emma's face. The black and blue welt above her eye marred an otherwise perfect complexion. Although Emma was much leaner than her sister, Julie found the physical resemblance to Sara to be uncanny. But her tone and her words were the complete opposite.

"I didn't really give you much of a chance to ask me questions. You look so much like her. It freaked me out."

"I'm sure it was a shock to you." Emma grinned and shook her head. "I mean, you punched me and knocked me to the ground. That wasn't a friendly greeting. You obviously don't have fond memories of Sara."

"Obviously," Julie said as she chuckled softly. "Maybe if I'd stopped to hear you out we wouldn't be here right now."

"Well, we can't change the past."

Julie nodded quietly and attempted to wiggle her feet free from the ropes that bound them to the chair. She knew it was a futile effort, but still did not want to give up hope. Julie looked over at Emma and studied the ropes that held her in place.

"I don't get it. If you brought me back, then why are you

tied up with me?"

"I found the candles. The ones you told me about. The ginger and sesame scented ones. There were several others. I called my mother out on it. Told her that I talked to you. She freaked out when I started questioning her. That's when Bobby attacked me."

"What's his story?"

"Oh trust me, I have endless stories about that monster." Emma lowered her head and closed her eyes. "I'm so stupid. I should have run the minute I knew he was still in the picture. I'm sure he was involved in a lot of what happened to you. The bodies at the beach. The candles. All of it."

"You mentioned there were other candles. What were they?"

"I don't know. Most weren't labeled. Only three were, including the two Asian ones."

"Was the other one called 'Seabreeze'?"

"Yes. That's the condo where you were attacked, wasn't it?"

"Yes. Our friend Marc owned it. He and his girlfriend Chris were the ones that disappeared that night of the blizzard."

"And you think they are in that 'Seabreeze' candle? Just like the Asian couple?"

"I know it sounds crazy, but your mother told me it was true. She admitted to it. I was tied up in the barn, and she was getting ready to kill me. She showed me the 'Seabreeze' candle and told me she always kept one for herself. She told me she wanted my tallow."

"The family recipe," Emma whispered under her breath.

"What?"

"I believe you, Julie. It's all making sense to me now. Again, I'm so sorry."

"Don't apologize for them. It sounds like you had no idea what they were doing."

"But it's my fault that you're here. I was a fool to trust her. I should have known better. But after so many decades I guess I just wanted to believe we could be a family again."

Julie studied Emma's despondent face. She found it so

odd to hear a voice and see a face that looked so much like Sara's but seemed so soft-spoken, caring, and well-meaning.

"Emma, can I ask you how your mother survived that fire?"

"There's an underground bunker on the property. That's where I found the candles. Tunnels connect it to the barn and house. She used that to flee the barn before it collapsed." Emma looked back and forth between the two doorways. "I don't recognize this room, but I know one of the rooms down here has a hidden door that leads to the bunker. If we can get free from these ropes, we might be able to escape through the tunnel that connects to the barn. Well, the rubble that used to be the barn. We can push through it and make a run for it."

"Didn't you say I was behind a locked door? What if it's locked from both sides?"

"We'll just break it down. We need to get out of here."

Emma started twisting her body back and forth, yanking at her arms trying to free her wrists. She tried pulling her legs up and down, but her feet were securely strapped to the sides of the chair.

"These ropes are impossibly tight," Julie said. "I feel like I've been trying to free myself forever. It's impossible. Unless … unless we were to work together."

Emma stopped yanking on her arms and looked Julie up and down. She could see that her feet were bound to the chair, the same as hers. Julie did the same. Slowly, their eyes met, and they each allowed a small smile to emerge.

"Do you trust that I won't try to drug you again?"

"Do you trust that I won't knock you on your ass again?"

Emma burst out laughing, and Julie quickly followed. The laughs were not of joy, but of anxiety and disbelief at the situation they were both in. It was an explosion of nerves, doubt, fear, and hope all jumbled and twisted together.

"So how do we do this?" Emma asked.

"I think if we can sort of hop and spin around we could …."

The creak of a door opening wafted through the room. The two women turned and looked through the doorway that led to the dimly lit room with the same walnut colored paneling as the room they were in. The muted sound of footsteps clapping against stairs quickly followed.

"Shit," Emma said.

After several seconds, a door lock snapped open, and Laura Johnson entered the room. Her arms were folded against her chest. She glanced up at the pale light cast from the overhead bulb. Almost as if on cue, the fixture started to flicker and buzz, creating a strobe effect in the room. She looked around the room, twitching her nostrils at the dank scent of mildew. Laura did not bother to acknowledge Julie and turned her attention to her daughter.

"I see you're awake," Laura said.

"Mother, you have to listen to me."

"No, Emma, I don't." Laura resisted the urge to step further into the room. The buzzing light stopped flashing and settled into a steady hum. "I'm sorry it has to be this way. You should have gone home when I told you to."

"Please let me go, Mother. Please."

"You are such a disappointment." Laura glanced over at Julie. "As for you, young lady, well, it's time to pay."

TWENTY TWO

Separation

1989 Sunday 25-Jun 7:00 p.m.

Susan ran the edge of her fork across her plate, meticulously collecting the last remnants of maple frosting. She then mashed the tines into a smattering of spice cake and scooped it into her mouth. Susan smiled at the intense sweetness of the sugar frosting, paired with the syrupy smell of maple.

"Another piece?" Jennifer asked.

"No, I'm full," Susan said as she snatched a bit more frosting from the cake plate. "For now."

"This cake is so good," Emma said. "You make the best desserts, Aunty Jen."

"It's Betty Crocker, Emma," Jennifer said. She downed the remainder of her chardonnay and pushed her chair away from the dining room table. "But it's Susan's favorite, and she's the birthday girl."

Jennifer left the room to head to the kitchen to refill her wine. Emma and Susan stood up and began to collect the plates and clear the table. Susan stole one last swipe of maple frosting before grabbing the cake pan and heading to the kitchen.

"Oh, I was going to clean up," Jennifer said. She opened a

fresh bottle of white wine and filled her glass. "It's your birthday. You shouldn't have to do this."

"We don't mind," Susan replied.

The kitchen counter was littered with take-out Chinese food bins – Kung Pao chicken, fried rice, chicken lo mein, and sesame beef. The scent of soy and rich oils filled the kitchen. Emma set about closing the tops of each of the boxes. There would be plenty of leftovers for tomorrow. Susan piled the dirty plates into the sink and grabbed the dishwashing soap.

"I'm sorry I couldn't make you a homemade meal tonight," Jennifer said. "The cake took most of my energy."

"It's fine, Mom. I love Chinese anyway. It was perfect."

Jennifer sipped her wine and leaned back against the refrigerator. She smiled as she watched her daughter and niece weave their way around one another to get things cleaned and organized.

"Do you mind if I head to bed?" Jennifer asked. "I know it's early, but I'm reading this fascinating book about religious cults in New England. I can't put it down."

"We've got this," Emma said.

"I want you to know how happy I am that you are with us," Jennifer said as she slid her arm around Emma and pulled her close, kissing her on the back of her head. "Just because Susan is going off to college soon, that doesn't mean you have to leave. You've been here six months Emma, but you can stay another six years if you want. OK? We're family."

Emma wiped her hands on the closest kitchen towel, turned around, and gave her aunt a long embrace.

"Thanks, Aunty."

Jennifer spun Emma around and aimed her back at the counter. She then gave her daughter a light peck on the cheek, grabbed her glass, and headed off to her bedroom.

Emma began moving the take-out boxes into the fridge, while Susan focused on the dishes. The two girls worked together in silence. After several minutes the kitchen counters were spotless, and the dishrack was filled with newly cleaned dishes.

"Have you picked a college yet?" Emma finally asked.

"No, not yet."

"What are you waiting for?"

Susan pointed to the two empty wine bottles on the counter.

"I don't know that I can leave her. Between her drinking and the pills she's taking, she keeps getting worse. Chinese food for my eighteenth birthday? Come on!"

Susan folded her arms and shoved her hands into her armpits. Emma put her arm around her cousin and pulled her close. The two tilted their heads together and sighed in unison.

"I thought it was quite tasty," Emma said with a slight chuckle.

"It was, but, you know what I mean."

"I know, Susan. Look, you don't have to feel like this is all on you. I live here too. Together we can help take care of her. I'm sure she'll get better someday. These things can take time."

"No, Emma, this isn't your problem. Besides, your grades are phenomenal. You can get into any college and get a scholarship. Nursing is your future. Leave this place and never look back."

"Bullshit. You guys took me in when my family abandoned me. I'm not turning away. I'm not running away. Like your mom said, we're family."

Susan walked over to the fridge and pulled out the bottle of chardonnay her mother opened earlier. She then grabbed two wine glasses from the rack hanging beneath the counter.

"What are you doing?" Emma asked, somewhat confused.

Susan smiled and filled the glasses halfway. She handed one of the goblets to Emma.

"She won't notice," Susan said. She raised her glass and smiled at her cousin. "To family. I'm glad you're here."

"Me too. Happy birthday, cousin." Emma took a sip of the wine and winced. "That's kind of gross."

"I know, right? How can she drink this shit?" Susan took another small sip and frowned. "Speaking of family, I invited her. Sara."

"You did? And?"

"She wouldn't talk to me. I called and talked to your mom. She asked Sara to come to the phone, and she refused."

Emma lowered her head, turned, and walked over to the sink. She dumped the rest of her wine down the drain and started to wash the glass.

"Give her time, Emma. I'm sure she will come around."

"No, Susan. For six months now she's snubbed me. And you. And your mom. I don't know what else to say or do. Sara's made her choice."

***

The wood slats on the bench outside the kitchen window creaked as Laura sat beside her daughter. Sara shuffled sideways a bit to make room for her mother. A soft breeze wafted by, carrying the mild scent of salt from the ocean far off in the distance. Laura unfolded a stone-blue and sage-green flannel blanket across her and Sara's legs. The 60 degree temperature, fading light, and windy evening conspired to make for a lovely setting outside the old Victorian home.

Laura slid her hand across the blanket and patted Sara on her thigh. Her daughter sat still, her sight set on the barn door creaking back and forth in the breeze. Laura raised her arm and took Sara by her chin, turning her daughter's face toward her own.

"It's not too late if you want to go see your cousin," Laura said.

"No," Sara replied. She pulled herself away from her mother's grip. "I told you I'm done with Susan."

"Sara, don't let my anger split the bond you have with your sister and cousin. I know Emma upset you, but you shouldn't take it out on Susan."

Sara looked around the yard, searching for the family Doberman. She clapped her hands three times. Apollo emerged from the barn with his head held high and ears erect. His nostrils flared as he took in the bombardment of aromas swirling around the property. He set his gaze on the side porch. Sara clapped her hands, and he darted across the driveway to be by her side.

"It's everyone, Mom." Sara leaned forward and pressed her face against her dog's snout. His cold, wet nose tickled her cheek. "Aunty Jen made such a scene because of what Emma told her. Everything's ruined now. Susan sided with Emma. I'm just done with all of them. It's just you and me now."

Laura ran her fingers across the back of Sara's head, dragging her nails through her daughter's thick brown hair. Sara abruptly stood up and tossed the blanket from her lap onto her mother's legs. She jumped off the porch, with Apollo matching her descent.

"Where are you going?" Laura asked.

"To the pond. I want to sit on the dock and watch the fireflies. They should be coming out soon." Sara reached over and scratched her dog's head. "Come on Apollo, let's go for a walk."

Sara and the Doberman headed off behind the barn, leaving Laura alone on the porch bench. She rolled the blanket off her lap and draped it along the back corner of the seat before heading into the kitchen. The counters were cluttered with various bowls and utensils from this evening's dinner.

Laura ignored the mess in the kitchen and made her way upstairs to the master bedroom. She stepped into the dark room and ran her hand along the top of the cherry wood dresser next to the doorway. Her fingers reached the textured bronze base of the faux Laburnum Tiffany lamp and followed the cord to the in-line power switch. The bulb fired to life, casting a warm glow across the walls and ceiling. The intricate mix of cascading leaves and flowers covering the lampshade shimmered in soft tones of rose, gold, fern, and teal.

The master bedroom was the largest room upstairs, taking up close to the entire back quarter of the second floor. Even in broad daylight, it was a room filled with shadows and little light. The garnet acrylic carpet and the burgundy and metallic gold brocade floor to ceiling drapes made every effort to keep the bedroom as somber and joyless as possible.

The only hint of pleasantry came from an amber glass bowl filled with cinnamon and vanilla scented potpourri.

Laura knelt beside the king-sized cherry four-post bed and thrust her arms deep beneath the frame. After a bit of fumbling, she retrieved the cardboard box Bobby gave to her a few months ago. She sat up on her knees and flipped the top open, revealing the cherry-red candle.

"It's time." Laura closed the top of the box and cradled Bobby's gift close to her chest. "Time to put you away."

Laura stood up and walked over to the exit, extinguishing the soft lighting. She descended the stairs to the main floor, and went back into the kitchen. After grabbing a flashlight from a utility drawer, she made her way down into the basement.

The overhead fluorescent lights hummed loudly, casting a stark, sterile white light across the maze of rooms that snaked throughout the underside of the house. Laura walked through three rooms before coming to a halt, stopping at a workbench in the far corner. She dropped to her knees and flicked on her flashlight. The yellow beam reflected off the small brass latch above the hidden doorway beneath the bench.

Laura yanked the door open, grabbed the box, and crawled through the entryway. After several feet, the tunnel widened, and Laura was finally able to stand up. She aimed her flashlight along the space above the narrow tunnel that led back to the basement. A four-inch metal electrical box was screwed to a wooden post that ran across the top edge of the opening. Laura opened the lid securing the box and flicked the switch hidden inside.

A string of lights hanging from the top of the tunnel sprang to life. The dull gray cement walls were littered with patches of green mold. Laura followed the lights until she reached a fork. The overhead lights continued to brighten both tunnels. She took the path to the left.

The bunker at the tunnel's end was dark and damp. Laura flicked another switch, located just inside the room. A different set of overhead lights came on. A second switch, next to the light switch, triggered a fan embedded in the back corner of the ceiling. The fan roared to life, quickly pulling fresh air from an air vent, and exhausting the stale pungent musk that filled the room.

Laura walked over to the coffee table and took a seat on the sofa. She unpacked the box and pried the metal latch of the mason jar open. The scent of pine brought a smile to her face. Two other candle jars sat on the coffee table, along with a book of matches. It took several strikes before Laura could get one of the damp matches to ignite.

The flat wood wick in the cherry red candle with Fred's remains crackled as the fire from the match brought it to life. Laura held the jar a few inches below her face. The heat from the flame, along with the sweet pine scent, felt comforting in the confines of the cool clammy bunker. She smiled and placed the jar on the coffee table.

This was not the first time Laura had burned the candle. The loss of her husband and Bobby were a difficult combination for Laura to manage these past few months. Many nights, after Sara was fast asleep, Laura would light the candle and hold it in her lap, talking to her late husband. Hours of burning had resulted in concentric layers of discolored wax surrounding the flat wood wick.

"I need to find a way to move forward, Fred. This family has been shattered, and it's not going to heal anytime soon. You must be happy that Bobby's no longer around. I dreamed of a future with that man, and now here I am alone. Wherever you are, I hope you are at peace. I'll do my best to maintain this home, and what's left of our family."

Laura glanced over her shoulder at the shelves filled with a mix of candles and canned foods. The fins in the ceiling fan sang as the edges repeatedly struck a rusted metal brace. The hum of the lights and the crackle of the candle's wood wick joined into the rhythm, softly playing like a three-piece band.

"Family." Laura sighed as she stared at the flickering flame. "I know you would take one look at what's become of our family bonds and simply scream in anger. There's been too much suffering, Fred. Too many accidents. Too much death. I need to focus on Sara. We need to heal."

Laura closed her eyes and bowed her head, taking a

moment to recall happier times with her husband.

"I can't spend my nights talking to you anymore, Fred. Rest in peace."

Laura leaned forward, pursed her lips, and gently blew into the top of the mason jar. The flame crackled and sputtered but refused to die. Laura frowned, took a deeper breath, and fired off a short, sharp blow. The light from the candle expired, leaving only the orange glow of the flat wood wick and a trail of smoke wafting into the air.

Two mason jars sat atop the uppermost shelf that ran along the far side of the room. Laura closed the lid on Fred's candle and carried it over to the ledge. The first jar was filled with a dark chocolate colored wax. The one next to it was sage green. The light from the overhead bulbs caused the edges of the mason jars to glow warmly. Laura placed Fred's candle next to the rosemary one.

"Each candle tells a story, Fred. Will you be the last one? Are there more stories to tell, or is it all finally over?"

Laura kissed her finger and slid it along the side of the red candle. "Goodbye, Fred."

Laura wrapped her hands gently around the green candle. "My dear, precious Rose."

After releasing the glass coffin with the remains of Rose and Mary, Laura glanced at the brown driftwood-scented candle. Her tone of fond remembrance turned to one of disdain. "Eddie."

TWENTY THREE

Hero

The clusters of towering spruce trees and low-lying shrubs thinned out as Tom approached the path that widened at the edge of the Johnson family's backyard. He was close enough to see the house and cars parked alongside the old Victorian. Tom dropped to his knees taking shelter behind an elderberry bush. He looked back at the path he'd just taken, hoping to see his dog, but Max was nowhere to be found.

Tom reached into his backpack and retrieved his binoculars. A quick scan showed three vehicles parked in the driveway – an old Jeep Wrangler, a white Ford F-150, and a green Subaru Outback Sport. Tom remembered the heavily customized Jeep from his last trip here. The sight of so many vehicles concerned him.

"How many people are in there?" Tom lowered his binoculars. "And, of course, still no cops."

Tom surveyed the property a second time, adjusting the zoom and focus ring as he searched the area. The oversized white propane tank was surrounded by the ashen rubble from the remnants of the barn. He paused to focus on the large home's back corner. A steel angled bulkhead door jutted out from the base of the property. The twin doors were open, but from his current position, Tom was unable to see down into the basement.

A branch snapped several feet from behind Tom. Tom spun around, ready to grab his backpack. He immediately exhaled a sigh of relief as Max emerged from the dense brush of the forest.

"Hey there." Tom sat up on his knees and held his arms out. Max limped across the patches of dead leaves and dirt and fell into his master's arms. "You doing OK? Why did you run off like that? You crazy dog."

Tom gently kissed Max on his head. The dog's right leg was covered in blood. The gash on his forearm was still bleeding, although not as bad as earlier.

"We need to clean this, don't we?"

Both Tom and Max flinched at the sound of the steel bulkhead doors slamming closed. Tom pulled Max close to prevent him from running off to follow the noise, taking shelter behind a cluster of large pine trees.

Bobby Mason picked up the oversized brown canvas tool bag he had brought up from the basement and tossed it over his shoulder. The contents rattled and banged together. He shifted the shoulder strap to distribute the weight better. Bobby glanced around the back yard, scanning the forest.

"Zeus!" Bobby called out. He waited several seconds and then whistled loudly. "Zeus!"

Tom's heart pounded as he pulled Max closer to his chest. Max resisted and started to whimper. Tom clamped down on his dog's snout and kissed him on his head.

"No, Max," Tom whispered into his dog's ear. "Sit. Please, please sit. Relax."

Bobby looked at his watch and frowned. He looked back at his truck and then into the forest. Bobby began to stroll further away from the house, toward the group of trees that Tom and Max were hiding behind.

"Zeus! I don't have time for this. We've got to go!"

The twigs and branches snapped beneath the heavy weight of Bobby's construction boots. Each crack of wood grew closer and closer to Tom and his dog. Tom wrapped his arms around Max, clamping down on the dog's snout.

Bobby paused several yards from the pine trees concealing

Tom and Max.

"Zeus!" Bobby let out another whistle.

Tom buried his face against Max's neck. His body was shaking violently as he desperately tried to control his dog and calm his nerves. Tom looked over at his backpack resting nearby and wondered how quickly he could retrieve a weapon. The bark of a dog shattered his thoughts. Max instinctively tried to pull away, but Tom held him close.

Zeus emerged from the far side of the property, near the path that led to the pond.

"There you are," Bobby said. He whistled again.

Zeus slowly made his way across the yard and past the blackened debris that used to be the barn. The dog's progress was slow, and he began limping as he approached the house. Bobby quickly jogged over to meet Zeus.

Tom let out a long sigh of relief as he heard the footsteps running away. He refused to turn to see what was happening and chose to rely solely on his ears to guide him.

"What the hell happened to you?" Bobby said. He bent down and inspected the scrapes and blood covering Zeus. Bobby shook his head and ran his fingers along the dog's snout. "We can get you patched up when we get to Cindy."

Tom waited patiently as he listened to the footfalls fade further away from him and Max. Eventually, the clatter of the failing engine of Bobby's Ford F-150 echoed throughout the forest. Tom kept a tight grip on his dog until the sound of the motor faded away.

Tom pulled his knapsack to his side, keeping Max's head comfortably in his embrace. It took several minutes for Tom to clean the bite wounds on Max's leg. The dog remained a trouper throughout the entire experience, never once recoiling or howling in pain. Tom used a small pair of scissors to cut the last piece of tape he would need to finish securing the gauze bandage. He kissed Max between his eyes, affixed the tape, and coached his dog to sit up.

Max jumped up to all four legs, his right front leg wobbling under his weight. He lowered his head and ran his snout across the bandages, studying the scent of the woven dressing and adhesives.

"Do *not* bite that off. We're going to have to get you to the doc when we get home." Tom peered around the pine trees sheltering he and Max, to confirm there was no activity happening around the house. "OK, Max, I need you to stay here, OK?"

Tom took Max's leash and looped it around a nearby evergreen tree. He then attached it to the dog's collar. Max knew the drill and dropped to his stomach, resting his head between his front paws.

Tom opened his archery case and retrieved the broadhead tips from their box. He set about securing three of the shafts with the deadly arrows. Tom glanced over at Max, who's piercing brown eyes studied his every move.

"What? Don't give me that look. Trevor was a no-show. I know what I'm doing."

Tom slid his hand into his backpack and searched for another hunting item his trainer Rick had recommended he buy. He let out a soft exhale as his fingers grasped the rubberized handle of the dagger resting in his bag. Tom gently stroked the leather sheath to be sure the knife was safely secured. He removed the weapon from his pack and withdrew the blade from its casing.

The compact weapon was less than seven inches long with a three-inch stainless steel blade. Tom gradually withdrew the knife from its sheath, exposing the bright mirror polished edge. The dagger was only a few weeks old, and its only use was when Tom tested it using a stick he found in his front yard. He was surprised at how little pressure was needed to sink the blade deep into the solid wood. Despite Tom's dedication to archery, he could never forget the weapon used to attack Julie, as well as take the life of his father. Tom shoved the dagger back into its sheath and glanced over at Max.

"This time I'm better prepared." Tom slid the small knife into his front pocket. "Stay here, and stay quiet, OK? Stay."

The most direct path to the bulkhead door was also the most exposed. Tom decided it would be best to backtrack several yards and approach the back of the house from the other side of the property. The vegetation in that area was much more dense, giving him better protection from anyone that might be looking out through a window. He did one final scan of the house with his binoculars. All was quiet.

Max sat up on his hind legs and whimpered as Tom jogged off into the woods. It took Tom several minutes to weave his way through the bushes, shrubs, and trees that blocked his way to the other side of the property. Eventually, Tom found himself propped behind a mature pine tree less than five yards from the steel bulkhead. The tree was surrounded by a group of gray dogwood shrubs, giving him ample privacy.

Tom used his binoculars to survey the back of the house. He paused at each window, looking for any sign of movement or activity from any of the rooms. Despite two vehicles being parked outside, the place seemed abandoned. He couldn't hear any sounds coming from the house. Tom looked back toward the propane tank and then at his set of arrows.

"I wonder if it still has gas in it," Tom said softly. "It might make for a distraction to get everyone out of the house." Tom used his binoculars to study the lines and valves connecting to the tank. He adjusted the focus ring and inspected the tank's rusted fittings. "Or I might cause a massive explosion and accidentally destroy the house. And us."

Tom rolled away and took shelter behind the towering pine tree, leaning his back against the rough penny colored bark. He closed his eyes and slid his hand into his pocket, letting his fingers stroke the handle of the hunting dagger resting inside.

Tom felt his heart begin to race as he sought the courage to approach the house. He recalled his last visit to this property several weeks ago, and the screams of his best friend crying out from the barn. He thought back to witnessing his dad's murder, and the devastating news of the discovery of the butchered bodies of Marc and Chris.

With a heavy exhale, Tom stood up and sprinted across the yard. He fell to the ground next to the bulkhead and waited several seconds for his nerves to settle. Tom was relieved to hear nothing but the chatter of birds and other creatures roaming the forest. The house remained silent.

Each steel bulkhead door weighed roughly 25 pounds. The brick-red paint covering them was faded and peeling along the hinges. The right-side door overlapped the other one. Tom hunched his body over the doors, placed his left leg on the underlying door, and used both hands to gently pull the right door upward. The steel hinges squealed and groaned as the door rotated. Tom took his time, trying his hardest to prevent the metal from screeching loudly. The fifteen seconds it took to quietly open the door and lower it to the ground felt like fifteen minutes to Tom. He did not bother opening the other half of the bulkhead and descended the cracked cement steps.

The wooden door at the bottom of the stairs was warped and covered in the same brick colored paint as the bulkhead. This entrance to the basement was not original to the house. Fred Johnson's father had constructed it back in the 1950s. It had been a less than professional installation job, and the poor condition of the door, frame, and cement structure reflected it.

Tom ran his fingers across the weathered brass handle, unsure if the door would be locked. A gentle twist of the wrist revealed it wasn't. Tom felt a mix of relief and terror as he pushed the door open. Thankfully, the hinges stayed quiet. Tom decided to leave the door open in case he needed to make a hasty exit, as well as cast some light into the basement.

Once inside, it took Tom's eyes a few moments to adjust to the darkness. He found himself in a large room with no lights or windows. He decided turning on the flashlight on his phone would be a bad idea. Tom slid his right leg out in an arc and waved his arms in front of him, testing to see if there was anything in his path. There was a doorway on the opposite side of the room. A faint light flickered on and off from beyond the opening.

Tom felt his knees quiver as he made his way across the room. He used his bow like a sword, waving it back and forth as he cautiously approached the door. Once Tom got to the middle of the room he heard a creak coming from upstairs. He stopped and waited, wondering if it was just the wind or his imagination. The sound of shifting floorboards rang out again. They were still coming from upstairs but from another part of the house. The squeaks and groans were moving away from him. Tom walked to the doorway and stopped.

Tom's heart was racing at a furious pace. His temples throbbed as adrenaline gushed throughout his body. His left hand kept a fierce grip on his bow. Tom slid his free hand into his pocket and grabbed his dagger. The rubberized handle brought him little security. He closed his eyes and focused on the direction the overhead creaks and groans were coming from.

The light in the doorway continued to waver. Tom surmised the shimmering light must be coming from a weak or faulty bulb. He pressed his jaw against the doorframe and angled his ear into the room ahead of him. The overhead footsteps were gone, replaced with the faint sound of mumbling voices. He couldn't make out what they were saying, but he knew they were coming from somewhere far beyond the other room.

The sound of shattering wood pierced the silence of the dark cellar. Tom jumped at the sheer volume of the discord. After several seconds Tom heard the murmur of voices making their way closer toward the doorway.

Tom took a few steps back and withdrew his knife. His left arm was shaking as he desperately tried to keep hold of his bow and the three arrows tucked between the bow's upper limb and the palm of his hand. His dread and fear grew deeper as a new light appeared against the paneled wall inside the doorway. A sweeping beam, most likely from a flashlight, ran along the wall and down to the floor, disappearing and reappearing.

Tom raised his knife to his face and bit down on the welted leather sheath covering the blade. He carefully pulled the handle back, leaving the cover jammed into his mouth. A bright white light abruptly hit the edge of the stainless steel blade, reflecting directly into Tom's eyes. Staring into the blinding light, Tom realized the beam was coming from behind him. Tom's jaw fell open, causing the sheath to fall to the ground.

"Don't move." The woman's voice from several feet back was firm and forceful.

Tom stood frozen in terror. His hand holding the dagger quivered as he kept a tight grip on the handle. The sweeping beam of light on the other side of the doorway came into the room. A blinding shaft of white LED beams shot straight into his face. Tom was now blinded by the light reflecting off the dagger, and the one ahead of him.

"Hold up." The voice in front of Tom was a deep baritone. "Tom, I need you to drop the dagger. Right now."

It took a few moments for the voice to register with Tom.

"Officer Stevens?" Tom said. "Trevor?"

Trevor lowered his flashlight and stepped forward. He shook his head in disappointment as he pried the dagger away from Tom. A pair of hands from behind Tom took his bow and arrows. Tom turned around to see two Wellfleet police officers standing behind him. Tom lowered his head and exhaled, relieved his heartbeat was slowly beginning to return to normal.

"Do you want to tell me what the hell you are doing here?" Trevor asked. "I was talking to you, like, half an hour ago. Wait. You were already here when we chatted, weren't you?"

"Sort of," Tom replied. "I was out by the beach."

Trevor took a moment to inspect the knife he removed from Tom. He aimed his flashlight at the two cops standing behind Tom. Officer Edmunds waved the bow and arrows back and forth and rolled her eyes.

"This here is Tom Leblanc," Trevor said to the Wellfleet officers. "He's the one that called this in." He aimed his light back at Tom. "What on earth are you doing with these weapons? Did you think you could just come in here and save the day?"

Tom lowered his head and slid his hands into his pockets. He and Julie never told Trevor the truth about the barn fire. Their explanation to the police was that the fire had started on its own. Tom wasn't about to admit that he'd been the one, arrows in flight, destroying the barn and saving his best friend.

"I had to try," Tom finally replied.

"You're lucky you didn't get your head blown off."

"All I wanted to do was save Jewels."

"The house is empty, Tom. We searched all the rooms upstairs, as well as this basement. You're standing in the last room for us to inspect."

"She has to be here. Are you sure you checked everywhere?"

"There was one locked room, Tom. Trust me, it's clear."

The light from the three flashlights the cops were holding cast an eerie white glow throughout the space. Tom looked around at the various shelves and tables covered in tools, boxes, and bins. He shook his head and looked at Trevor.

"The GPS signal died here," Tom said. "So, where's Jewels?"

TWENTY FOUR

Time to Pay

The cauldron that once sat inside the Johnson family barn was a tight fit in Bobby's narrow shed. Ten years ago, Bobby expanded the size of his shed by creating an addition along the back section of the existing structure. The end result was an L-shaped building with triple the storage capacity of the original space. A propane tank fed a makeshift rack and burner assembly beneath the heavy iron pot. The solution boiling away inside the cauldron was filled with the bones, meat, organs, and fat of the last of Bobby's goats.

Bobby used a pair of cooking tongs to adjust the angle of the burners beneath the pot. The crude assembly was made from an old dismantled outdoor grill. He twisted the valve on the propane tank to lower the heat, allowing the pot to settle into a gentle simmer.

Bobby turned his attention to the brown canvas bag resting on the floor next to the cauldron. He reached inside, and one by one removed the contents, spreading each item out onto a small table. The collection of tools from Laura's bunker included a handful of daggers, as well as the charred machete and jagged tooth saw. Bobby ran his thumb across the nickel and turquoise inlaid handle on one of the knives.

"Fred certainly did quality work," Bobby bemused. He

looked over at Zeus. The dog was tied up in the corner and sleeping. "Don't you worry, boy. We'll get you properly cleaned up soon enough."

The phone in Bobby's pocket buzzed briefly, indicating there was a new text message. It was from his fishing buddy, Nick Lawson.

Cindy is ready and waiting for you.

Bobby smiled in approval and replied with a thumbs-up emoticon. He opened his photo app and scrolled through his most recent pictures taken during a fishing trip he spent with Nick last week. The sun and wind that day were close to perfect, as was their luck in reeling in a variety of striped bass, scup, and winter flounder. Bobby let his eyes wander across the sleek lines of Nick's boat. Scrawled along the back of the old Boston Whaler 28 Conquest was the vessel's name – Cindy.

***

"It's not too late to end this," Emma said. Her voice and tone were calm as she tried to reason with her mother. Emma approached the situation as if she were at work at the hospital trying to convince a difficult patient to do what's best. "You can still turn yourself over to Jeff. Just put the blame on Bobby."

"Blame Bobby?" Laura replied. She shook her head and walked over to the shelves behind Julie. "No, Emma, if anyone is to blame it's you. I don't know what I'm going to do with you now. Once again, you've disappointed me."

Laura rifled through several tattered cotton rags clumped together in a pile next to a rusted can of ceiling paint. The bottom rag was from an old oversized T-shirt that had been sliced into four sections. She shook it several times, whipping dust into the air.

"Mother, please. You need to ...."

Laura shoved the rag into Emma's mouth and tied the ends behind her daughter's head. Emma coughed from inhaling the dust particles littered within the fibers of the old shirt. She tried to scream, but her cries were now completely muffled.

Julie looked on in repulsion as the old woman made her way back toward her. Laura walked behind Julie and parted her hair, exposing Julie's neck. She lowered her head until her nose rested on Julie's nape. Laura inhaled and smiled.

"Cocoa butter it is," Laura whispered into Julie's ear. She looked over at Emma, bound and struggling to free herself. "You wanted to learn the family recipe, Emma. You're going to have a front row seat."

The worn hinges on Bobby's exterior basement door screeched as the door swung open. The blackened room off to the side was suddenly aglow with sunlight pouring in from outside. Bobby strolled into the room carrying the scorched twelve-inch jagged tooth saw. Julie screamed in horror at the sight of the familiar tool. Laura quickly wrapped a rag around Julie's face, gagging her mouth shut.

"The shed's ready," Bobby said.

"Take her first," Laura said as she pointed at her daughter.

Bobby walked over to Emma and grabbed the back of her chair. Emma screamed through her rag as Bobby tipped her chair back and dragged her into the dark room that connected to the basement door.

"I haven't forgotten about your friend Tom," Laura said as she turned to glare at Julie. "Months from now, when he's fraught with misery wondering what happened to you, he will get a package in the mail with a cocoa-butter-scented candle inside. Maybe I will even send him my Seabreeze one. Then he will have all his little friends to cherish. A lifetime of torment awaits him."

***

Tears ran down Emma's face as she stared at the cauldron bubbling away in the middle of the shed. The scent of stew wafting through the air brought her no comfort. All she could think about was how much time and effort she had spent the past several weeks trying to rebuild the family bonds of trust with her mother. Her heart ached with regret over the choices that led her to this place and time. She tried to call out to her mother, but the gag only permitted a muffled cry to escape her.

Several copies of "Urban Legends of Cape Cod," along with the mason jar candles from Laura's bunker, sat atop the workbench near the cauldron. Laura smiled as she admired the row of colorful candles. She intended to take them with her when she and Bobby escaped on the boat. She slid her thumb into her mouth, coating it with saliva and used her spit to polish the glass lid of the cherry red candle. Laura pried open the metal closure, releasing the rubber seal from the top of Fred's glass urn. She inhaled the sweet pine scent and brought the candle over to Emma.

"Say hello to your father," Laura said. She held the rim of the jar beneath Emma's nose. Emma looked at the candle and then back to her mother. "Yes, Emma, he's in there. Just like Rose and Mary. Well, not exactly like them. It's a slightly different recipe."

The front door of the shed swung open, slamming against the rack of shelves behind it, knocking a pair of gardening shears to the ground. Julie wailed helplessly, crying through the gag that cut across her mouth as Bobby dragged her chair into the room. She shook her body violently, but the ropes that bound her were simply too tight. She stared up at the corrugated metal ceiling and cried, confused as to where she was being taken. Julie's head fell forward as Bobby released her chair, setting it upright aimed at the cauldron.

Julie's eyes widened at the sight of the iron pot that had burned and melted Sara. Exhausted from struggling, she screamed a muddled cry of "no" through the T-shirt crammed in her mouth. She looked across to Emma. Her fellow captive's face was covered in tears. The two women locked panic-filled eyes with one another, their bodies shaking as they fought to break free from their bonds.

Zeus momentarily awoke from his slumber to see what the commotion was all about, but quickly rolled over and fell back to sleep.

Laura opened a book of matches and used one to light

Fred's candle. She carefully put the mason jar onto the seat of a chair next to the propane tank.

"You and your father can learn the recipe together," Laura said to Emma. She turned and faced Julie. "The death of a loved one can haunt you. It can change you forever. That's a lesson your friend Tom will learn soon enough."

Laura looked over at Bobby and smiled. He nodded in approval. Bobby desperately wanted this day to end. He understood how important Julie's death meant to Laura and was happy to know that Emma would also be out of their lives. But the hours were passing quickly, and he knew he and Laura needed to leave soon.

"What are we going to do with her?" Bobby pointed to Emma. "She's seen too much. She knows too much."

"Emma will also have to pay." Laura ran her fingers across the lump on Emma's head. "You can knock her out again. She'll wake up to find Julie's dead. She can tell the police whatever she wants, but by then it won't matter. We will be far away."

Bobby glared at Emma and shook his head in disgust.

"That's not good enough, Angel. They'll still come looking for us. The only people that know you're alive are in this room. No loose ends, remember?"

"I remember." Laura nervously twirled the silver chain around her neck, darting her eyes back and forth from Bobby to Emma. Her mind raced as she tried to resolve the situation. But every option came to the same conclusion. Laura lowered her head and closed her eyes. "There must be another way."

Emma could not believe what she was hearing. She repeatedly cried, calling out for her mother over and over again. The gag muted her words, making them unintelligible.

"We don't have to kill her, Laura." Bobby sighed as he realized Laura would never allow him to do what was necessary. "I can hit her hard enough so that she doesn't remember anything. She'll live. Enough."

Laura opened her eyes and turned her attention to the iron pop bubbling away. She exhaled a sigh of relief and convinced herself that Bobby was right. Laura walked over to the two tables next to the cauldron. One table contained her candles, the other the bladed weapons. She smiled at the sight of the tools her husband had crafted decades ago.

"Thanks for running back to the house to get these." Laura glanced over at Zeus, resting in the corner. "And my dog."

Laura ran her hands across the daggers and knives spread out across the table next to the candles. She stopped to let her fingers caress the charred handle of the machete. The nickel and turquoise inlay of the weapon was scorched and cracked.

"Where is it?" Laura asked. She scanned the collection of knives one more time before turning to Bobby. "The saw?"

"I gave it to you."

"I must have left it in the basement. Can you get it for me?"

Bobby exited through the front door of the shed, slamming it behind him. Laura grabbed a ladle from the workbench and set about stirring the simmering contents of the iron pot. Her stomach rumbled at the aroma of stewed meat. Emma and Julie continued to struggle to free themselves, but their movements were now much less strenuous than when they were in the basement.

Laura placed the spoon back on the table and picked up one of the books piled next to the candles. She flipped through the first few pages, reading the table of contents that listed the different myths and mysteries. She couldn't help but grin when her eyes reached her own story set in Wellfleet. Laura held the copy of "Urban Legends of Cape Cod" in front of Julie's face.

"Remember, dear, legends never die." The hinges on the door to the shed creaked as it slowly swung open. She kept her ice-blue eyes peering deep into Julie's. "It's about time. This girl needs to pay."

Laura turned around to get the saw from Bobby. Her smile faded as she dropped the book to the floor. Truro Chief of Police Robert Grant was standing in the doorway with one hand resting on his holster.

"Laura Johnson, I presume?" Robert said. He glanced at the two women bound and gagged in their chairs and withdrew his pistol. "And you two must be Emma and Julie. Don't worry, you're safe now."

Officer Grant aimed his gun at Laura and motioned her away from Julie. Laura stepped backward until she was against the workbench with her candles. She slid her hands into her pockets.

"Hands where I can see them," Robert said forcefully. Laura obliged and raise her arms in the air. Robert walked over to Emma and untied her gag. "Are you OK?"

Emma spit out the rest of the rag from her mouth and gasped for air. She nodded and lowered her head as tears exploded from her eyes. Robert kept one hand on his gun as he began to loosen the ropes binding Emma's hands behind her back. Across the room, Julie began to stammer and scream and shake her body.

"I'll get to you next," Robert said.

Emma kept her head between her knees. Her lungs burned as she continued to cough. The soot and dust from the rag covered the inside of her mouth and her upper throat. She spat twice to clear her airways. Emma began to sit up when Officer Grant collapsed on top of her, falling into her lap. She looked up to see Bobby standing behind him, holding a gun with blood dripping from the blunt end of the handle.

Robert rolled off Emma's lap, dropping his pistol as he fell to the ground beside her. He groaned as he rubbed his hand along the gash running across the back of his head. Bobby knelt down next to Emma and drove his knee deep into Robert's back, pinning him to the ground. Bobby's right hand quivered as he raised his gun above his head. He took aim at the fallen police officer and delivered another punishing blow to his skull. Robert immediately succumbed to unconsciousness. Bobby wiped the blood from his hands and slid his gun behind his back, tucking it within his waistband. He then placed the twelve inch saw along the back of Robert's neck.

"Wait, Bobby." Laura marched across the room and grabbed Emma by her chin. "How did he know we were here?"

"I have no idea," Emma replied. "I don't even know where we are."

Bobby stood up and dusted his knees off. He checked his hands, noting that his right one was splattered with blood from Officer Grant. He wiped it across Emma's shirt.

"Laura, we need to go. Now. And we need to kill this cop. He's seen you."

"This is getting out of control, Bobby." Laura jammed the rag back into Emma's mouth. "Who else knows we're here?"

"It doesn't matter anymore. Let's just burn everything to the ground, including the bodies." Bobby looked down at Emma. "All of them."

Laura slowly lowered her gaze and looked into her daughter's eyes. Emma's cheeks were bright red and stained with tears. She stared back at her mother, hoping, searching, and praying for salvation. Laura looked back up at Bobby.

"Then let's finish this." Laura snatched the saw from Bobby's hand and walked over to Julie. She smiled and placed the jagged blade on Julie's thighs. Laura leaned forward until her nose was less than an inch from Julie's. "I'm going to watch those pretty hazel eyes of yours as the life drains from your body. You killed my Sara. Time to pay."

Julie cried out as loudly as she could. Her life flashed before her as she fought to rip her hands free from the heavy ropes that strapped her to the chair. Julie screamed louder as the jagged teeth of the saw bit into her legs.

"That's far enough." The voice took everyone by surprise. Officer Jeff Jones, having entered from the far end of the shed, was standing with his gun drawn and aimed directly at Laura. "Drop the weapon. I won't ask twice."

Laura released the saw, allowing it to tumble to the floor. The tool came to rest at Julie's feet, some of the teeth dripping with blood. Jeff waved his gun, motioning Laura to step away from Julie. Laura lowered her head and went and stood beside Bobby.

Tears ran down Emma's face as she tried to call out Jeff's name through the gag cutting across her mouth.

"Thanks for telling me their plan, Aunty."

Officer Jones took three cautious steps forward and

quickly surveyed the situation. His anger shot up threefold at the sight of his boss lying unconscious on the ground, blood running from his head. Jeff tightened the grip on his gun as he slowly approached the cauldron.

"Emma," Laura said angrily. "I knew I couldn't trust you!"

Jeff paused beside the cast iron pot. He took a moment to check on Julie. Her left thigh was cut and bleeding, but it did not appear to be that severe. Julie's face was flush, her wide eyes filled with fear and confusion. Jeff gave her a reassuring nod.

Emma quickly set about yanking her wrists through the ropes that were binding her. Officer Grant had loosened them just enough that she could finally start to free herself.

Laura leaned back against Bobby and slid her hand to take hold of his. Bobby pulled her close and stepped behind her.

"I need your hands up," Jeff said. "Both of you. Now."

Laura let go of Bobby and raised her arms above her head. Bobby slid his left arm behind his back and slowly withdrew his pistol. He raised his other arm until his hand was level with Laura's left shoulder. With one swift move, he shoved Laura to the side, aimed his gun and fired at Jeff. Laura crashed to the ground in front of Julie, her head slamming into the jagged teeth of the saw.

Jeff winced as the bullet penetrated his left shoulder. It was a clean shot, running directly between his scapula and clavicle bones. He immediately fired back at Bobby, the round dealing a deadly blow. Bobby clutched his chest and fell to his knees, dropping his gun. He looked at his blood-soaked hands and then over to Laura.

"Angel," Bobby said with bewilderment. His eyes closed and he collapsed face first onto the floor in front of the cauldron.

"Bobby!" Laura cried as she crawled to be by his side.

Jeff maneuvered around the cauldron and quickly kicked Bobby's gun toward the side of the shed, beneath the workbench covered with the mason jar candles and books. He turned and knelt down next to Officer Grant and checked for a pulse. He let out a sigh of relief once he realized his boss was still alive.

Zeus was now wide awake, having been woken by the gunfire. The dog immediately began to bark and tug viscously on his leash. The short chain kept him well isolated in the corner of the shed. His baritone growls and snapping echoed throughout the room.

Emma finished undoing the ropes binding her legs to the chair and ripped the rag from her mouth. She collapsed to the ground and threw her arms around Jeff.

"Thank you, Jeff," Emma cried. Jeff gave her a quick hug and released her. "I thought we were dead. Will he be OK?"

"You tell me. You're the nurse." Jeff glanced back at the barking dog. "So, that must be Zeus."

Julie groaned and yelled through her gag. She jumped up and down causing her chair to rattle. Emma looked up over Jeff's shoulder and screamed as Laura plunged a dagger into the police officer's right trapezius muscle high up on his back.

Jeff cried out in pain and dropped to his hands and knees, releasing his gun as he struggled to keep from falling all the way to the ground. Both of his shoulders throbbed from their wounds. He reached back to try and extract the blade but ending up collapsing onto his right elbow.

Emma stared in disbelief at the handle sticking out of Jeff's back. The nickel and turquoise inlay glistened in the shed's dim lighting She looked at her mother in complete horror. Emma's eyes wandered over to the cherry red candle crackling atop the chair beside the propane tank, expelling the sweet scent of pine.

"You've been such a disappointment, Emma," Laura said.

Laura turned and dropped to her hands and knees and crawled under the workbench. She found Bobby's gun and picked it up. Laura grabbed the edge of the table and pulled herself upright. The legs of the beaten workbench wobbled as she struggled to hold it for support. Blood dripped down her face from the gash the saw left on her cheek. Laura took one last look at the row of candles spread out in front of her.

"I'm sorry it has to end this way," Laura said with a regretful tone. She turned to face her daughter.

"So am I," Emma replied. She raised Jeff's pistol, closed

her eyes, and pulled the trigger. The explosive crack of the gun immediately silenced Zeus, plunging the shed into silence.

The bullet hit Laura's mid-section, ripping a hole in her stomach and severing her spine. She fell backward, crashing against the workbench. The front left leg of the table snapped, sending the collection of mason jars tumbling to the ground. One by one they slid off the pine tabletop and crashed into one another, the glass caskets shattering and cracking with each impact. Two of the urban legend books spun to the ground, coming to rest atop the broken candles.

Laura cried out and gasped for air. She looked down at the blood stains covering her dress and couldn't understand why she couldn't feel the pain from the bullet wound. She slowly realized that there was no feeling at all below the entry point of the bullet. Laura fell forward onto her hands and retrieved the rosemary candle from the pile of splintered memories sprawled out before her. With all her will, she used her elbows to pull her body across the dirt covered floor. She slid the candle in front of Bobby and took his lifeless hand into hers, cradling the remains of their precious Rose by their side. Laura pressed her head gently against Bobby's face, closed her eyes, and exhaled.

Emma pushed her way past Jeff and sat beside Bobby and her mother, running her fingers across her mother's face. She checked her pulse, and then Bobby's, confirming they were no longer alive. Emma crawled over to the chair beside the propane tank and pulled the cherry red candle into her lap. She gently inhaled the sweet pine scent, closed her eyes, and extinguished the flame.

***

Officer Jeff Jones groaned as he struggled to exit the shed. Julie and Emma did their best to keep him propped up over their shoulders with his arms draped around their necks. The angle of his arms brought intense pain to his wounds. Chief of Police Robert Grant remained unconscious but breathing inside the shed, not far from the bodies of Bobby and Laura.

The late afternoon weather greeted them as they stepped outside. All three tilted their heads back to take in the fresh air and warm rays of the sun. The stench and darkness of the shed were finally gone. Julie and Emma worked with Jeff until the three were in lockstep as they made their way to Bobby's front yard. Julie's blood-soaked left leg quivered under the weight of the police officer.

"How are you doing?" Emma asked Jeff.

"Considering I have two holes in me? Not too shabby, Aunty Em."

"Aunty?" Julie asked.

"It's a long story. This old gal and I go way back."

"I swear to God, Jeff, I will drop you right here," Emma said.

Jeff started to laugh but instantly regretted it as waves of pain shot through his body. He paused to steady himself.

"See what you get?" Emma added.

Once at the front of the house, Julie and Emma guided Jeff to the narrow set of wooden stairs across the front door. They gently lowered him so he could lean back against the house. Jeff's eyes were heavy, and he was getting light headed from the loss of blood.

"Em," Jeff said, "I have to ask you something. Were you caring for your mother this entire time? Is that why you've been so distant?"

Emma nodded and lowered her head.

"It's a long story, Jeff. I'll explain it when you are feeling better."

"That day I came to see you at your house in Chatham. You knew she was alive, didn't you?"

"I did."

"So, all that talk about inheritance and the dog was for nothing?"

"No, Jeff. Those things were bothering me. They just weren't as pressing as my mom secretly being alive."

"Oh, right." Jeff started to chuckle but winced from the pain. He leaned back against the house and closed his eyes. "Can I still have the dog? I think I'd like having a dog."

"Sure thing, Jeff." Emma turned to face Julie. "How's the

leg? You should let me check that for you."

"I'm OK," Julie replied. "I think it looks worse than it is. I don't know how to thank you. Both of you."

"You have no reason to thank me, Julie," Emma replied. "I'm the one that got you into this mess. I'm at fault."

"No. This started long before you. It started in the candle store with your sister last December. Since then, your mother's been obsessed with getting her revenge. If it hadn't been this weekend with you involved, it would've been some other time." Julie looked at Officer Jones' blood-stained uniform and then down at her injured leg. "This nightmare is finally over."

"Jeff, how the hell did you find us?" Emma asked. "I told you to go to the house in Wellfleet. That was their plan."

"They must have lied to you, Em. Or maybe they changed their mind at some point. After I listened to your voicemail, I checked the timestamp and realized almost two hours had passed. I went into a panic, worried that it might be too late. I asked Robert what to do, and he told me to have the Wellfleet police check it out. They were closer. He thought we should investigate Mr. Mason's place, due to his involvement. Robert has had multiple run-ins with Bobby Mason in the past. Besides, the police station isn't too far from here. The funny thing is that when I called Wellfleet to have them go to your mom's house, they told me they already had it covered."

"That's weird," Emma said.

"I wonder why," Julie added.

The rumble of rolling tires could be heard coming down Bobby's crushed stone driveway. Julie turned around just as the Provincetown Police Interceptor came into view. Emma sat next to Jeff and pulled two rags from her back pocket. She then began to apply pressure to his two wounds. He winced but exhaled a sigh of relief knowing he was in the hands of a skilled nurse.

The Ford SUV came to a stop next to Jeff's Dodge Charger Pursuit sedan. Julie took a few steps forward at the sight of the familiar vehicle. The driver's door swung open, and Officer Trevor Stevens emerged and came around to the passenger's side.

"Trevor!" Julie cried out as she tossed her hands to her face to catch the tears flowing from her eyes. "It's so good to see you. I can't believe you are here."

"It's good to see you too, Julie," Trevor said. "But don't thank me."

Trevor opened the back door of the Explorer and swung his arm as if he were presenting a pop star to a group of paparazzi. Tom stepped out, smiling and waving. He held his hand up telling Julie to hold on. Tom turned and reached into the backseat. Julie looked on with confusion as Tom lowered Max to the ground.

"Max, Max, Max!" Julie yelled.

Max turned and looked around, somewhat baffled. Once he spotted Julie, he attempted to sprint. The dog quickly stumbled and slowed to a halt. Julie noticed his bandaged leg and ran ahead to meet him, clutching her blood-soaked thigh. Max limped several feet before stopping and waiting, his tail swirling with excitement.

"Oh my God, what happened to you?" Julie flung her arms around Max's neck. He yanked his head back and began to nibble on her nose. "Aunty Jewels is very happy to see you."

"Hey Jewels," Tom said. He knelt down on the ground next to Julie and Max.

"What the hell are you doing here?"

"We're supposed to be at the beach."

Julie let out a slight chuckle before bursting into tears. She fell against Tom's shoulder and began to shudder uncontrollably. Tom held her tight and rocked her back and forth. He would hold her for several minutes until her trembling finally subsided.

TWENTY FIVE

Memorial

The strong rays from the sun belied the cool 65-degree temperature today. In typical New England fashion, the air was over twenty degrees cooler than it was just three days ago. The maple trees scattered along West Shore Road created patches of shade, allowing the cool temperatures to buffet the occupants inside Tom's Jeep. Julie adjusted the HVAC to blow warmer air from the vents in front of her. Max was sitting in the backseat, undaunted by the brisk wind cutting through the cabin. Tom checked his mirror to make sure Robin's car was still following him.

"Do you think my mom will freak out that I'm bringing three extra people, including a small child?" Tom said to Julie. "I didn't bother to tell her."

"Yes and no. Behind their backs, she will worry she doesn't have enough food. But to their face, she will turn on the sparkle and try to impress them."

"Probably."

"I give her no more than ten minutes before she makes some racially inappropriate comment."

"Jewels, my mom isn't a racist."

"I didn't say that. But you have to admit she can, at times, make some rather, well, unsuitable observations."

"I think she'll be fine."

"Five bucks?" Julie extended her arm toward Tom and opened her palm. "If she says something offensive in the first ten minutes you owe me five dollars."

"Deal." Tom shook her hand and let out a chuckle. "And I'll double it to ten if she fucks it up in less than five minutes."

Max whimpered from the backseat and laid down.

"Whoops. F-bomb. Sorry, buddy." Tom glanced back at Max. The dog was resting his head on his freshly bandaged leg. Tom then looked over at Julie's hands lying in her lap. Her wrists were covered in a variety of bracelets, ranging from half-inch multi-colored plastic rings to gold and silver chains. "How are your wounds today, Jewels?"

"Mental or physical?"

Tom pointed to the overabundance of jewelry adorning her wrists. Julie smiled and wiggled her arms back and forth, causing the mix of materials to jingle and jangle. She slid a few of the larger pieces back to expose the bruises on her wrist.

"These will heal," Julie said somewhat assuredly. She gingerly ran her hand across her left leg, caressing the soft blue denim of her jeans. "The same with the cuts in my thigh. I just don't need your mom giving me the third degree about the bruises."

"You could tell her it's from some kinky sex thing. That would totally shut her up."

"Right?"

"Sorry Mrs. Leblanc, but I moonlight as a dominatrix. They call me Fluffy Valley."

Julie and Tom burst out laughing. Max stuck his head through the front seats as Tom slowed Ruby to make the turn off West Shore Road. Julie gave the dog a big kiss on his snout and looked back behind them at Robin's car. She waved to them, and Robin and Darryl waved back.

"I'm so glad you invited them along. I'm surprised, too."

"Why?"

"Because you're finally listening to me."

Tom looked over and raised an eyebrow.

"Don't give me that look, Tom. I told you we needed new friends. I told you we needed to move forward."

After a few minutes, Tom made the final set of turns to get to his mother's house. The wide driveway was filled with cars, and several more were parked along the edge of the roadway. Tom pulled to the far end of the property and parked beneath a red oak tree that towered over seventy feet into the air. The leaves would stay green until the fall when they would take on beautiful tones of crimson and butter. Robin pulled her BMW sedan in front of Tom's Jeep.

Robin and Darryl removed a few canvas bags from the BMW's trunk while Julie and Tom grabbed what they needed from the back of Ruby. Tara was thrilled when Tom handed her Max's leash and asked her to lead the way to the side gate. Tom couldn't help but grin as Tara and Max marched side by side across the front lawn.

"I think you have a future dog sitter," Darryl said to Tom.

Tara waited patiently by the gate for the adults to catch up to her.

"Now?" Tara asked Tom.

"Now," Tom replied.

Tara removed the latch from Max's collar just as Tom opened the side gate to the backyard. Max tentatively stepped through the gate, cautiously surveying the yard. The vast space, normally filled with nothing but grass and trees, was occupied by over two dozen people wandering around, laughing and talking. Max flared his nostrils at the onslaught of aromas bombarding him.

Dorothy Leblanc emerged from a cluster of four older women that were engaged in a heated discussion. She squinted at the group of people entering her backyard. Her eyes descended to Max, bringing a smile to her face. That smile quickly turned to a look of shock when she noticed the bright white bandage wrapped around his leg. She excused herself from her guests and hurried over to the gate.

"Tom?" Dorothy asked as she knelt down and took Max's injured leg in her hands. "What happened?"

"He got in a fight, Mom. He's fine."

"Where?"

"At the dog park."

"Which one?"

"Does it matter?"

Dorothy stood and dusted bits of dirt and dead grass from her knees.

"Well, you can't bring him there anymore," Dorothy said adamantly. "It's obviously not safe."

Robin was well aware of the sudden jolt of tension in the air. She pushed her way between Tom and Julie and extended her hand toward Dorothy.

"Hi, I'm Robin. Tom's told me so many wonderful things about you."

"Oh. Oh, well thank you."

"This is my daughter Tara and my brother Darryl. Tara and I just moved in above Tom."

"Oh. You're the new owners?" Dorothy forced a smile as she did a quick inspection of the three surprise guests.

"Pleased to meet you," Tara said as she stepped forward with her arm out."

Dorothy grinned and shook the young girl's hand. Tara held up a canvas bag and presented it to Dorothy. Dorothy opened it and withdrew a nine by thirteen foil pan filled with brownies.

"Oh my goodness! These look lovely. Did you make these?"

"I stirred the bowl, but my mom was in charge of the oven."

Tom smiled, relieved that a spat with his mother appeared to be averted. He glanced over at Julie and raised an eyebrow and nodded. Julie responded by tapping on her wrist as if she were keeping time.

"Your hair is quite ... unique," Dorothy said. She focused on one of Tara's locks and studied the bright red and white beads. "Are they tribal?"

"And that's ten," Julie deadpanned.

"No," Robin replied. "They're detachable. Would you like to wear them?"

"Oh, my, no. No thank you." Dorothy felt her cheeks redden. "I'm sorry if I offended you."

"No apologies needed." Robin laughed, stepped forward, and gave Dorothy a hug. "I was just messing with you. Can we bring our stuff inside? I have a few things for the fridge."

Darryl held his arms out with the remaining bags they'd brought. Dorothy raised her eyebrows and clasped her hands together.

"Of course! So much food." Dorothy turned to Julie and inspected the bags in her hands. "And did you bring that Mexican dish?"

"Mexican?" Julie closed her eyes to try and remember what she was supposed to bring. The cookout had been the least of her concerns this weekend. Her bags were filled with nothing but chips and dips. She opened her eyes and looked over at Tom. "You mean the empanadas? Sorry. No, I didn't have time. The Colombian deli was closed. Colombian."

"Oh, well. Perhaps next time." Dorothy smiled and put her arm around Robin and took Tara by the hand. "I'm sure we can find room in the fridge for everything. Let me show you around."

Tom groaned as he handed Julie a ten dollar bill.

"Ten?" Julie asked. "I think you owe me twenty. Veinte!"

***

The Memorial Day cookout was proving to be a huge success. Dorothy was in her glory, running from guest to guest to make sure everyone's glass was topped off and their stomachs were full. She dragged Robin and Tara around endlessly, introducing them as her son's new friends.

Tom and Julie were relaxing in matching teak Adirondack lounge chairs tucked in the back corner of his mother's yard. Between them sat an umbrella stand with a faded blue umbrella, lowered and wrapped up tightly. The cool breeze coming in from Greenwich Bay contrasted with the sun's rays, resulting in an idyllic mix of warm and cool temperatures alternating with each passing cloud.

"Who *are* all these people?" Julie asked.

"Some are neighbors," Tom replied. "But most are old friends of my mom's. Plus my Aunt Judy."

Julie glanced across the yard until she spotted Dorothy and Judy. They were strolling beside the garden, laughing and talking.

"It's great that she flew in to surprise your mom. They seem to be very close."

"They most definitely are."

"How come none of your childhood friends are here? I think we're the only people under thirty. Excluding Tara."

"I only had a couple of close friends growing up. They both went off to college and never returned."

"Just like me. I can appreciate that."

Darryl was hard at work at the outdoor grill. He'd kindly offered to take charge of cooking the chicken, burgers, sausage and hot dogs. The grill was at the far end of the deck that ran across the back of the Leblanc family home. Tom watched from his Adirondack chair as Darryl laughed and joked with everyone waiting to get a fresh helping of grilled delights.

Darryl finished placing two Italian sausage links on someone's plate before looking out across the yard. The raised deck gave him an excellent view of the party-goers. He spotted Tom and Julie tucked away in the back corner and waved to them.

"He likes you," Julie said. "I hope you can see that."

"I can."

"And?"

"And ... I think I like him too."

"Oh my God. Houston we have a breakthrough." Julie popped a chunk of cheddar cheese into her mouth and looked down at her empty paper plate and frowned. She flicked the plate onto the ground. Max, resting quietly by her side, rolled over and began to lick the bits of cheese and salami grease from the surface. Julie turned to her side and looked at Tom. "Wait. Are you actually thinking of going out with him?"

"I think so. I mean, I want to get to know him more, first. But, sure."

"Wow, try and calm your excitement."

"Honestly, Jewels? I look back and think of the mistakes I

made with Marc. Things I should have said. Things I regret."

"You have to move forward, Tom. Darryl is insanely sexy. And he seems super sweet. You never know where life will lead."

Tom shoved the last of his hamburger into his mouth and washed it down with a gulp of pinot noir. He looked at his empty plastic cup and exhaled. The comfort food, sunshine, and friendship surrounding him felt amazing. He couldn't remember the last time he felt so relaxed.

"So, Jewels, we both agreed that yesterday was our day of recovery from the shitstorm that happened on the Cape. Can we talk about it now? Is it OK if I ask you about her?"

"Her? You mean Emma?" Julie sat up and folded her arms defensively. "I told you everything on the ride home Saturday night."

"I was just wondering if you were reconsidering pressing charges. I mean, she abducted you."

"She also saved my life. Look, Tom, we need to move forward, OK? You weren't there. That old witch completely fucked with Emma's head. Besides, I assaulted her first. She was trying to have a conversation with me in my driveway, and I wailed on her."

"I know, but ...."

"But what? The ones that killed Marc and Chris are dead. It's over. Can we please move on? We've all suffered enough. Everyone."

Julie pitched her head back, emptying the last of her red wine from the acrylic cup. The clear plastic was already stained a light shade of garnet. She tossed the glass to the ground. Max gave it a brief sniff before returning to the plate he was now eating.

"I'm sorry, Jewels. You're right. I didn't mean to upset you." Tom reached over and took Julie by her hand. He used his thumb to part the cluster of bracelets covering her wrist and exposed her bruise. Julie stared blankly across the yard, lost in her thoughts. "Come on, let's go for a walk."

Tom stood up and helped Julie out of the Adirondack chair. He tapped his thigh and waited for Max to spit the pieces of paper plate from his mouth and join him by his side. The three made their way through the people standing and lounging throughout the yard.

Darryl was still busy working the grill. Tom walked up behind him and tapped him on the shoulder. Darryl spun around and flashed Tom a brilliantly white smile.

"I didn't bring you here to cook all day," Tom said. "Have you eaten yet?"

"I'm fine for now. I love to cook, so I'm enjoying this. My building has a rooftop garden area with amazing views of downtown Boston. I bring my electric grill up there and make dinner and soak in the night sky as often as I can. Maybe someday I can have you up for a home cooked meal."

"I'd like that."

"You would?" Darryl sounded both surprised and thrilled. His smile somehow became even more exuberant. "Great. It's a date, then."

"It is." Tom realized he was suddenly blushing. "Darryl, I'm going to take a stroll with Jewels and Max. If my mom comes looking for me, do you mind covering for us?"

"I'd be happy to." Darryl looked across the deck at Julie. She was busy wrapping what seemed to be half a pound of cheese cubes into a plastic freezer bag. "Tom, I know something happened this weekend. Robin was awake when you two got home Saturday night. She said she heard Julie crying on your front steps. Is she OK? Are you?"

"I'll be fine." Tom glanced back at Julie, who was busy inspecting wine bottles lined across the back of a folding table. "So will Jewels."

***

Tom and Julie took their time as they strolled through Tom's childhood neighborhood. The cool late afternoon air was filled with the chatter and laughter of families and friends enjoying the Monday holiday. Smoke rose from backyards, carrying the scent of greasy burgers, butter-soaked corn on the cob, and syrupy baked beans. Max kept close to his master, taking care to keep a watchful eye out for any demonic squirrels.

"Is this walk too long for him?" Julie asked as she eyed the dog's right front leg.

"No, he'd stop if he was in pain. My mobile vet came by yesterday and gave him a clean bill of health. It will sting for a bit but should heal up just fine. He's a trouper." Tom pointed at Julie's thigh. "How about you?"

"Fine. I should have worn baggy jeans. These are a bit tight, but I'll survive."

The trio turned down a dead-end street lined with vehicles parked along the sides of the road. Once they got to the end, Tom led Max and Julie through a small cluster of rhododendron bushes blocking a narrow dirt path. After several dozen yards they emerged at the edge of Greenwich Bay.

"Wow, this is beautiful," Julie said. "You've never taken me here."

"I used to come here in my teens before there were houses here. Technically we're trespassing."

Tom took Max off his leash, and the dog quickly descended the rocky slope in front of them. The bay was too far inland to allow for any waves along the shoreline. Instead, shifting tides and the wake from boats would send small ripples along the sandy, rocky shore.

Julie pointed to a pair of wide flat boulders and headed toward them. Once there, she took a seat and set the plastic bag down and went about removing the wine, cups, and snacks packed inside. Max watched, licking his lips, as Julie pulled out a few pieces of cheese. Tom's back was to them. She tossed the dog a chunk of cheddar.

"I saw that," Tom said without turning around.

"Do you have eyes behind your head?"

"Maybe." Tom took a seat on the boulder beside Julie and poured two glasses of wine. He passed one to Julie and held his glass up next to hers. "Cheers, Jewels."

"Cheers." Julie took a small sip of wine and stared at Tom. "Speaking of eyes behind your head, how did you end up out in Wellfleet? You still haven't told me."

"Is it enough that I saved your life?"

"No. Spill it."

Tom tapped his thigh, and Max walked over to the base of the boulder and whimpered. His leg ached too much for him to jump up. Tom leaned back and tapped the back side of the rock. Max walked up the sandy slope so that he could easily step onto the boulder. Tom spun the dog's collar around until he found the GPS tracker. He palmed it and looked at Julie and smiled.

"You tracked me?" Julie looked at her wrists and ran her hands across her legs, chest, and neck. "How?"

"I dropped a similar one in your handbag. It's bigger and has much more range. I was going to play a joke on you with it."

Julie shook her head and managed to chuckle.

"I should be angry, but I'm not." Julie grabbed two chunks of Havarti cheese and tossed one in her mouth. "And for the record, Tom, you didn't save me."

"Excuse me?"

"Officer Jones did. And his boss. The cops saved the day."

"True, but I was the one that led them to you."

"No, Tom. Emma did. Emma called Jeff after she got back to Wellfleet with me. She told him what her mother and that whack job Bobby were planning. The police decided to cover Bobby's house *and* the old Victorian home. You sent Trevor to the Victorian. If Emma hadn't called Jeff, the cops never would have gone to Bobby's. And Emma and I would both be dead right now."

Tom stared into his plastic cup of pinot noir and frowned. He closed his eyes and tried to play back the sequence of events from two days ago. Julie did not bother to wait for him to draw his own conclusions.

"Tom, I appreciate that you went running out there to play the hero. You risked your life to save me. I'll never forget that. But in the end, the police saved me. The system worked."

"I guess."

"What did Trevor have to say about you playing the hero?"

"He wasn't too happy."

"You told me you ran into him at the old house."

"Sort of." Tom grabbed a handful of crackers and popped

one in his mouth. He turned and looked out at the bay, dreading the reaction he knew he would get from Julie. "The run-in was sort of unexpected. And in the dark. To be honest, Jewels, I'm lucky I wasn't shot."

"Oh my God! Are you serious? You didn't tell me that."

"Because I knew you'd get mad. I went in through the bulkhead door. I was in a total panic, but I was convinced you were in there. Someone came up behind me. Then Trevor came around the corner in front of me. I was surrounded by cops with their guns aimed at me."

"And did you go in there with your bow and arrow?"

"Yes," Tom said softly. "And a dagger."

"What? No wonder you almost got shot. Where would that have left me? Or Max?"

Tom reluctantly nodded in agreement and turned his head away, letting his gaze drift across the bay.

Julie topped off their cups with more red wine and waved for Max to come over to her. The dog complied and patiently waited to be rewarded. She ran her fingernails between his ears and gave him half a slice of cheddar. Tom's head was hung low. Julie leaned over and kissed him on the cheek.

"Thank you for caring so much, Tom. I love you, but you could have been killed. I know your dad's murder haunts you, but the police came through this time. You've got to learn to trust in others. They may surprise you."

"I know."

"I mean, I never expected Emma to shoot her mother."

"Emma killed her?" Tom sat up and wiped his cheeks dry. "I thought the cop did. Jeff. That's what you told Trevor and me."

"Shit." Julie lowered her head and sighed, nervously fidgeting with her overabundance of bracelets. "I wasn't supposed to tell anyone."

"Jewels, what happened in that shed?"

"Everything we told Trevor was true, up until the end. Her mother was about to shoot Jeff, but Emma fired the gun, not Jeff. Jeff was face down when it happened."

"So you lied. To the cops."

"That was Jeff's call. He didn't want Emma to have to deal

with the fallout. She saved his life. Mine too." Julie paused to study Tom's face. She could see the gears turning in his head. "We've all suffered enough, Tom. Let it go. Emma's not filing assault charges against me. I'm not going after her for abduction. Jeff's not charging Emma with killing her mother. The guilty ones are gone. We all need to move forward."

Tom exhaled loudly and nodded in agreement. He gazed over at Julie. Max was half asleep, draped across her right thigh. Julie was staring out at the bay while slowly caressing Max's ears.

"You're right, Jewels."

"Of course I am. The legend is over, and the killers are dead." A wry grin spread across Julie's face as she turned to look at Tom. "Wait. I've got a new one coming, Tom. I'm thinking ... Legendeady!"

Tom chuckled at his best friend's never-ending desire to create her own words. He closed his eyes and downed half his wine. He placed the cup by his side and leaned back, propping himself up by his elbows. The wind coming in off the bay carried damp salt air across his face. Far offshore a boat raced by, the muted buzz of the engine barely drowning out the laughter of the passengers onboard. The sun was low on the western skyline, partially masked by the wispy strands of cirrus clouds floating above.

"When did you get so wise, Jewels?"

"Wise? Hardly. I'm just tired, Tom. Things need to change. I've been close to death too many times lately. These past several months have been a rollercoaster. For both of us. We need to move our lives forward."

"Cheers to that, Jewels." Tom held up the bottle of red wine and wiggled it at Julie. She extended her cup and Tom emptied the rest of the alcohol, splitting it between their two glasses.

"We can't change the past, Tom."

Julie pulled out her phone and flipped through her photos. She stopped at the picture taken of her, Tom, Chris and Marc at the Seabreeze condo last December. Julie held her phone out so that Tom could see the image. Tom's eyes welled up as he studied Marc's face.

"I loved him, Jewels. So much."

"I know you did."

Tom held up his half-empty cup of pinot noir. Julie tapped her glass against Tom's and downed what was left of her wine. Tom did the same as Max came over and placed his head on Tom's knee. The bay was quiet once again. Tom held Max close, enjoying the calming sound of the water brushing up against the rocks and sand lining the edge of the shoreline. Julie closed her eyes, leaned back, and soaked in the last bit of sun before it set. Several minutes passed as Tom, Julie, and Max sat in silence, each lost in their own thoughts.

"So what's next for you, Jewels?"

Julie smiled, sat up, and pulled her knees to her chest, resting her head sideways on her kneecaps.

"Believe it or not, I think I'm going to go back to school to finish my law degree."

"Holy shit, Jewels. That's fantastic. What brought this on?"

"My yaya. Oh my God! I didn't tell you. We talked Saturday morning, right before everything went to hell. She sort of laid into me for not pushing myself to have a better life. Really hit me with the guilt trip."

"Grandmothers can be great at that."

"She got me thinking. Where is my life going? What would I have accomplished had I been killed? I need to focus on my future."

"How will you juggle work, school, and the apartment?"

"There you go, diving into the details again. I haven't planned that far ahead. My yaya was right. I deserve a better life." Julie let her eyes wander across the bay, taking in the twinkling sparks of sunlight dancing against the rippling sea. "She wants us to visit her."

"Us? As in you and me?"

"Yes. I haven't been to see her in, like, forever. Several years ago she got this stunning cliffside villa in Santorini. Every time we chat she shows me different parts of it." Julie sat upright, as the excitement about a trip to see her grandmother flooded her mind. "Tom, the place is amazing. I think it has four or five bedrooms."

"Wow. Greece? I don't know, Jewels. It sounds, well, far away. And expensive."

"You're only half right. It's far away. But it will be free."

"Free?" Tom studied Julie's beaming smile and couldn't help but grin and shake his head. He was so happy to see her so excited. "How so?"

"Because of the amazing Adrian."

"Who?"

"He's family. Long story. What matters is he's gorgeous and insanely wealthy. My yaya told him about what happened, and he wants to fly us out there. On his private jet."

"What?" Tom slid off the boulder and landed on the sandy beach. He wiped the dirt off the back of his jeans and spun around to face Julie. "Are you kidding?"

Julie jumped off the rock she was on and put her hands on Tom's shoulders.

"No. It's like we hit the jackpot! We will spend a week staying in the villa of the fabulous Helen Perez, courtesy of the stunning Adrian .... Shit, I don't even know his last name. But he's hot. He's also supposed to have a sexy brother. Maybe we can each have one?"

Julie pushed Tom away and covered her face as she burst out laughing. Max took the long way down around the back of the boulders and came and stood between Tom and Julie. Julie ran her fingers along the dog's snout.

"Well, Tom? There's no reason for you to say no to this."

"Excuse me, but do I need to remind you that I hate heights and you hate the ocean. I mean, a seaside villa on the other side of the Atlantic is the last thing we should consider, right?"

"Tom, that's *exactly* why we need to do it. Besides, it's a private jet!"

Tom sighed, realizing there was no point in challenging her on any of this.

"When did you want to go?"

"Well, my birthday is in November. It's the big Three-O." Julie paused and sighed. "Shit I'm getting old. Maybe we go then? Or sooner? We'll have to check the weather and stuff."

"OK, Jewels. I'm in. How can I say no to a private jet and luxury villa?"

Julie kissed Tom on the cheek and flung her arms around him. He held her tight, leaned back, and spun her around. Julie laughed as Max barked with confusion over the acrobatic undertaking happening before his eyes. Tom lowered Julie to the ground as they continued to laugh.

"Oh my God, Tom, this is amazing. I'm so glad you said yes. This will be an epic vacation. I just know it. A stunning house. Gorgeous men. Amazing weather. A private jet!"

"But Jewels, if this hot guy Adrian is family then how will you bag him?"

"We're not blood-related. Again, long story. Stop digging into the weeds! It's a private jet flying us to stay in a massive house overlooking the Aegean Sea. It won't cost us a dime. Max can stay with your mom. We just need to get the time off from work."

"Sounds like you've got it all figured out, Jewels."

"I do. See, your planning skills continue to rub off on me."

"You're welcome."

Tom made his way to the bay several yards away. The sun had taken shelter low in the sky, obscured by silver and white clouds. Bands of yellow and amber sunshine sliced through the clouds as the sun slowly began to descend below the horizon. The blue sky slowly began to take on tones of purple and gold. Julie and Max joined Tom near the water's edge, enjoying the quiet sounds of the water gently washing against the sandy shoreline surrounding them.

"It does sound amazing," Tom continued. He turned and gave Julie a cynical grin. "Just don't bring along any creepy urban legend books for the private jet ride."

Julie chuckled as she knelt down and surveyed the small rocks scattered across the beach surrounding her. She picked up a flat oval stone and chucked it out into the bay. The rock skipped several times before descending into the dark gray ocean.

"Trust me, Tom, this will be a vacation of sun, fun, and men."

"And no blizzards."

"Right? Oh, and no candle shopping. Or *any* gifts for your mother."

"Good point. Better to be safe than sorry."

Tom slid his arm around Julie's shoulder. She grabbed onto his waist, allowing her to take some of the pressure off her injured leg. Max sat in front of Tom and shoved his snout under Julie's hand. They watched as the sun finished disappearing below the horizon across the bay.

"No myths or legends on this trip, Tom."

"Ditto on that Jewels."

"Ditto on that, Leblanc. Ditto on that."

EPILOGUE

He glides across the deep blue waves.
Beneath his smile he misbehaves.
He will tempt you with his trust.
And seduce you with his lust.
But in the end he will send you to the graves.

Mythical Poems of Greece

Author – Helen Perez

.

ACKNOWLEDGEMENTS

I have learned so much since publishing my first two books. Wrapping up The Tallow Series has been an inspiring undertaking. What literally started as a nightmare back in 2017 has spawned a trilogy of stories that I am quite proud to share with the world. I was fortunate to be able to dedicate myself full time to writing this final novel.

Time to Pay would not be possible without the support from my family, especially my mom and my sisters Lori and Debra. Lori was the first person to read my completed draft. Her insight into my early drafts has always been spot on. I highly value her encouragement and feedback. Debra encouraged me to pursue writing full time, coaching me to believe in myself and to move forward.

A special thank you to Merrie Myers, my primary editor. I was fortunate enough to connect with Merrie earlier this year. Her background in journalism and communications proved to be quite insightful in shaping my storytelling. My skills in character and storytelling will continue to grow with great friends like Merrie coaching me along.

One more shout out to my friends Shawn and Jacob and their pointers and direction on nursing and medicine.

I love the "World of Tallow" I have built with my first three novels, and hope to one day revisit it. Tom and Julie do need to get to Greece, don't they? Even if Helen's poetry foretells the trip may not go as planned.

ABOUT THE AUTHOR

MJ Howson was born and raised in Providence, Rhode Island. He spent many summers enjoying Cape Cod as well as the local state beaches of his home state.

Ever since college, MJ always thought he would write a book. There is a saying: "Life is what happens when you are busy making plans." After a successful career in IT, MJ finally decided to pursue his dream of being an author. The advent of print-on-demand and e-books made this goal something he could somewhat easily pursue. The Tallow Series is the first set of stories to be published. He has a long list of story ideas and looks forward to sharing them with the world.

MJ adopted the tag line "The Terror is Real" as the focus for his books. Escapist, paranormal, and supernatural stories are always good for a scare. The tales that run the risk of being able to come true, however, are the ones that can really haunt you.

You can connect with MJ via his website. From there, you will find links to his different social media accounts.

mjhowson.com

www.ingramcontent.com/pod-product-compliance
Lightning Source LLC
Chambersburg PA
CBHW072236190626
46809CB00018B/2314